CURSED ICE

PARANORMAL FANTASY

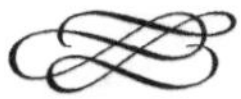

ANN GIMPEL

CONTENTS

Cursed Ice   v
Book Description, Cursed Ice   vii
Books in the Ice Dragon Series   ix
Author's Note   xi

Chapter 1   1
Chapter 2   17
Chapter 3   33
Chapter 4   47
Chapter 5   63
Chapter 6   81
Chapter 7   97
Chapter 8   113
Chapter 9   129
Chapter 10   147
Chapter 11   163
Chapter 12   177
Chapter 13   193
Chapter 14   209
Chapter 15   225
Chapter 16   241
Chapter 17   257
Chapter 18   275
About the Author   293
Primal Ice, Dragon Time   295

CURSED ICE

ICE DRAGON SERIES, BOOK TWO

Paranormal Fantasy

By
Ann Gimpel

Tumble off reality's edge into myth, magic, ice, and dragons

By his own admission, Johan's always been one stubborn bastard. He's wedded to his freedom, and the thought of bonding with a dragon has some pretty serious downsides. If he doesn't sign on to become magical, though, he'll be left behind—also not an acceptable outcome.

Distant relatives to dragons, sea-serpents are gaining strength shockingly fast. Breeding farms spring up on distant outposts, spitting out all manner of evil. Banished eons ago by the dragon god, the serpents are making a comeback. As the dragons seek allies, they uncover still more atrocities.

Katya, dragon shifter and twin to the dragon prince, thought she wanted Johan as her mate, but he has more rough edges than she counted on. Besides, the serpent problem supersedes everything. She's used to dragons being in charge, but when a serpent almost steals her will, it's quite the wakeup call her magic isn't as potent as she always assumed.

Is the age of dragons drawing to a close? If that's true, what will come next?

BOOKS IN THE ICE DRAGON SERIES

Feral Ice, Book One
Cursed Ice, Book Two
Primal Ice, Book Three

Ice Dragon is a trilogy, so a long tale split into three books that need to be read in order. I was fascinated by Antarctica long before I visited there, and my two trips were so incredible, I still stumble over words to describe the awe I felt at the vista of ice-crusted ocean, hardy mosses and lichens, and the proliferation of wildlife. Tame critters who are as likely to peck at you or sit on your lap as they are to put on an amazing show—as if you weren't even there.

A story about ice dragons has been percolating for a few years now. It was time to breathe life into it.

CHAPTER 1

My name is Johan Petris. I'm not entirely certain how it happened, but I've fallen off a cliff. Not a physical one, but one separating what I always believed was real from where I am now. I'm a metallurgical engineer, for chrissakes, and a Dutchman to boot. We're a bit of a dour lot. Hell, we don't even encourage our children to engage in flights of fancy.

I admit to a closet fascination with science fiction and fantasy, but it wasn't anything I'd ever have confessed to anyone. Not out loud. My work fellows would have had a tough time taking me seriously if they thought I entertained myself with tales of alien visitation.

Or werewolves. Or vampires.

I'll spare you the details of how I ended up kilometers underground in a dragon shifter lair. That's a tale for another day. Let it suffice to say I'm here, along with Erin Ryan, a doctor and biochemist. We're deep in discussions with our dragon shifter hosts to determine what comes next. Not surprisingly, radical differences in our belief systems have turned our chat into a contest of wills.

I feel for Erin, but I admire her spirit. She's having a much rougher time than me absorbing the idea of magic being anything other than an abstract construct. Too nervous to remain seated, she's pacing around the room asking questions. Blonde hair is billowing around her tall, spare body, and her blue eyes hold a worried cast.

I'm not sure why accepting magic is real hasn't been harder for me, but people are different that way. I have half an ear on Konstantin, one of the dragon shifters, as he describes several iterations of magic wielders. Only half, though. The rest of my mind is busy—reeling might be more accurate—with information about other worlds. Lots of them.

Apparently, we're headed toward a constellation of borderworlds to secure assistance from other magic wielders. Sea-serpents, a distant relative of the dragons, have invaded Earth. We're the only ones who know about them, so, presumably, we have to act as the first line of defense—

A brilliant flash I've come to associate with dragon shifter magic made me squinch my eyes tight. When I opened them, Konstantin had crossed the kitchen and grabbed Erin. She was writhing in his grasp, trying to get away.

I wasn't anxious to confront him. Richly muscled, he

probably stood six feet six with shiny copper-gold hair cascading around his shoulders. But I couldn't just sit there and let him manhandle Erin, either. She'd been one of my shipmates on an Antarctic research expedition. It's how we ended up in the Southern Ocean.

The dragons' cozy kitchen stretched around us. Carved out of earth, its walls sported rich veins of gold, silver, and other precious metals. Most of the kitchen's contents were tucked behind magical panels at the far end of the rectangular room. We'd been sitting at a good-sized table, one that could easily accomodate twenty, before Erin jumped up and began pacing.

I hustled to where she and Konstantin stood and asked, "Is that really necessary?"

"I won't hurt her," Konstantin growled.

I'm certain he meant to dissuade me from further words —or action—but I didn't back down.

While I was considering what to do next, Katya, Konstantin's twin and another dragon shifter, materialized next to me and hooked an arm beneath mine. "Come with me. We shall talk. Erin is safe with my brother."

Katya is stunning. About the same height as Erin, she has masses of copper-colored curls. Most of the time, she's naked, which is a huge distraction. I admit I'm weak, but I'm a man, and we tend to be diverted by bare breasts and acres of leg. Both she and her brother have golden eyes with deep-green centers. In dragon form—she's golden, and he's black —their eyes spin, casting a hypnotic net.

I felt power spilling from her, but I was helpless to do

anything except acquiesce. It was a damned uncomfortable spot to be in. I value my free will, and it's been in short supply lately. My mouth opened, seemingly of its own accord, and I murmured, "Of course. Where would you like us to sit?"

"Can't you see what Konstantin's doing?" Erin squawked. "Whatever he left out, we all need to hear it. Together. In the same room."

I heard Erin, but her voice was coming from a long way away. Her complaint seemed petty, unimportant. When I twisted my head to look for her, she and Konstantin were gone. It should have worried me, but Katya's warmth, pressing the length of my side, was paramount.

Somehow, Katya and I ended up one flight above sitting on one of the pallets scattered through a number of sleeping areas. She seized a length of fuzzy fabric and wound it around herself, almost as if she divined how much trouble her nudity created.

Whatever she'd done to get me to follow her upstairs dissipated. Worry for Erin filled me. "Where has Konstantin taken Erin? And for what purpose?" I asked without preamble. I tried for a stern enough tone Katya wouldn't blow me off.

Or muffle me with magic again.

She nodded. "It's understandable you'd be concerned, but my brother would never harm her."

I folded my legs beneath me and said, "Konstantin indicated the same thing. That he would not hurt her, but you did not answer either of my questions."

"No. I did not."

"Why? I still know nothing about his intentions."

Katya curved her fingers and raked them through her thick, unruly hair. The motion stretched the fabric tight across her breasts. I forced my gaze upward with firm instructions to keep my eyes on her face, not on the outline of her nipples.

After a pause, one that dragged out so long I was crafting what to say next to encourage her to talk, she said, "We're in a precarious predicament. We have no time to waste while I dispel your fears about Erin."

I opened my mouth, but she shook her head. "Hear me out. We cannot leave you here in our home while we travel to various borderworlds seeking allies. If something unexpected happened, and we were unable to return, you and Erin would be stuck down here. There is no way to reach the surface without magic."

She spread her hands in front of her. "It's far too dangerous to stumble around the universe with two humans in tow. For you and for us. We might end up fighting for your survival instead of lobbying for the help we so desperately need. Absent aid, Earth will be lost to the sea-serpents."

"How can you know?" I asked, startled by the adamant tone of her statement.

"Because they're like us. It means I understand how they think, how they operate." She cast a sidelong glance my way.

"All right. You ruled out several options. We cannot accompany you, and we cannot remain here. What is left?"

She traded looking askance at me for raking me with an

astute gaze that probably missed very little. "Only two options. We leave you on the surface—where you would be vulnerable to both the sea-serpents and the elements if we were gone overlong."

"Or?"

"Or we make a bid for each of you to become a dragon shifter." Her golden eyes never left my face.

"What? But neither of you is even certain such a thing is possible." I felt as if a mule had backed up and kicked me in the guts with both its rear hoofs.

"No. We're not," she agreed. "Konstantin intuited Erin would be a harder sell than you. Fear lives in that one, although she covers it well. It's why he took her to a more private location. He will lay out her options, and then she will choose."

"What happens if she says no to becoming a dragon shifter?" It was an easier question to ask than one about me because it was a step removed from my own fate. But I bet the answer would be the same.

I ground my teeth in irritation at my cowardice. I didn't usually avoid tackling difficult situations, but this one was so bizarre I didn't have a place to slot it.

"Konstantin will probably deliver her to that Polish research base the two of you have mentioned."

Understanding flooded me, right along with guilty relief. Erin would never opt to become a dragon shifter. Not in this world or any other. "We are here until she decides, right? Because both of us have to make the same choice."

"No. We're here for two reasons. To move us out of the way, and for you to think about what you want to do."

I frowned, remembering an earlier conversation, one of the first we'd had with the dragon shifter twins. "But Erin and I are ruled by a single fate, correct?"

Katya shook her head. "No longer true." She offered me a soft smile. "For a transformation to have a ghost of a chance of success, you must want it with everything in you. The same is true of Erin. Neither of you can ride on the other's coattails."

I turned the information over, considering it. "If I demur, you will see I end up at Arctowski, the Polish base?"

"Yes. It will be a death sentence. Not right away, but quite soon. The nearest humans will be the first targeted by the sea-serpents."

"Mmph. So I would be better served having you leave me in Europe?"

"You would, indeed." She paused long enough to take a measured breath. "I would erase your memories. While I would be as careful as possible, you would lose some that are bound up with your time with us."

"I understand. Some of my memories of Erin would be at risk too."

Katya nodded solemnly. "Would that be a problem?"

Her tone was studiedly neutral, so I couldn't read what might lie behind it. Part of me hoped she might be a tiny bit jealous, but I was being ridiculous. "Not a problem so much as it pokes my control freak buttons," I mumbled.

"What exactly are they?"

I chuckled. "Humans are an odd lot. We nurture the illusion we are masters of our own ships." I took a breath and blew it out, my amusement fading. "Every time you or your brother uses magic to force an outcome, I resent the hell out of it. I am used to living in a world where people make requests, and I am free to accept or decline."

She knitted her coppery brows together. "Does that mean you never have to do things that bother you? Or that you disagree with?"

"Of course not." I stopped before blindly blundering forward. Perhaps the freedom I'd cherished wasn't anything beyond a carefully constructed illusion.

"So you're not truly free?" she pressed.

"I guess not, but..." My voice faltered. How could I explain the nexus between manners and social expectations and outcomes?

"Never mind. It's not important. You know your choices. What is your decision?"

"Just like that?" Time shrank around me until I felt physical pressure compressing my chest like a steel band.

"Yes. Just like that. I'm happy to answer questions, but when we leave this room, it will either be to travel to the place between worlds where we shall petition Y Ddraigh Goch for a dragon of your own or to a spot on earth of your choosing. Which shall it be?"

She'd said she welcomed questions, and they bombarded me from all sides. "What if I try and cannot, uh, transform into something like you?"

"Then we retreat to Plan B, and I deliver you somewhere on Earth."

"Minus my memories."

Katya nodded. "Of course." She tilted her head to one side, and I couldn't look away. No one had a right to be as beautiful as she was. Her skin glowed golden, almost begging me to reach out and stroke my fingertips over its surface.

She dropped a hand on top of my thigh. The heat from her fingers and palm traveled through my thick, polar outerwear and prickled the skin beneath. "I'm not being cruel. Humans are a fragile lot. Your minds can only absorb so much. Holding memories of a failed attempt to bond with a dragon would eventually drive you mad. You would replay it over and over. You would blame yourself. You would want to try again, but once shut, that gate will never reopen."

"So, either way, I would lose my memories? If I fail at a transformation, or if I do not try at all?"

Katya nodded.

"I understand." It was the prudent response, although privately I wasn't certain she knew what she was talking about. How could she? From what she and her brother had said, they'd spent almost zero time with humans. Perhaps she was underestimating me. I rolled my mental eyes. Overconfidence had nearly been my undoing more than once.

It was how I'd ended up chucked in the chromium dig site with my femur broken. Erin set it, but Katya had healed me with magic. At the time, I'd had no idea how I'd recovered so fast, but I hadn't questioned my fortune, either.

"Questions?" Katya pressed.

I wrenched my mind back to the ones uppermost in my mind. "This transformation. If it works, won't it take really a long time for me to learn to control my magic?"

"Your dragon would help with that. The main problem will be maintaining control over the dragon." Breath rattled through her teeth. "They're an independent bunch. When they're not in your mind—or in their dragon form sharing your consciousness—they're free to travel where they will."

"But we have only one body?" I clarified. "Either the man or the dragon."

"Yes and no." She tossed an errant clump of hair over one shoulder. "The dragons have their own world. I suspect they're corporeal in their own place."

"Why would you not know that?"

"It's a good question." Katya's nostrils flared. "Even though we're bonded, the relationship is lopsided. My dragon knows everything about me, but the only things I know about her are what she wants me to know."

"You've never traveled to the dragons' world?"

"No. None of us have. It's barred to everyone but dragons."

My forehead scrunched into a mass of lines. Obviously, we didn't have hours and hours for me to quiz Katya. What could I ask that would cut through several layers of my ambivalence?

If Erin had asked me if I wanted to be a dragon shifter

even a few hours before, I'd have answered with a hearty affirmative. But now that the choice actually lay before me, I was of so many minds it was bewildering.

"What are the advantages of this...lopsided relationship?" I focused on Katya, wanting to pick up on her nonverbal cues as well as her words. For once, I wasn't half-aroused by her curves.

Probably because I was zeroed-in on the most critical decision of my life.

She met my straightforward gaze unflinchingly. "It's a hard question to answer. Since I was born with a dual nature, my dragon has been part of me forever." She closed her teeth over her lower lip. "It's like having a beloved companion. One who knows all of you, the good and the bad, and holds your feet to the fire when you've done something wrong.

"My dragon has been my closest friend—and my worst enemy. I hated her when she abandoned me after I refused to leave Earth. In retrospect, if I'd listened to her, Kon and I would be better off."

It seemed she had more to say, so I waited.

"When my dragon left, first I was angry, but then I was desolate. I missed her terribly. It was as if someone had cut off my right hand. Not the greatest metaphor, but I felt a critical part of me was missing."

"Did you ask her to come back?"

Katya's golden eyes skittered away. "Not for a very long time."

"What stopped you?"

She still didn't look at me. "Pride. The dragon left me. I figured she could find her own way back. Truth was, I thought she owed me an apology." Bitter laughter bubbled. "Doesn't work that way."

"How did she find her way back to you?" I was curious to hear what had finally turned the tide.

"Kon's dragon did something. I have no idea what, but she returned as abruptly as she'd left. And we took off running as if we'd never been apart." Katya stole a glance my way. "It's good to have her back. I'm whole again."

I pinched the bridge of my nose between a thumb and forefinger. Nothing Katya had said made me want a dragon of my own. I was fiercely independent, and the thought of another being telling me what to do—or even weighing in with an opinion—made my skin crawl.

But the specter of being dropped off in the Netherlands —if I chose to go home—didn't hold much appeal, either. Right now, I had knowledge of a serious threat to all life on Earth. Once Katya got done with me, I wouldn't remember any of it.

Fat, dumb, and happy, I'd molder on the sidelines, fiddling while Rome burned. Maybe not quite that bad, but I had an uncomfortable premonition about the serpents. "Once the sea-serpents develop momentum," I asked Katya, "roughly how long will it take them to establish control over Earth?"

"Not long at all. Men have nothing at their disposal that will make the slightest dent in a magical war. They'll fall by the wayside in a single generation. Perhaps less. Depends how many serpents their leader, Surek, imports from wherever they came from."

Her response didn't surprise me, but neither did it make my choice any simpler. If I had her return me to my human kin—and that would happen even if I made a bid for a dragon and failed—I'd find out about the threat to Earth along with everyone else. We'd mount what defense we could, and fall flat on our asses.

Not how I'd envisioned myself ending up. Taking the coward's way out.

I was in a position where I could make a difference. If I pulled my head out of my rump and acted like a man.

I stumbled to my feet and stood as tall as I could, vertebrae cracking as I pushed my shoulders back. "I wish to become a dragon shifter."

Katya rolled to her feet and regarded me. Magic prickled where she jabbed me with it, no doubt testing my words. My resolve.

"Not quite good enough," she said. At least she had the grace to sound disappointed, but she didn't sugarcoat her words.

"What do you mean?" I sputtered. "Of course I harbor doubts. I would be a right fool not to have them, but—"

She made a chopping motion. "You must want this with every fiber of your being, or you're wasting both of our time. The dragon will sense your hesitation"—she blew out a tight breath—"if we even got that far. Our first stop is Y Ddraigh Goch. If the dragon god is not convinced of your purity of heart, he'll send us packing."

I turned my hands palms up. "I will offer the best within me."

Her harsh expression softened, but not by much. "I'm sure you will. For now, take a walk outside. Perhaps down by the lake. I will confer with my dragon, and I want to visit the surface to keep an eye on the serpents. In roughly one turn of the glass, I shall return, and we will see which direction opens before us."

Before I could protest I was as certain as I was likely to get, the air around her turned glistening and liquid, and she was gone.

I blinked stupidly at the place she'd stood before I turned and trudged up another set of risers to the large stone door that led outside. Taking a walk was a good idea. It was easier to problem solve when I was on the move. Somehow, she'd known that about me.

As the heavy door swung shut behind me, I thought about Erin. Should I try to locate her? I shook my head. I couldn't help her any more than she could help me. Determined to find a way to mute my concerns, I set off through an unusual underground paradise carved deep beneath Antarctica's ice cap. It was warm down here. I'd mapped this string of subterranean lakes from my lab on the *Darya*, the research vessel I'd been dragged away from by Russians intent on stealing what they could of Antarctica's mineral wealth.

I may have mapped these lakes, but I'd had no idea they'd be so beautiful.

Not much point looking back, though. That life was lost to me.

Besides, thinking about Erin or the *Darya* were diversionary tactics. What I had to do was dig deep and figure out if I could open my metaphorical arms to a dragon and mean it.

Unsure what the result would be, I set off at a trot for the nearest lake half a kilometer distant. I was a proud man. Maybe too proud, verging on arrogance. And independent as hell. Peeling back the layers of a persona I'd cultivated for my entire adult life wouldn't be easy.

The prospect scared the holy crap out of me, but the alternative—the one where I forfeited my memories and returned to the world I'd left behind—held very little appeal.

Maybe I was making this too hard, but I had to carve out a spot for my dragon. One where it would feel cherished. A short bark of laughter startled me until I realized it had come from me. I wasn't used to sharing anything with anyone.

How in the hell would I share my innermost everything with an arrogant, critical dragon?

A snort followed the laughter. Might not be as impossible as all that. When you chopped the fluff away, dragons were a lot like me.

Short-tempered. Opinionated. Sure of themselves.

I reached the lakeshore and dropped onto a flattish rock. As I stared at the mirror-bright surface, a plan took shape.

The longer I gazed at the lake, the surer I was I could pull it off.

"Serious alterations in the status quo," I mumbled.

But what else was new? My previous circumstances had vanished when Russians forced me off the *Darya*. I'd be an idiot to long for the impossible. My past was deader than dead. The sooner the reality of that sank in, the better for everyone.

Especially me.

CHAPTER 2

Katya forced herself to leave. Her heart went out to Johan, but she couldn't help him. He had to figure this out on his own. Her presence wouldn't do anything but muddy the waters. Lust spiraled between them, too obvious to ignore much longer. He wanted her, and she longed for him as well. Sex could be their undoing at this point, though. She'd done her best to muffle her sexuality, covering herself when she could to make herself less an object of heat and need.

Despite her efforts, she'd caught Johan gazing at her several times, undisguised desire sheeting from his blue eyes. Men were so transparent. And they thought with their cocks. It was one of the most annoying parts of them, yet endearing as hell at the same time.

Konstantin had startled her when he draped Erin over one shoulder and spirited them out of the room. Katya hadn't expected him to be quite so Draconian, or to leave at all. She'd assumed they'd talk things out as a group and have a definite plan before breaking into dyads.

Konstantin had wrenched matters out of her hands, though.

Her brother cared about Erin. More than cared, he was smitten with her. So smitten, desire clouded his judgment. Katya reached the Earth's surface but maintained an invisibility spell around herself. She wasn't done dissecting her brother's actions, and his usual cool, detached approach to everything had deserted him. She hoped his attraction to Erin wouldn't destroy everything. Just as with Johan, Erin had to want a dragon of her own for the dragon—not to open the door for her to become Konstantin's mate.

Surely, he'd make that clear.

Katya pounded a fist into her open palm. She wasn't at all certain reason would prevail. Her brother had been mightily aroused the last private moments they'd had together, so aroused, she'd left him to slake his lust as he chose. Hopefully with his own hand.

If he'd waited until he had Erin alone, all bets were off. Erin didn't appear nearly as taken with Kon as he was with her, but dragon shifters were incredibly persuasive. If her brother wanted Erin in his bed, he had ways to make it happen.

A low growl rumbled from her throat. Smoke followed. Her dragon was making its disapproval clear. She sank to a crouch. Whatever did—or didn't—happen between Kon and

Erin was out of her hands. She'd been stupid not to talk with her brother, but what would she have said?

They might be twins, but they'd never interfered in one another's love lives. There'd never been a need. Neither of them had ever found another who'd felt like mate material.

Until now.

She rolled the thought around. Unlikely as it seemed, two strong perfect humans had fallen out of the ether into their domain at just the right time. Normally, neither she nor Kon would have given the humans a second glance, though. So it wasn't just Erin and Johan's proximity.

Katya chewed on her lower lip. Maybe the sequence of events wasn't as arbitrary as it appeared. She and Konstantin had remained on Earth after their dragon shifter kin left. Sheer stubbornness was behind their decision. Neither of them liked to lose, and they'd staked a claim to their subterranean home. This wasn't like Mu where the world became unstable. The dragons had been forced to abandon it before it imploded, scattering particles throughout its distant universe.

They'd been on the verge of leaving Earth—finally—but were waiting for Katya's dragon to return. Wherever they relocated, chances were she'd need to be able to fly. Flight required her bondmate. About that time, when she'd grown serious about coaxing her beast back to her side, she'd become aware of Erin and Johan—amazingly alive in the midst of a sea of dead companions.

The pattern of incidents held a choreographed feel, yet

no one, not even Y Ddraigh Goch, could have known the serpents would invade Earth...

Katya drew her thoughts up short. Of course the dragon god, once deity to the serpents as well, would have ways of keeping tabs on his banished minions. If that were true, he'd have known they were headed for Earth.

The implications staggered her.

Offering homage to Y Ddraigh was one thing. Suspecting he'd been playing them like pieces on a chessboard, quite another. She batted her annoyance aside. It had no place here, but if the dragon shifter god had plans for them, she'd appreciate a simple heads up.

Not a cloak-and-dagger tactic steeped in crafty manipulation. She wrapped her arms around her knees. She wanted Johan to choose transformation. It was another reason she'd had to leave. She couldn't influence him, no more than Konstantin should have played on Erin's loneliness and fear to persuade her to become like him.

Besides, even if both humans turned into dragon shifters, nowhere was it written they'd fall into her arms—or Konstantin's. They'd be independent entities, capable of choosing to mate.

Or not.

They might be so intent on saving Earth from the serpents, mating would be the last thing on their minds.

Fire flashed from her mouth. It made her smile. "I know what you think," she told her dragon.

"If that's so, stop mollycoddling yourself. Get up, and let's figure out what the serpents are up to. It's why we're here, isn't it?"

"One of many things I love about you," she told her dragon. "You keep me focused."

"I do, indeed," she retorted. *"Come on. Up and moving. You've wasted half the time you said you'd be away on useless mental chatter."*

"Do you know where Kon and Erin are?"

"Yes."

Katya waited, but her dragon didn't add anything. "Are you going to tell me?"

"No."

Well, there it was. The lopsided relationship she'd attempted to describe to Johan. She didn't squander breath arguing. Once her dragon said no, that was it. Her bondmate might come up with the information eventually, but not here and not now.

Nothing for it but to get moving.

"We will shift," the dragon informed her.

Katya hadn't been planning to, but she couldn't come up with a good reason to remain human, either. She let go of the coverlet she'd draped around herself, and opened her magical center. Power poured through her along with the stretching, tearing, breaking sensation that accompanied shifting. It was more intriguing than uncomfortable, and she rode it out as she welcomed wings and scales and rows of sharp teeth gnashing together.

Talons were still forming when the dragon spread her wings and let gale force winds carry her high above the desolate stretch of icy beach. She closed the transparent protective membrane that kept dirt, grit, and wind out of her eyes and surveyed an endless vista of gray and white. The bay around their headlands had turned into a sheet of ice—unusual given it was summer in Earth's southern hemisphere.

Wind buffeted her, but wasn't a match for the powerful sweep of her golden wings. After a quick assessment, she didn't sense sea-serpents anywhere near. A magical scan confirmed her findings. Maybe after their last confrontation where they'd killed a few, Surek had moved his minions elsewhere.

It was too much to hope he'd abandoned his plans to take over Earth. Not many borderworlds offered the rich biodiversity Earth did. Never mind it was slowly dying. Left to its own devices, the planet could last another few hundred years. Or more. As temperatures and oceans rose, and humans died off, the issues wreaking havoc would lessen.

If enough humans died, Earth might very well survive. Katya liked the idea of an emptier planet.

Dragons adored heat, so a warming world wasn't a deterrent to them—or their sea-serpent cousins. Keeping her magic subtle, Katya sent pulses ahead of her flight path, and off to both sides. She let her dragon take the lead. Its magic was stronger than hers, and its senses far more acute.

"There." The dragon angled a wingtip after they'd flown a few kilometers. *"And over there too."*

Katya directed her attention to the iced-over ocean—and cursed. Borrowing from a strategy they'd employed earlier, the serpents had forced a layer of ice to form and hidden beneath it. Or maybe the ice had developed on its own, and the serpents were merely taking advantage of its presence.

What a bunch of lazy bastards. Originally, they'd planned to excavate caves, but apparently it had been more work than they'd anticipated. Water was their native environment. Ice wasn't, but they must have decided to live with the cold.

Black lightning crackled from the frosty sea. Katya feinted to one side, evading it easily. *"They know we're here,"* she told the dragon.

Her bondmate didn't waste time with words. It bugled ferociously, a challenge if Katya had ever heard one.

Goddess damn dragons to hell. She'd waited too long to rein hers in, and now the beast was hellbent on destruction.

"No!" she shouted into their shared consciousness.

More bugling, followed by fire that scorched a path across several ice floes. As far as the dragon was concerned, they were under attack, and they'd meet aggression with violence of their own.

Breath mingled with smoke and flames, creating white furrows snatched away by the wind. Puffing and wheezing between gouts of fire, Katya battled her beast for ascendency.

She couldn't lose. If she did, the creature would never forget its victory, and her tenure as a dragon shifter would be seriously tarnished. If not damaged beyond redemption.

Forever.

She gnashed double rows of teeth until her jaws ached with the pressure. If the dragon couldn't open its mouth, it couldn't bugle. Nor could it toss fire about. Katya wanted to turn them around, but she didn't have enough energy to fight on more fronts than she already was.

"I. Am. Not. Your. Enemy," she ground out. "*You weaken us with your antics.*"

The dragon fought back harder, wrenching its jaws open. A single strangled bugle escaped before Katya slammed them shut again.

Softening her tone, she tried again. "*I love your spirit and your determination, but you are not in charge. You cannot be, or you will pervert our bond. Y Ddraigh Goch will force our ties asunder. You will not only be mateless, you will be forbidden from ever forming another bond.*"

Holding her mouth firmly shut despite her aching facial muscles, Katya waited. Would her dragon listen to reason? Or was it too far gone in battle lust? Such things occurred, but she did not want it to happen to her. She loved her dragon. The beast was part of her. If they couldn't be bonded anymore, she would wander bereft the rest of her days.

As quickly as it had grabbed the point, the dragon ceded it. More lightning flashed all around them as the serpents did their damnedest to blow them out of the skies. Katya started to thank her bondmate but stopped herself. The beast had been out of control.

It should thank her for reining it in.

A sharp pain along one flank, followed by the stench of burning scales, told her she'd been hit by magical lightning. "*Get us out of here!*" she shrieked.

"*Oh, so now you want my help,*" the dragon snarked.

"Yes. Your magic is stronger than mine. I command you to—"

The dragon wheeled, flying higher, beyond the reach of the serpents' lightning strikes. Katya recognized teleport magic a few seconds before they traded Antarctic shores for her lair deep within the earth. She added her own power to the dragon's to obliterate all traces of their destination.

The dragon's magic was good for big, flashy things while hers was more adept at dealing with subtleties. Her side ached, but it would heal. She hoped. She had yet to get a good look at the damage. Wounds forged by magic could be tricky to treat. The dragon brought them out in the great room. Katya waited for the teleport spell to fade before calling shift magic.

Her side burned with a fury of its own as her body reformed itself. The coppery smell of her own blood burned her nostrils before she felt a hot trail dribble down her ribs. Lifting an arm, she swiveled her head to assess her injury. Smoke steamed through clenched teeth as she regarded a long, jagged cut running from the midway point of her ribs to hip level along one side.

The edges of the gash had turned black, and they pulsed with dark magic. She could heal herself, but it would require time and concentration. First, she'd have to neutralize the sea dragons' poison. Once that was done, her flesh would knit back together.

A wave of nausea told her she needed to hurry. Right now, the venom was localized, but it would spread. It wouldn't kill her, but the longer she did nothing, the harder it would be to counteract.

Reaching up, she dragged her hair to the other side to reveal the length of the injury. It looked worst at the bottom, so she focused a beam of power on where the creeping black place was thickest.

And recoiled fast.

Her own magic shouldn't hurt, but it felt like she'd flayed open flesh with a dull knife. What the unholy hell?

Breath caught in her dry throat, and she clenched her teeth. Her magic was similar enough to the serpents' to have fed the putrescence, and the black horror was spreading fast. Katya switched spells and steeled herself as she tossed a different mix of power at the sinister enchantment dissolving her flesh.

Pain speared her, but she didn't quit. It was like controlling the dragon. She couldn't give in. If she did, the injury would outstrip her ability to corral it. Konstantin wasn't here. If he were, he'd have sensed her distress and come running.

Sweat gathered, running freely down her body. Where it dripped into the wound, it stung worse than if a wasp nest had disgorged its residents, and all of them had attacked. Still, the pain from her magic outstripped it a hundredfold.

She'd never had to deal with anything remotely near this level of agony before. It stole everything. Attention. Energy. Magic.

Her vision hazed at the edges. Desperate, she felt for the Earth's power beneath her bare feet and sucked it into her body. It didn't help nearly as much as she'd hoped it would.

The gash in her side was growing. Panic added a fine edge to her struggle.

She was working as hard as she could. And she was losing.

Hands gripped her shoulders from behind. She screeched, outraged to be beset by yet one more enemy.

"Katya!" Johan's deep voice held a sharp note. "What the hell did you do to yourself? Hold still a moment."

The room swam back into a crazy partial focus. Had she been so out of it, she hadn't heard Johan approach? Apparently. Because here he was. She struggled to make her tongue cooperate. "You can't help."

"At least let me try. What you are doing is making it worse. In just the seconds from when I first saw you to now, the wound is bigger."

A cascade of something wet gushed down her side. She bit her lip, but the pain she was certain would follow whatever he'd poured on her never materialized. She jumped on the respite and focused more earth power at the lesion. Her earlier mistake had been to use fire. Fire was part of the serpents' workings, which was why she'd reinforced their attack on her.

Maybe the fucking serpents weren't as dumb as she'd always believed. They must have anticipated her drawing on fire, her primary element, and known it would amplify their destruction.

Probably right now, they were laughing their pointy heads off. At her expense.

Johan hovered, worry stamped into his rugged features,

but he didn't get in her way. Or try to talk. Somehow, he instinctively recognized she didn't have the energy to do anything beyond working on clearing her wound of taint.

Her breathing had devolved into panting gasps, but the blackened edges were smaller. She was certain of it. A walloping gust of magic shot through her.

The dragon.

For whatever reason, her bondmate had decided to help. Once it added its power to the mix, the margins of her injury lost all trace of taint. Puckery and white, they began to draw closer. Exhaustion dragged at her, but she remained on her feet, determined to keep going until the flesh had knitted together. At least the pain had receded from stabbing knives to a manageable dull ache.

The walls of the great room faded in and out of focus. She swayed on her feet. Johan's voice sounded like he was a lot farther than half a meter from her when he said. "I am no doctor, but I believe your work is done."

Before she could protest she had to be certain, he'd put an arm around her and led her to a pile of cushions. She fell heavily onto them, whimpers catching in her throat.

He handed her a half-empty flask. She drank from it, feeling an immediate lift from the magic Kon used when he brewed the mildly alcoholic infusion.

"I take it you located the serpents," Johan said.

She nodded. "I got into a power struggle with my dragon. Because I was focused on keeping her from taking on however many serpents hid beneath the ice—and losing—I wasn't as maneuverable as I would have liked."

Smoke and ash puffed from Katya's tired mouth. The dragon apparently didn't care for her assertion they would have lost.

"But you were in the air, right? How far does that poison of theirs spread?" He shook dark hair out of his eyes. "I thought you were immortal. How could you have been so gravely wounded?"

Katya scraped the heels of her hands down her cheeks. She was weary to her bones, but she'd been tired before. This wasn't any different. "They sent lightning bolts into the sky. One hit us. I had no idea how bad it was until I was back in my human form. If I'd known, I'd have stayed a dragon."

"Do they heal faster?"

"Yes." Katya upended the flask and drained it. "Was this what you poured on me?" At his nod, she went on. "Brilliant move, but how did you know to do it?"

"Beginner's luck?" He shrugged, but the corners of his eyes crinkled with pleasure at her compliment. "I would love to claim I knew precisely what I was about, but I did not. In my world, alcohol cleanses injuries like yours. Why did the drink help?"

"Because this particular batch contains Konstantin's magic. Lucky for me. He and I trade off brewing our drink, and his magic augments mine."

Johan drew his brows together. "You did not look like you were doing very well when I ran in here. Could you have died?"

"No, but I might have wandered long in dark places before finding my way back." Katya sat up straight, reminded just how precious time was. "The serpents would love it if I dropped out of sight for even a few days. Months or annums would be even better. Every single day allows them to grow stronger."

"I am starting to see the need for more dragon shifters—or at least more magical creatures."

"Does that mean you still plan an attempt to transform yourself?" Katya was too tired for subtleties. If they were going to petition Y Ddraigh Goch, they needed to get on with it. On the other hand, if she was returning Johan to wherever he wished to wait out Armageddon, she wanted to get that over with too.

She would miss him. A lot. But humans had no place in magical warfare. She rolled her eyes. She'd barely come through in one piece, and her magic was robust.

"What was all that about?"

"All what?" She quirked a brow, shocked how much energy such a small thing absorbed.

"Not sure. You appeared beleaguered. Understandable after what you just went through."

"How'd you know to look for me?"

His mouth twisted downward in one corner. "I heard you screaming."

Her eyes widened.

"You did not know?"

She shook her head. "I was immersed in a critical battle to save myself." Katya rolled to her feet, still feeling shaky but much better than before. "We should go."

Johan raked her from head to toe with a frank gaze that,

for once, didn't hold dual intents. "We will leave, but you will feel better if you wash the blood off."

Katya snorted. "And you'll probably like it if I don't stink of serpent poison." She crinkled her nose at the acrid, rotten reek. "I can smell myself. You'll wait here?"

"Close enough. I will be in the kitchen."

She motioned for Johan to stand. When he did, she said, "Food is in the far corner of the room. You can't see the cabinets but if you get close enough, you'll stumble into them. Once you touch one, they'll become visible."

"I remember. I am looking forward to the magical part of becoming a shifter."

Katya narrowed her eyes. "And the dragon part?" Smoke puffed through her mouth. Her bondmate was interested in his answer as well.

"It is something I will have to experience—" he began.

Katya felt burning as fire rose from her chest. She averted her head before it blasted out her mouth. *"Be nice,"* she told her dragon. *"He helped me."*

Fire ceded to steam. Billows of it puffed around them. The heat eased the residual ache in her side. "I'll meet you in the kitchen," she told Johan.

"I shall find something for us to eat. And then we will leave."

He sounded resolute, determined. Before she picked his intent apart, she summoned magic to take her to the lake. A quick rinse, and she'd join him inside.

"I don't know," her dragon muttered.

"You can't know everything," she told her bondmate.

"Some things require faith. If we believe he can manage the transformation, it'll help him a whole lot more than if we're nattering nellies casting doubt in a wide net."

For once, the dragon didn't reply.

Katya waded into the lake. When it hit her at waist level, she ducked all the way beneath the water. Surfacing, she sputtered, blowing out bubbles and tossing her wet hair across her shoulders. The dunking had a salutary effect, but it was time to go inside.

"Please," she murmured, not addressing anyone in particular, "Johan is a good man. Help him find a way through what lies before us."

"I will do everything I can," her dragon said, surprising her.

Cantankerous and uppity, the dragon could be compassionate too. Love for her beast filled her, wiping out her annoyance its highhandedness had nearly landed her in deep trouble.

That was the thing with loving someone. You loved all of them. Not just the easy-to-swallow parts. A smile curved her lips, and she teleported back inside.

CHAPTER 3

*D*espite stumbling about locating the hidden cupboards, I managed to have a few things ready by the time Katya materialized in the kitchen. I'd be lying if I didn't admit to wanting to be able to think a location and pull a "Beam-Me-Up-Scotty" trick to make it happen.

She and I made small talk as we ate, and I was grateful she wasn't grilling me about my residual concerns. How could I not harbor at least a few? I was leaving everything I've ever known and embracing a very different life.

"Where are we headed?" I asked and pushed back from the table. She'd rinsed off the worst of the bloody residue streaking down her side, and we'd eaten enough for now.

Katya laced her fingers together and rested her chin on them. "I've been thinking how best to proceed."

For some reason, her words surprised me. I'd assumed

this was like any other project with a set number of steps, but perhaps magical undertakings weren't like that.

"What did you come up with?"

"Konstantin and Erin aren't here. I'm fairly certain he moved her to the liminal space between worlds."

I held up a hand, not wanting to interrupt but needing to understand. "Why there?"

"It's easier for the dragon god to intervene." After a pause, she went on. "Sorry, I'm searching for a way to explain something that's happened so rarely I lack a method to describe it."

I recalled earlier conversations among the four of us where either Katya or her brother had said something to the effect that humans turning into dragon shifters were the stuff of myth and legend.

"So will we go to this liminal area too?" I pressed. Now that I'd made up my mind, I wanted to get moving. To see if I was going to pass muster or be kicked to the curb.

Katya angled her head to one side and regarded me, her golden eyes reflecting serious consideration. "Kon picked a traditional route. First the space between worlds, and then a borderworld of the dragon god's choosing."

I should have kept my mouth shut, but asking questions was as natural as breathing for me. "How do you know they made it as far as a borderworld?"

The corners of her mouth twitched. "They'd be back by now if they hadn't travelled beyond the liminal space."

"One if by land, two if by sea," I muttered.

"What?" She shot an odd look my way, and I didn't blame her.

"Nothing. Your deductive logic makes perfect sense."

"Another term I'm not familiar with." She shrugged. "Anyway, you wanted to know my thoughts. Here they are. We can mirror Konstantin's journey, but it might take longer. When we are in the place between worlds, we aren't in anyone's way. Y Ddraigh Goch can wait as long as he wishes to respond to our petition."

"What option do you recommend?" My question was more formal than I wished, yet it was familiar ground. I'd asked variants of that same query hundreds of times through my engineering career.

She blew out a tight breath. "If we begin on a borderworld, we'll be in someone's gunsights immediately. The presence of strangers on borderworlds doesn't pass without notice."

I frowned. "What have you left out?"

She thinned her lips. "Insightful of you. If we pick the wrong borderworld—or a string of them—we'll waste even more time than if we'd begun in the liminal boundary."

"What would happen on these incorrect worlds?"

"We'd be run off, forced to leave."

Confusion swamped me. "Weren't you and Konstantin planning to visit a chain of borderworlds to solicit aid?" She nodded, so I went on. "How is this different?"

"We're dragon shifters."

"Which means they would tolerate you, but not someone like me."

"Yes. It's been a long while since I've visited any other worlds. Things may have changed, but on the ones where humans coexist with magic, it's much as it is here where humans don't know creatures like us exist. Your kinsmen wouldn't bother us, but nor would they do anything beyond slow us down."

She unlaced her fingers and stretched them in front of her. "I talked myself out of taking a shortcut. We'll follow Kon's lead and begin in the place between worlds."

Katya stood and gestured for me to come close. Before I did, I patted the open front of my insulated suit. "Will I need anything this heavy?"

"I don't know. Is it uncomfortable?"

"I'm too warm with it on." Without waiting for her to answer, I toed off my boots and skinned out of my polar one-piece suit, draping it over a chair. I still had plenty of clothing. Dual layers of long johns and a down jacket and pants. I slid the green, triple-layer neoprene boots back onto my feet over double socks and positioned myself next to Katya.

Her scent changed depending on her mood. Right now it was an alluring mix of sunbaked clay, vanilla, and cloves. Steam puffed from her mouth, and the distinctive feel of dragon shifter magic made the small hairs on the back of my neck prickle. It wasn't unpleasant. Far from it. Anticipation swept through me. I may have dillydallied a bit, but I was ready.

The plan I'd hatched while staring at the lake was a simple one. When it came to where I lobbied the dragon god

—or the dragon—I'd opt for absolute honesty and tell them I always followed through on my commitments. This wouldn't be an exception. I offered a pure heart and a willing spirit.

In my imagined conversations, I stopped shy of asking what more could they possibly want? In truth, probably a whole hell of a lot. Like a man who'd always nurtured a secret desire to fly or breathe fire. I couldn't lie, though. If I did, it would go worse for me. They'd know, and I'd be finished.

The feel of Katya's magic intensified, turning the air warm and golden. She wrapped her arms around me. "Hang on," she instructed. "I don't want to lose you."

Although we were in one another's arms, it wasn't anything like my fantasies of holding her. I'd spun plenty of them where I settled my mouth over hers. Imagining how her lips would feel beneath mine, how her breath would quicken once our kiss took off and developed a life of its own... I cut that train of thought off fast. Having her close enough I felt the jut of her breasts against my chest was tantalizing, but none of this was about sex.

It was about transforming me.

Katya was going well out of her way. Because of me. Was she doing all this because she was fond of me? Or was she desperate to grow an army to defeat the serpents, no matter where the soldiers came from?

I told my cock to stand down, but it never listened to what I wanted. Surely, she could feel the length of me pressing into her belly. I was embarrassed, but I'd tossed fuel onto the pyre with my kissing imagery.

I gave myself a good mental shake as the kitchen walls shimmered into black nothingness. What lay ahead would require 110 percent of my concentration. I had to convince first myself, and then whoever examined me, of the purity of my intent.

That I wanted to become a dragon shifter for myself, not so I'd be more attractive mate material for Katya. She was so close, though, she was all I could think about. My cock twitched, harder than it had been a moment before. To divert myself, I drew out a few calculus equations in my mind and set about solving them. When that proved too easy, I went through the periodic table, listing the elements in order with their respective atomic numbers.

Katya's rich contralto rose and fell around us. Her words were in a language I'd never heard before. I was certain I'd be able to pick it up, given half a chance. One of the advantages of growing up in Europe is we all speak several languages with a few dialects tossed in on the side.

I didn't detect any sense of movement after the kitchen vanished. We appeared to be suspended in a black void. In defiance of the laws of physics, I could see Katya. The warm glow that surrounded her was far more pronounced here. When she fell silent, I asked, "Is there anything I should be doing?"

"I don't believe so. I have petitioned the dragon shifter god on your behalf. Now we wait."

"How long?"

She tilted her head and looked at me. "As long as it takes. You humans are a literal bunch. Time isn't nearly as important as you believe."

"It is if you only live eighty years or so—give or take a decade."

"True enough. Quiet your mind. It may speed things up."

I nodded. I was nervous, although men hate to admit such things. When I'm edgy, I fill in with talk, but Katya had all but ordered me to remain silent. I tried closing my eyes, but that didn't last long. Control may not be much more than an illusion on the best of days, but I liked to believe I had the upper hand.

Except in this situation, I didn't. I was the greenest of neophytes, and I'd do well to hold that knowledge front and center.

A buzzing grew around me until my ears complained. Pulsing, pounding, shrill. I raised my hands to clap them over my ears and realized Katya wasn't there anymore

"Katya!" I yelled her name, but she didn't answer.

When had she left?

Why hadn't she told me?

Without her, why wasn't I plummeting down through blackness? What was keeping me suspended in this void?

Aw shit. Without her, how would I get back? Was I destined to float in this alien place forever?

If I was, how long would forever entail? Maybe not long since I'd die without water in short order.

Except this wasn't Earth. Maybe things were different here. Maybe—

"Stop!" I shouted the word. My mind was on a rampage when what I needed was calm. No one—magical or otherwise—would want anything to do with a raving madman.

The buzzing stopped as abruptly as it had begun, leaving my ears ringing.

I've never been much for frou-frou things like meditation, but I sucked in a breath, a big one, all the way to the bottom of my lungs. After holding it there, I blew it out slowly and repeated the process.

I focused the entirety of my consciousness on breathing. When I had a handle on it, I added a few bits like imagining peace and tranquility filling me when I inhaled, and uncertainties leaving with every exhale.

I feel sheepish to admit this, but it did make me feel better. More settled. More balanced. Maybe there was something to that meditation crap after all. I've always respected the Dalai Lama, and I felt ashamed for doubting the cornerstone of Tibetan Buddhism. I have no idea how long I floated, but long enough to become resigned to nothing ever changing.

This wasn't all that bad.

I'd been in worse places, like when the Russians broke my femur and left me for dead. Guilt pricked. I wanted to help save Earth from the serpents, but I couldn't do it from here.

More time passed. I might have dozed off and on. The next time my eyes flickered open, I said, "I'm ready. I wish to become a dragon shifter."

Nothing changed. The endless vista of black didn't even flicker.

"I'm ready," I repeated, my voice louder this time.

"Are you?" An amorphous voice echoed around me.

It startled me, but I kept right on floating. What choice did I have? I started to ask who'd spoken, but didn't. Somehow I understood this wasn't a juncture for me to question anyone. I opened my mouth to say, *I think so*, but changed it out for one word. "Yes."

I had to project confidence.

Doubt would be my undoing.

The buzzing rose again, following by a crackling like sheets of aluminum foil rubbing together. My womblike existence shattered, and I was swept into another dark place, except this one lacked air. I longed for my thick suit; it might have held a few residual oxygen molecules within its weave. As it was, I tucked my nose into my down jacket. It didn't help much.

My lungs first ached and then burned. The ringing in my ears grew louder, and my vision narrowed. I shouldn't be able to see anything, not without a light source to reflect back, yet I could see my body. I sucked at the airless ether reflexively. My lungs were on fire.

Christ!

If I was going to die, I'd have preferred drowning. From everything I've read, it was easy after that first sweep of water entered your lungs. Suffocation, on the other hand...

Shut up, my inner voice shouted. Dead was dead. What difference did the manner of its making matter?

A cavalcade of everyone who'd ever meant anything to me marched through my fading mind. I should fight, but what could I do? After three minutes, my brain would begin to die. Once it checked out, nothing else would work, either.

Something like a giant horse's hoof kicked me in the rump. I catapulted through a barrier that cut through layers of fabric, shredding my clothing, and landed sprawled on my belly, gasping like a gutted fish.

It took a moment for me to understand I was breathing again. Wherever I was had air. I got to my hands and knees and rolled to my feet remembering the voice that had come out of nowhere asking if I was ready.

I winced. I'd made a horribly poor showing. If a dragon was out there somewhere, I was certain it had left in disgust. A quick look around convinced me I wasn't beneath Antarctica anymore. This place had ancient evergreens, but they weren't any variety I'd ever seen before. Their needles were shades of blue and silver. Brush grew beneath the trees in the form of a manzanita-looking plant with shiny orange bark and red leaves.

The dirt was normal color. So were the rocks. Rolling land extended as far as I could see. From overhead a sun shone in an ochre sky, but didn't produce any warmth. It wasn't cold, not by Antarctic standards. Perhaps minus two Celsius.

My oxygen-starved brain was coming back online. If I wasn't at Katya's, and I wasn't in the void between worlds, it had to mean I'd passed the first test. I was on a borderworld.

Elation filled me, rolling upward from my toes.

I wanted to whoop, to cheer, but after making an arse out of myself during the transit from where I'd been separated from Katya to here, I opted for a more dignified approach. I started by tucking shreds of my tattered down jacket into holes the barrier had sliced through it. Feathers floated around me.

Where was Katya?

I didn't believe she'd have left me unless something forced her away. In her own way, she was as much of a control freak as me. I couldn't envision her embarking on a project and abandoning it partway through.

I turned in a full circle, checking to make certain I hadn't missed anything. My ears had quit ringing, and the tempting sound of running water reached me. I was thirsty. God only knows how long I'd hung in the place between worlds. Nothing else was happening, so I angled toward where I was certain I'd find water.

Would it be safe to drink?

I grimaced. What a twenty-first century question. Men had been drinking water out of creeks, brooks, and lakes forever. It was only during the past hundred years or so anyone had questioned the practice.

I ducked beneath a particularly lush tree, and a small, babbling brook skittered past my boots. The water was clear. I squatted and cupped my hands. The sight of them, dirty and stained, brought me up short. Rather than using my hands as a cup, I lay on my belly and dropped my mouth into the flow. After a tentative swallow, where I determined it tasted like water, I drank until I wasn't thirsty any longer.

If the stream contained some stray microbes that did me in, so be it. I couldn't carry on with whatever my life had turned into if I suspected everything was out to get me. Nothing would be familiar, and I had to suck it up and get used to it.

I got my hands and knees under me, moved back into a crouch, and spied a reasonably flat rock. This was a peaceful spot. If I had more waiting to do, it was as good a place as any. After brushing dirt off the front of me, I settled on the rock.

The rushing creek was mesmerizing, but I did my damnedest to remain alert. I had the oddest sense something was lurking unseen watching me. But maybe I'd imagined it. My eyes wanted to close in the worst way. I fought the sensation, but my lids grew heavier and heavier.

Just when I was starting to wonder if I'd stumbled into a reenactment of Rip Van Winkle—at least he woke up eventually—images took on a kaleidoscopic quality behind my half-closed lids. When I gave up and let them fall, an emerald-green dragon took shape. Huge and beautiful, its wings were spread, and its golden eyes whirled.

"Are you my dragon?" I flinched at my presumptuousness, but I couldn't take the words back.

"*Are you my human?*" it countered, its words resonating inside my head. Understated humor laced its question, and I knew it was mocking me. Strangely, I didn't care.

I felt humble in the creature's presence. Everything Katya had cautioned me about, including the importance of maintaining the upper hand, frittered to dust.

"I'd like to be," I replied.

"Take off your clothes and stand in my presence."

I hastened to comply, but it felt like I was swimming through thick honey. My motions were slow and clumsy. Finally, I stood naked and shivering a little. My eyes were open, so of course the dragon had disappeared.

"Open your mind to me," thundered through my head.

I held an image of the dragon and imagined dropping all my boundaries. It was hard. I'd always held a part of myself aloof from everyone. To rip myself open down to my very foundations required a leap of faith.

Either I did this or begged the dragon to help me return to Earth. A half-assed attempt would be worse than none at all. Several times, I reached a place where I was certain I'd done everything I could. When nothing happened, I dug deeper and peeled back one more layer.

I discovered parts of myself I'd forgotten about. Parts I hadn't fully known existed. Regardless of today's outcome, I understood myself a whole lot better. If by some miracle Earth survived, I hoped I'd be less of an arrogant jerk when the tide wasn't running in my favor.

With no warning, something sharp blasted into the center of my chest followed immediately by what felt like hundreds of razor-sharp knives piercing my skin. I wasn't imagining it. Blood spurted from gashes all over my body. I smelled it and felt its thick heat gushing down my flesh.

I ground my jaws, did everything in my power to hold back the scream in my throat. Men didn't screech. The sharp thwack of bones cracking undid me. I hollered, bellowed, squealed. I fell to the dirt since my broken legs wouldn't hold me upright.

Had the dragon found me unworthy? Was that why it was killing me?

"Visualize me," it shouted into my mind. *"Jump into my body."*

"How?" The word tore out of me, drowned by the next scream. How much more could I hurt before I blacked out?

My eyes were scrunched shut, but I couldn't see the dragon any longer. Had all this been a hallucination? Not the pain part. My body was truly broken beyond hope of redemption. No one could be hurt this badly and survive.

Maybe there'd never been any dragon at all.

"If you do not believe in me, you will die, human."

A ringing slap across my cheek forced my eyes open. Katya bent over me, her face contorted by fury and horror. "Goddess damn everything. Johan. Reach for your dragon. Do it now."

"I cannot see it. Not any longer."

She gripped the sides of my face; her power flooded into me. I had no idea if my eyes were open or closed, but the dragon hovered in front of me, forelegs extended and fire blazing from its mouth.

With the last dregs of my strength, I reached for the green behemoth, imagined blending my consciousness with it. It was the hardest thing I've ever done. Every part of me hurt. The only thing holding me steady was Katya's magic wrapped around me.

And then it too departed, and I plunged into blackness.

CHAPTER 4

Short While Earlier

Katya still floated in the place between worlds, but a different spot from where she'd been next to Johan. The dragon god was here. He'd spirited her away. Knowing it was probably useless, she raised her mind voice and called Konstantin, but her brother didn't answer.

"What are you doing?" she screamed at Y Ddraigh Goch. "Johan's helpless in a magical world. He needs me."

"His dragon must ensure he is worthy of the bond," the god replied.

"I don't care. You had no right to drag me from his side. He won't understand what's happened."

"You forget yourself." Y Ddraigh Goch drew himself up to his full height. Despite him being in his dragon body and her being human, their heads were level with one another. His scales were silver and gold, and his eyes held an endless collage as they told one story after another, chronicling dragon shifters from the beginnings of time.

Katya recoiled. She'd always had a temper, but the god was right. Even if she didn't agree with what he'd done, she'd overstepped her boundaries by a good big bunch.

"I'm sorry, but he trusted me—"

"And now, he will have to trust me," the god cut in.

Hot words bubbled from her throat, but she bit her tongue. Johan wouldn't have understood why she suddenly wasn't by his side, arms wrapped protectively around him. Worse, he'd have no idea what to do.

"Look at me, daughter."

Katya tilted her head back, regarding the dragon god.

He nodded. "Better. You came to me, requested the human become a dragon shifter. Do you not have faith he is strong enough, resourceful enough, to find his own path?"

She tried to look away but couldn't. The question was a two-edged sword. If she didn't have faith in Johan's courage and ingenuity, she had no business petitioning for his transformation.

"It's not that I don't have faith..." She faltered, but then more words forced their way through. "I didn't instruct him sufficiently, mostly because I had no idea how the process would unfold."

"It hasn't happened often," Y Ddraigh Goch agreed.

Katya chewed her lower lip and chose her next words with care. "If I give you my word not to interfere unless it is absolutely necessary, will you tell me where he is?"

"Do you offer a blood bond?"

"Absolutely." She would have done anything to return to Johan's side.

"Hold up your hand."

She did. He dipped his mouth until he nicked her fingers with his sharp teeth, binding her with her blood. Katya drew her hand back and waited. She'd done her part. Time dribbled past; she remained floating in the liminal space, eye to eye with the dragon god. She didn't wish to anger him, but worry bit deep.

Finally, she couldn't stand it any longer. "I gave my word."

"I understand."

She wanted to ask why she was still here and not where she could keep an eye on Johan. Instead, she tempered her question. "When will I be allowed to keep watch?"

"Soon. I am orchestrating this venture."

"So you're watching over him?" It was the first piece of maybe decent news she'd had since being yanked from Johan's side.

The god's eyes zeroed in on her, reminding her she'd overstepped herself—again. "Keeping him safe isn't my job. He must be strong. The first transformation is very difficult."

Which was precisely why she wanted to be there. If the lore was correct, many humans had died. Katya couldn't hold the words back. "Why am I still here? I gave you my word. My blood."

"He may not need you."

But I need him.

The thought cut through her like a knife, sobering her. It

was the first time she'd admitted to herself how much Johan had come to mean to her. When she'd floated the idea of him becoming a dragon shifter, she'd assumed she'd be there, overseeing every step along the way.

If the other dragon became unruly, she'd planned to shift to her beast and— And what? Browbeat it into submission? The bond didn't work like that. She had no control over any shifter binding beyond her own. Guilt left a foul taste on her tongue. She'd been a fool, and Johan would be the one to pay for her hubris.

"Please." Her voice wavered. "If he dies because he trusted me…"

"He would have died had you returned him to anywhere on Earth," the god reminded her. "Perhaps not as quickly, but the serpents are intent on establishing dominion." He shook his great head; fire flew from his jaws. "I should have expunged them from all worlds when I had a chance. Once I banished them—misplaced mercy, if ever there was such—I lost the opportunity."

"I see." Katya nodded.

"Some outcomes are worth risking everything for, Daughter."

Steam puffed from the dragon god's mouth, surrounding Katya. He meant it to be soothing, but she couldn't let go of worry cutting a path through her. It wasn't a lack of faith in Johan. He was plenty competent.

In his own world. With his own people.

Her domain was brand new for him. She hoped to hell he remembered everything she'd said about starting out in control with his new bondmate. If the dragon thought it could run wild, bit in its teeth, the partnership would be doomed from the gate.

The liminal space shattered around Katya, and she catapulted through blackness. She knew this place, had been here many times. It was unpleasant since there was no air, but that part was always short-lived. A barrier brushed past and she dropped onto a borderworld. A hasty glance told her she'd never been here before, but it wasn't surprising.

There were thousands of borderworlds, perhaps tens of thousands. She'd only visited a bare handful. She stilled her uneasiness and sent a questing thread of power outward. If Y Ddraigh Goch had released his hold on her, it must mean Johan's transformation was complete.

Or he was in trouble.

A tortured scream filled her ears, echoing all around her. She forgot about magic and sprinted toward the agonized bellowing. Johan sprawled on the ground. From the looks of things, most of his bones were broken. Blood pooled around him. She kindled her power and looked through her third eye. A green dragon hovered nearby, regarding Johan's shattered remains.

"What have you done?" Katya demanded.

"Not me," the dragon said indignantly. *"Him. He gave up too soon. I cannot help him."*

She didn't waste any more words. Bounding to Johan's side, she squatted next to him and called his name. He was too far gone to hear her. Hating herself for what came next, she slapped him. The last thing she wanted was to hurt him further, but she had to get through. It worked. He opened his eyes, and they seared her soul. She'd seen eyes like his in Hell. Tortured. Persecuted. Desperate.

"Goddess damn everything. Johan. Reach for your dragon. Do it now."

"I cannot see it. Not any longer."

She gripped the sides of his face and forced magic into him, determined to augment his waning strength. Had Y Ddraigh Goch waited too long before releasing her? Moments passed, and she feared Johan had moved beyond where even an infusion of magic could help him bond with his dragon.

Her heart seized in her chest, and she moaned low in her throat. She felt her dragon's presence. *"In Y Ddraigh Goch's name,"* her beast intoned, *"you will help this human join with you."*

She would have thanked her bondmate for trying to wring some effort from the green dragon, but she had nothing to spare. Every shred of power at her disposal was focused on Johan.

He rallied, but she didn't slack off. What she was doing was helping.

Would it be enough?

Come on, she urged silently, willing him success with every last particle of her being. The tattered lump of flesh that had been Johan wavered. Had she imagined it because she wanted it so desperately? Katya directed her third eye at him, sharpening her senses.

All in a rush, his body faded to nothing. In its place, the green dragon stood, fully corporeal, fanning its wings.

Too angry to savor her victory, Katya leapt to her feet and shook a fist skyward. "You could have done more. He almost died."

"Like what? I told him to reach for me. And I told him he had to try harder, that he would die." The dragon's voice rumbled through her head.

Bright light seared her corneas. Y Ddraigh Goch appeared in the center of a nimbus of blue-white illumination. The dragon god looked from her to the green dragon and nodded. "It appears we snatched victory from the jaws of defeat." He focused his next words at Katya. "Shift and fly with them."

She was still furious at how close a call they'd had. "Should we make certain Johan is even in there?" she retorted.

Fire roared from the god. She sidestepped it nimbly. "I deserved that, I suppose, but I kept my word."

"You had to," the god observed acidly. "I did not release you until—"

"Johan was nearly dead," she muttered.

"I am all right. I think," Johan spoke up. *"I may never want to shift again, but I made it through. Thank you. If it hadn't been for your magic—"* Fire shot from the green dragon's mouth, followed by ash. It was obviously annoyed by Johan's gratitude being aimed at her.

"What?" Katya planted herself squarely in front of the green dragon. "You wish to take all the credit?"

"No, but it appears you would," the dragon replied coolly.

"Will you quarrel or fly?" the god inquired. "There is cause for celebration. We have a new dragon shifter in our midst."

Katya shoved her temper aside. Y Ddraigh Goch was correct. She bowed, not low, but enough to indicate acquiescence. "Thank you for bonding with Johan Petris," she told the dragon, keeping her tone formal. "I appreciate your willingness to take a chance on an untried human."

The dragon inclined its head. *"Will you fly with us?"*

She felt her dragon champing at the bit. It had stood up to the green dragon when Johan was dying, and now it wanted to make peace. Her magical well was low, but she kicked what was left of it open and trusted her beast would do the rest. It did. The familiar stretching moved from her head downward. It took a little longer than she was used to, but soon enough, her golden scales shone brightly in the muted light of this world.

For once, she was amenable to turning things over to her bondmate. She was giddy from relief Johan had made the leap into the dragon. When reading through the lore books, she'd always assumed the tales of humans dropping dead were overblown.

Apparently, they'd all been true.

The green dragon spread his wings and let the air currents lift him into the skies. Her dragon leapt skyward, joining it. For a time, they flew gently this way and that. *"What do you think?"* she asked Johan.

"I am still recovering, but this is amazing. Will my body, the human one, ever be habitable again?"

"Oh yes."

"How?"

"Our magic is repairing it right now," his dragon cut in.

Its words were a sharp reminder to her that she was no longer the only one interested in Johan's welfare. If she was wise, she'd back off enough to let the bond between man and dragon grow and deepen. When they overflew the spot they'd begun, Y Ddraigh Goch was gone.

Of course, he would be. His task here was done. Perhaps Johan hadn't had as close a call as she feared. She'd gotten there in time, hadn't she?

She started to suggest they'd flown enough for a first flight but decided to let the green dragon make that call. It bugled and angled toward a herd of something that looked a bit like striped deer. She watched as the dragon singled out its prey, cutting it from the crowd.

"We shall hunt as well," her dragon informed her.

Katya didn't contradict it. She needed energy, and feeding would help replenish her magic. Their animal was nice and fat. Her dragon snatched it in powerful jaws before rising back into the air. The first bite of succulent flesh woke every nerve ending in her mouth. Flying and chewing weren't a good mix, though. Too many food bits dropped out of the sky. Her bondmate settled to earth and proceeded to consume flesh and organs, crunching through bones and hoofs last.

The delightful, copper smell of blood was thick in her

nostrils, and she slid her tongue over her scaled lips to capture the last of it. Not surprisingly, the rest of the herd had made themselves scarce.

Next to her, the green dragon finished the last of its kill.

"How are you doing?" she asked Johan.

"He is fine." The green dragon regarded her balefully.

"I can answer for myself."

Katya hooded her eyes, delighted Johan wasn't going to sit back and let his bondmate determine his every move. Perhaps some of what she'd told him had sunk in.

"What would both of you like to do?" she asked brightly.

The green dragon, who stood half a head taller than her, lowered its head so their eyes were on a level plane. *"My bondmate has done well for today. It's time for him to shift back to his other form. He requires practice with shift magic."*

A muted squawk rose from Johan. *"Is there a step-by-step instruction manual? I do not wish a repeat of my transition from man to dragon."*

Katya waited, not wanting to annoy the green dragon any more than she already had. This dragon could well end up being their mate. Maybe. She had no idea what her dragon thought of him. There certainly hadn't been a plethora of oohs and aahs, though.

If her dreams materialized and Johan longed for her the same way she desired him, her bondmate would have to agree with her choice of a mate. At least so far, their time with the green dragon hadn't been particularly auspicious.

Katya kicked herself. They had significantly more in front of them than her misplaced desire for a mate. Getting back to Earth was paramount. Finding Kon and Erin ran a close second. Had Erin bonded with a dragon of her own? Or was she even now sitting among humans at the Polish base?

Erin's fate aside, they still had an unimaginable amount of work ahead of them. Every day they burned through to better prepare themselves, the serpents' magic was strengthening. Soon they would no longer be vulnerable in their human form. Once they couldn't be killed, there'd be no way to defeat them.

"The transition is simple." The green dragon belched steam.

"A few pointers would be appreciated." Johan's dry humor shone through. For some reason, it heartened her. He wasn't blaming his dragon for the last shift—the one that had nearly killed him.

"Hold an image of your other body," the dragon began.

"Which one?" Johan cut in.

"You only have one." The dragon corrected him.

"All right. Before or after most of my bones broke?"

"Before, of course," the dragon replied stiffly.

Katya thought Johan might be stalling. Made sense since he'd been in excruciating agony when she found him. *"Simplest thing in the world,"* she spoke up. *"Imagine your human form and fall headfirst into it. Like this."*

She summoned power, saw the characteristic flash, and tumbled into her other body. The deer-like animal had boosted her energy. She wasn't quite back to full strength, but near enough fingers replaced talons quicker than she expected. She stood in front of the green dragon and appealed to it.

"We can help him through this. Tell me when you're ready, and—"

"He does not require your magic. Mine will be sufficient." Smoke and ash rained down on her.

She batted it aside, along with the dressing down she longed to shout in his face.

"Hopefully, I will not need anything beyond my own ability," Johan said. The confident, resolute note was back in his voice. Katya wanted to applaud, but it would truly offend his bondmate.

Light flickered, brightened—and died. Johan tried again. This time, the flash was brighter, but it didn't yield the transformation, either.

"Take your time," Katya urged. "Think it and let it happen. No hurry."

Magic built around her—not hers. She knew better than to interfere after the green dragon had warned her off. The air thickened with the scents of sunbaked clay and burning wood. The scorched cedar smell intensified, rich and earthy. Katya bundled positive energy into belief in Johan, adding his dragon as an afterthought.

The next time brilliance glittered all around the clearing, the dragon shimmered to nothing. Johan stepped from the middle of a cloud of magic. His eyes still whirled, and his hands and feet still sported talons, but they were ceding to fingers and toes. Fine red lines crisscrossed his body, the remnants from his injuries.

Katya wanted to run to him, throw her arms around his broad shoulders, but she held back. It wasn't just the two of them. Their dragons hovered nearby. She bowed her head. "Thank you, Johan's bondmate, for seeing him safely back to his other form."

Johan nodded. "My dragon appreciates your acknowledgement." He shook himself from head to toe and looked down at his body. "I still cannot believe I am whole again."

She wanted him to come to her, but he didn't.

"How are you?" she asked.

"Not certain. It is a lot to take in."

"I bet you have questions. Maybe not right this moment, but consider me a resource—in addition to your dragon." She smiled encouragement, pleased she'd included his dragon in her comment. Bondmates you were born with didn't require ongoing acknowledgement. Apparently, the ones who volunteered to take on projects—like fully grown humans—were an entirely different breed.

Was it just dragons? Or did all varieties of shifter pluck a page from the same rulebook?

"We should return to Earth," Johan said. "But I need to locate my clothes, first."

Katya clasped her hands in front of her. "Excellent. Your second magical project. Think about how you piled them wherever you left them."

He shut his eyes. "Got it. Now what?"

Katya hesitated. How did you start from nothing? "Air is best for seeking spells. Instruct it to show you the way."

Johan set his mouth in a tight line. Annoyed crinkles formed at the corners of his eyes. "Come here and show me, please. It is simpler than me floundering about making one mistake after another."

It wasn't quite how she'd envisioned standing next to him again, but she walked to him and turned so they were both facing the same direction. "Raise one arm," she said, demonstrating. "Open your hand. Tell the wind to flow across your palm. When you feel the air moving, close your fist around it. Toss the ball of air while telling it to find your garments."

"How will that help?"

She quirked a brow his way. "Try it and see."

It took three tries before a small wind tunnel formed. Johan knew to follow the air current without her telling him to. She stood next to him and waited while he hurriedly got into his many layers of clothing. He was quiet, and she wasn't certain what to make of it.

She debated a peek into his mind, but his dragon would know and probably resent the hell out of her intrusion.

"I can teach you how to warm yourself without all those garments," she ventured.

"No need for it," he replied. "With so much to learn, that is a very low priority."

Katya moved nearer him. "What's wrong?"

He zipped his jacket while feathers fluttered around them from places the coat was torn. When he finally turned to face her, his expression held a closed-off aspect. "I do not feel very good about this, but being at the bottom of the heap is not a comfortable spot. I have traded competence and skill for the inability to accomplish the simplest tasks without someone watching over me."

Katya narrowed her eyes. So much for Johan being steeped in wonder at his transformation to a magical being. Where was his enthusiasm? The way his face had lit up when he'd discovered magic was more than the purview of books and movies?

"You haven't lost any of the skills you had," she pointed out.

"Maybe not, but they are not much good anymore."

Something inside her snapped. For the second time that day, she slapped him, but not nearly as hard as she had when life was fading from him.

He recoiled and rubbed the side of his face. "What the hell did you do that for?"

"When you're done feeling sorry for yourself, we can talk. Meanwhile, we're going home. You can pay attention and learn something new, or you can sulk. Your choice."

Breath hissed through his teeth. "Of course, I wish to learn. I do not know what is wrong with me. Tell me the steps to move us from here to Antarctica. If I can help in some small way, I am willing."

His tone was strained, formal. She cursed herself for an impatient fool, but she didn't have time to coddle him. Magic was new to him. Shifting was scary, but he had to hit the ground with all burners engaged.

The serpents wouldn't wait for him to come to terms with his new ability. They'd prefer him timid and insecure.

Beyond that, his dragon would abandon him if he didn't pull his act together better than this.

"All right." She kept her voice even. "You will control our teleport spell. The first step in virtually all magic is visualizing what you want to happen—"

"And believing you can do it," he broke in.

She stole a glance at him, encouraged he was trying. She'd feared him so mired in negativity, he was just along for the ride.

"Yes, that too," she agreed. "Faith in yourself as a magic-wielder is a cornerstone. Now, for teleport spells, we use mostly fire mixed with a smidgeon of earth..."

She'd taught young shifters before. It was comfortable ground. All she had to do was forget she'd ever entertained the idea he might be her mate. Nothing had passed between them. Not really. It should be easy enough to switch roles. If being by herself was her destiny, she may as well embrace it.

"Did I get that last part right?" I prodded Katya with an elbow since my hands were busy holding a fledgling spell together.

She seemed preoccupied. I was sure I'd been a huge disappointment to her during my brief tenure as a dragon shifter, but I needed to know if I was on the proper track. One that would spit us out on Earth.

Magic shimmered around her as she assessed my efforts. "Almost. Try blending in a very small puff of air."

"But you said fire and earth."

Katya's gaze slid over me. "So I did. Each of us brings something unique to our magic. No two shifters cast the same spell in precisely the same way."

I grinned. It was the first piece of welcome news I'd heard. So far, I had an imperious dragon nattering away in the background, and Katya tiptoeing around it. To hear I had to work things out on my own washed through me like a balm.

Still smiling, I said, "Thanks for making the leash longer. If I blow up the lab, save the pieces."

She probably wouldn't understand either metaphor, but my plate was too full to explain. I dithered about, first adding air then withdrawing it and adding water. The whole of magic—at least so far—appeared to be mental gymnastics and trial and error. Since I'm not actually trotting to the stream and pouring real water into my spell.

With no notice or fanfare, the borderworld shattered around us. My grin broadened. Not an elegant transition, but not bad for a first try. We shot through blackness as if we'd been blasted from a cannon.

I may have whooped, but this felt like a victory. I deserved to savor it.

"Pay attention to our destination," Katya reminded me.

"Thanks. I have not forgotten. I visualized it before we left."

She nodded, more reserved than she'd been before. "It's the hardest part of teleporting. You have to keep nudging the spell toward your end point."

"What happens if I slack off?"

"What would you expect?" she countered.

"We will end up somewhere else, but how far off could we be?"

She chuckled. "You'd be surprised."

I'd learned the feel of her magic, and it flickered around me, joining my spell. I sensed her enter my magic smoothly.

She felt right joined with me like that. I started to tell her but was suddenly shy. I hadn't heard much from the green dragon lately, but I detected his presence.

It seemed perverse, somehow, to say anything personal in front of an audience.

It was eerie in a way. Like having opened myself to a permanent extra resident. One who would always be there with his own thoughts, ideas, and opinions. Except I wouldn't be privy to them. This was a one-way street with the dragon knowing everything about me, and me knowing nothing about him. He'd been vocal enough so far, I didn't doubt he'd be the first to chastise me if he felt I'd made a mistake.

With reality laid out in those terms, I wasn't at all sure I hadn't made a mistake. I was warming to the magical part of things, but the price of having sold my soul to a dragon might prove higher than I was willing to pay.

Deep within me, the dragon rolled restlessly. Fire heated my chest and found its way out through my mouth. I altered my thoughts until they mirrored the restless, pitching South Atlantic. Nothing more. Nothing less.

"There." Katya's voice surprised me. "We're back on track."

I remembered the teleport spell. I'd been focused on how I felt about being shackled at the hip to a dragon. "Sorry. I got distracted. It will not happen again." Feeling through the bones of the casting, I located where she'd set markers.

To avoid her asking why I'd been distracted, I posed a

question of my own. "Why is there a breathable atmosphere here, but none between the liminal space and the borderworld?"

"Teleport magic uses its own channels," she replied. "When you were ejected from the space between worlds, it wasn't a teleport spell but Y Ddraigh Goch's will that propelled you."

"So if I'd teleported to the borderworld, I'd have been able to breathe?"

She nodded. "Yes. If I'd had any inkling the dragon god would yank me away, I'd have warned you. As it was, I wasn't certain we'd ever leave the liminal boundary."

"Information is disseminated on a need-to-know basis," I murmured.

"Sort of. Yes." She hesitated. "Why were you pleased when I told you magic was specific to the wielder?"

I kept part of my consciousness linked to the teleport spell, determined not to drop the ball again. "Because it meant I was free to find my own way."

"I still don't quite understand."

"I have never been a good soldier. I prefer to figure things out myself, rather than being force-fed a set of rules."

She scrunched her eyes thoughtfully. "Your need for independence, it's linked to the dragonfire from a little bit ago."

She hadn't posed it as a question, so I didn't treat it as one. If anyone understood about having a dragon as a permanent associate, she would. I reached for her hand, lacing my fingers with hers. "My new bondmate knows all my thoughts and expressed displeasure at a few of them."

"It's to be expected. You're still getting to know one another."

I shook my head. "The dragon is getting to know me. Will I ever find out anything about him?"

Katya looked away. "I don't know. With our dragons, it's more a matter of accepting them for what they are—and making double damn sure they don't grab the point. It will happen, but your job is to haul them back by whatever means you have."

"What if I fail?"

"The bond will become perverted. Sometimes they can be salvaged, but not often. Rogue shifters eventually end up before Y Ddraigh Goch, who severs the bond."

"Doesn't sound too bad," I ventured.

"Don't underestimate it. The dragon is forbidden from ever entering into another bond, but the human will long for its missing dragon forever. A forever that's far shorter than it might have been since you lose your immortality."

I looked at my spell again. If I read the signs right, we were nearly back to Earth. Clearly, I'd made a commitment on the borderworld, one that would be permanent. I'd known as much up front, but knowing and being confronted with the reality were two different things.

"You're quiet," Katya observed.

"Just working through things," I hedged. No reason to share my woes with her. She probably already saw me as weak and pathetic. Nothing like kneeling over a man's busted up remains with him whining in pain to kill off any romantic inclinations.

Still, having her as my teacher was better than not having her at all. If I was an apt pupil, maybe there'd be a chance of resurrecting the desire I'd sensed when we'd been near one another. I wanted her to see me as a man, not an object of pity.

Waves of approval rolled through me.

The dragon.

I buried my thoughts and bit back a sharp retort that sat in the recesses of my throat. I'd been an adult for a long time. I did not require anyone's endorsement for my choices.

Katya's magic slid in next to mine again. "Just checking," she murmured, followed by, "We're nearly there. Stand ready to cut the flow of power or we'll bounce right past the beach."

The teleport spell was ticking down. If I listened hard, I could almost hear the beats of a metronome slowing. But when was the time to call it?

"On my count of three," Katya said. I was grateful for her help and embarrassed I needed it, but I fixed my entire concentration on the casting. It was beginning to unravel around the edges. The pulse of magic that it emitted had definitely changed in both pitch and cadence.

When she got to three, I wrestled with the spell. It was like trying to turn rusty taps that wanted to remain open. For some reason, I hadn't realized it would require magic to shut the spell down, just as power had been vital to kindle it.

Her magic wove in with mine, fluid and graceful, just like

her. Between the two of us, we passed a barrier, kind of like an airlock in a submarine, except this time it didn't shred my clothing.

Clothing. I'd be cold on that ice-shrouded beach, but we wouldn't remain there long. We emerged a good ten feet in the air, but Katya did something and we floated gently down. Brine-filled air seared my lungs, cold and salty. Wiped out from the magic I'd commanded, I sat on the chilly sand.

It was cold. Below freezing. The wind cut straight through my down garments. I wrapped my arms around my tented knees to protect my core.

"Nice work." Katya looked down at me. Still naked, she wasn't even shivering.

"Mmph. You did most of it there at the end. Can we go below?"

"Yes. I wanted to take a look around. Kon and Erin have been here." The corners of her mouth curved into a smile. "She found a dragon too. Kon must be thrilled."

"Are you? About me, I mean?" I winced and scrambled to my feet. "Never mind. I should not have asked."

"Sister!" Konstantin's deep voice nearly deafened me. Moments later, he and Erin bounded out of a rent in the air that sewed itself shut behind them.

Katya threw herself into his arms and hugged him. They talked excitedly back and forth in their dragon tongue, except now I could understand them. Was that courtesy of my bondmate?

"Who else?" The dragon's question echoed through my skull.

"Thank you."

My chest swelled from pressure just before smoke, ash, and a tongue of fire found their way out. Was the beast pleased? Or had I pissed it off again?

I ran to Erin and extended a hand, intent on shaking hers. She swept me into an embrace. "Perfect timing! We'd just left to hunt you down, but the blood vectors turned a one-eighty as soon as Kon set his spell in place."

Before I could inquire just what a blood vector was, she pulled back out of my arms. "You're bonded?"

"Yes. I am." As I looked at her, it sank in she was naked, just like Konstantin and Katya. Whatever the trick was to keeping warm, I'd have to prioritize learning it.

"Congratulations!" Erin gushed. "Isn't it just the most amazing thing. I adore my dragon. She's a brilliant, beautiful red."

"Um, mine is green and quite special." I couldn't bring myself to say much beyond that, even though I was certain my beast was listening to every word and had noted my distinct lack of enthusiasm.

Erin, however, hadn't noticed a thing. "Tell me what you've used magic for so far."

"Most of the teleport spell back here. And shifting." I wondered if it had damn near killed her too, but didn't want to let on how bad it had been for me. We men have our pride. It might be stupid and misplaced, but it's part of what makes us men.

She rolled her blue eyes, except now they had broad golden rims around the irises. "Oh my fucking god, what a hideous experience that first shift was. I was certain I was dead." She shook herself. "It's the curse of being a doctor. You can name every single thing that's broken or shattered or crushed."

A snort pushed between my lips. "I am far from medically trained, yet I had no doubt I hovered very near the veil."

"So, it was hard for you too?"

"Hard would be an understatement." I stopped there, not wanting to relive my agony.

"It's impressive you managed a teleport spell," Erin went on. "I'm still letting Kon do all the tough things. After we first got back, I spent hours in that library of his, but there's so much material, I could spend years and not delve much beyond the surface."

"Books? There are manuals here that will help us learn about magic?" Cold as I was, a delighted thrill ran through me. I was used to learning from printed materials. Most were electronic nowadays, but the concept was the same.

"Yes. Scrolls, actually, but some very ancient books too. In a whole lot of languages."

"I am literate in many languages—" I began.

She held up both hands. "I wasn't, but it's not a problem. Something about the bond gave me the ability to read and speak a whole bunch of arcane languages. Probably modern ones too, but I haven't had time to test that theory. Maybe we could switch to Dutch?"

"Of course, but not right now."

I glanced over at Konstantin and Katya. They still stood,

heads together, chattering like a small flock of magpies. I trotted to where they stood, my boots slipping on the ice-coated rocks. "Can we go inside?"

Konstantin clapped me on the back hard enough to knock the wind out of me. "Welcome to the fold," he boomed. "Can't wait to see you in your dragon form."

Steam puffed from my mouth. And from Konstantin's. Apparently, our dragons were cooing to one another. I'd figured out steam was good, whereas the other elements, like fire, ash, and smoke, could cut either way.

"*We will shift. Now.*" My dragon's words weren't a suggestion. More of a command.

Konstantin trained his golden eyes on me but didn't say a word. He was waiting to see what I'd do. Katya looked as if she wanted to offer advice, but her brother shook his head.

"We shall shift," I told my beast, not bothering with telepathy, "but not right now. A library lies within. I must educate myself about magic as quickly as I can before we leave for distant worlds seeking allies."

Fire roared from my mouth in plumes that rose half a dozen meters into the still air. The pressure in my chest transferred to the rest of my body, and I felt the stretching, tearing sensation I'd come to associate with shifting.

Could the dragon force his way through?

He was a hell of a lot stronger than me, but maybe I had an edge because we were in my form. I instinctively reached into the earth beneath my feet, letting its power strengthen me as I fought my dragon's will. Because targeting the entire transformation felt beyond me, I focused on each part where the dragon tried to break through.

Fire continued to pour from my mouth, along with streams of ash. I let them roll. They weren't hurting anything, and they were keeping me warm.

When a finger turned into a talon, I forced it back. When wings tried to poke through, I layered magic over them and instructed them firmly to retreat. I may not have gained ground, but neither was I losing any.

Konstantin dropped his hands onto my shoulders and focused his whirling gaze right at me. His dragon's eyes, yet he still wore his human body. "Enough!" The word made my ears ring and resonated through my head at the same time.

"But you invited us to shift," my dragon protested.

"You misunderstood, and I withdraw the invitation," Konstantin said in the same dual-toned communication that was both telepathy and spoken out loud at the same time.

My dragon departed so abruptly, I almost fell over. When I looked within, I couldn't find him. "Where did he go?"

"He is furious because I pulled rank and censured him," Konstantin replied. "Don't worry. He will return."

"Why did your words make a difference?" I was blithering, but there was so much I didn't understand.

"My beast is one of the elders," Konstantin told me. "The other dragons are not bound to listen to him, but they all recognize he'll exact retribution if they do not."

"Thank you." I tried to stand tall, but the wind kept me hunched over.

"It was my fault. I should never have said what I did."

"You did really well," Katya chimed in. "Exactly the right approach."

Her praise warmed me. "Should I apologize when my dragon returns?"

"Oh hell, no," she and Konstantin said almost in unison.

Katya continued. "It made a bid for freedom, you said no, and it pushed for what it wanted despite your refusal. Such behavior must not be condoned."

"Or even acknowledged," Kon added.

Alrighty. I could pretend the last sequence of events had never happened. A well-known children's movie series about training dragons popped into my head. I made short work of that memory. It was one thing to not mention our confrontation, quite another to rub salt into the dragon's loss of face.

Erin made her way to Konstantin's side and threaded an arm around him. Surprise ran through me. So they were a couple now? I wanted to ask, but it would be rude. And it was none of my business.

"May we go inside?" I asked. "I wish to explore the library Erin told me about."

Katya nodded. "We don't have much time, but we need sustenance, and you can look through Kon's books while you eat."

"I'm afraid I left the library in a horrible mess," Erin said, "but there's a method to my pile system."

"I am looking forward to digging in. You can tell me which pile is which."

"Happy to."

Konstantin's magic, different from Katya's, bubbled around us. The chill, windy shore gave way to the familiar great room. I felt grateful for the warmth deep beneath Antarctica. My frozen fingers and toes began to thaw.

"I'll round us up some nourishment," Konstantin offered.

"Library is this way," Katya said. She rattled off a string of words peppered with "illusion" and "begone."

The far wall of the great room peeled back, revealing another space beyond. Erin hustled forward. I followed her. Normally, I'd have wanted to dig through the library at my leisure. Even a cursory glance told me the books and scrolls were very old, and probably worth millions. Not that their monetary value mattered. The piquant scents of tanned leather and vellum pricked my nostrils.

"Where should I begin?" I asked Erin. She'd spent hours in here. Presumably, she'd offer pointers so I could be as efficient as possible.

Katya joined us, her gaze scanning the stacks of ancient lore books.

"Perhaps you should advise him," Erin said.

Katya shook her head. "He'll benefit from what you found more than my opinions."

"All right." Erin started at the far end of the shelf-lined room. "This stack describes working with elements. This one delineates other varieties of magic wielders. The one over here is specific to dragon magic, its strengths and weaknesses..."

Before she was done talking, I crouched next to the element pile and plucked the uppermost scroll from the stack. My eyes widened. It was penned in Linear A, an ancient Minoan runic script. Even more surprising, I could decipher it.

Maybe my dragon was good for more than throwing tantrums. I grimaced, waiting for pushback, but it didn't come. When I checked, my beast hadn't yet returned. Good. I needed to either temper my mental chatter or find a way to shield my thoughts.

"Before I retreat to where I left off educating myself," Erin said, "you both need to know we were set upon by serpents."

"It appears you won," Katya growled, sounding like the feral creature she shared her skin with.

"We killed two. Kon forced them into their human bodies with magic, and then we burned them."

A long, whistling breath steamed through Katya's clenched teeth. "Good. They're not gaining strength as quickly as I feared they would."

"Your brother said the same," Erin agreed. "Yet we can't assume our good fortune will continue. We were going to hunt you down and then hit up that borderworld system for allies."

"Fleisher," Katya muttered.

"Yeah. That one," Erin said.

I was only listening with half an ear. I'd begun reading the scroll. It did a most excellent job separating out the elements and delineating the strengths of each. Soon, I'd dug into the next item down, a book so old it was handwritten in Old Greek.

Blessing my eidetic memory, I plowed through as much as I could before Konstantin showed up carting an enormous platter. Katya tried to talk with me. So did Kon and Erin, but I was determined to absorb as much as I could.

Finally, a hand closed around my upper arm. I turned to find Katya regarding me with a bemused expression. "Who would have guessed you were such a bookworm. Time to go."

I closed the book I'd been deep into, not worried about losing my place. These magical books had their own ways of interacting with me. When I said, "I'm ready," I meant it. I was far better prepared than I'd been when I entered the extensive lore collection.

"When did you come by all these?" I stood and swept both hands to the sides.

"They belonged to all the dragons who used to live here," Katya replied.

"They didn't take their source materials when they left?" Erin raised both brows.

Konstantin shook his head. "No, but they took their respective hoards. If you were to ask any dragon, they would tell you human bondmates have no need of books."

"Because the dragons can teach you everything you need to know," Katya added.

"I can see a clear advantage in holding my own knowledge," I muttered, still fresh from the power struggle with my beast.

Katya laughed, high, pure notes that heartened me, gave me hope. "I bet you can," she said.

Konstantin herded us into the living room and sealed up the library, hiding it behind illusion once more. "Gather close," he instructed.

The air developed a liquid, glistening aspect as his magic built around us. Quiet pleasure filled me because I was able to isolate the parts of his spell, understanding how they worked together. The great room fell away, and we floated in darkness.

It would take time—and a whole lot of hard work—but I'd master the magic at my command, no matter how high the cost. I vowed to turn myself into a man my dragon would respect, not one he'd waste energy playing silly games with.

"It's a good goal," Katya said very near my ear.

I startled. "You were inside my head?"

"Of course. How else will I know what you're thinking."

Before I could protest, say a man needed some privacy, she went on. "The nature of dragons is to dive into conflict. Yours will engage in skirmishes for the fun of it, but if you don't take him seriously, his attempts will lessen over time."

She floated near me but not touching. I reached for her hand. When she took it and squeezed lightly, I squeezed back. The dragon and I would begin anew when he returned. Perhaps Katya and I could as well.

Far quicker than I'd anticipated, Konstantin brought us out into something that looked like an overgrown jungle version of primordial Earth. Deep fissures reminiscent of canyonlands in the southwestern United States cut the landscape into furrows. Screeches, bellows, and grunts filled the humid air. Dinosaurs, heavy, lumbering beasts, formed a circle about us. Others flew in circles around our heads, toothed beaks open in a challenge.

Why weren't we leaving? Surely, this couldn't be the right spot.

Konstantin and Katya began to chant. The air developed a silvery hue and, one by one, the primeval beasts shifted into humans. Naked, they looked a lot like indigenous tribes from South America with dark hair, copper skin, and sharply defined cheekbones. Or they would have if the native tribesmen had been seven feet tall with silver eyes.

One of the men stepped toward us. He didn't bow or smile or look particularly friendly. "If you have come for help with dragon problems, leave."

"Aye, plenty of dragons you could solicit," another yelled.

The lot of them erupted in shrieks, squeals, and raised fists.

Konstantin shifted between two breaths. One moment, he was a man, the next his black dragon stood, fanning its wings. "Silence." Fire punctuated the word in dragonspeak. "You will do me the courtesy of listening. I, Konstantin, prince among dragons, have spoken."

CHAPTER 6

Katya was ready to shift in case her brother needed reinforcements, but the mob quieted and took a few steps back, offering a respectful distance between themselves and her twin.

Good. They should defer to him. Like everything else, magic was built on hierarchies. Dragon shifters had far stronger ability than these primitive beasts. They'd been around since the dawn of civilization, though, a date far earlier than when similar creatures had roamed Earth.

"My goal," Konstantin was saying, "is to build a cadre of magic wielders. Sea-serpents must return to wherever they originated, and—"

"They're not here," a man with silver hair pointed out. In contrast to his companions, he was the only one whose hair wasn't black.

"Not our problem," someone else shouted. He must have

concealed himself because Katya was damned if she could identify the speaker.

"Aye. Not our problem. Good enough for me." Another chap, this one sporting a riot of black curls, agreed with his fellows.

A huge, broad-shouldered man with straight black hair braided into many plaits planted himself in front of Konstantin. "If we help you drive them away from Earth, who's to say they won't end up here? It's the nearest group of habitable worlds."

"We would kill them." Konstantin fanned his wings. Ash fluttered from his mouth.

The man, who stood only about a head shorter than the black dragon, tossed his shoulders back. "I don't think so. We are not overly fond of killing, not being dragons and all."

Katya strode forward. "What happened to the dragons? As I recall, some used to live here."

"We were too dull for them," the silver-haired man muttered.

Something about his statement didn't quite ring true. Katya narrowed her eyes and wove magic into a subtle truth spell. "What do you mean too dull?"

"They're not here," the man in front of Konstantin repeated what his companion had said. "They didn't deign to tell us their reasons."

His words pinged cleanly off her spell, and they made sense. Dragons weren't in the habit of sharing their plans or intent with anyone outside their immediate circle. She glanced at Konstantin, meeting his whirling eyes.

He intuited her meaning and summoned shift magic. After a brilliant flash, he resurrected his human side and walked toward a gnarled willow-esque tree several meters removed from the shifter pack. She followed, along with Erin and Johan.

Roaring and stomping behind her told her the men and women had taken their beast forms once again. Unlike most shifters, this batch spent most of their time as animals.

"How long have they lived here?" Erin asked, keeping her voice soft.

"As long as any of us can remember," Konstantin replied.

"They were here long before our kinfolk," Katya added.

"Would dragons leave a place because it ceased to entertain them?" Johan knit his dark brows into a thick line.

Katya shook her head. "No. That part wasn't true, yet I have no idea why they'd lie to us."

"They were pretty damn protective," Erin murmured, "but I don't blame them. Guess humans aren't the only ones who fall into the NIMBY trap."

"What the hell is that?" Johan asked.

She muffled a snort. "It's an acronym."

"I guessed as much," he said, "but I am not familiar with that one."

"Means not in my backyard," Erin clarified. "Happens a lot when, say, someone has the bright idea about putting in low income housing or a rehabilitation center for addicts. Everyone agrees conceptually, but no one wants it near them."

Konstantin sliced a hand in front of them. "Not

important. We need to move to the next world, but not before we do a better job searching this one."

Something inside Katya twisted into an uncomfortable knot. "What? Do you suspect dragon shifters are here but instructed the others to send us packing?"

"Wouldn't be the first time," her brother muttered, and his mouth curved into a frown.

"If they went to all that trouble," Johan cut in, "we would be better served leaving them alone."

Konstantin puffed out his chest. Fire shot from his mouth. "They owe allegiance to me."

Katya resisted the urge to roll her eyes and tell her brother to stand down. Any social structure dragon shifters once had was long gone. She settled for saying, "You're living in the past, Brother. The distant past."

He whirled to face her, anger streaming from him, but she didn't flinch. "I am not the enemy," she reminded him. Her dragon pushed hard, wanting out. Her response to confrontation was fire and teeth and wings.

"Not now," Katya said firmly.

"But you need me."

"It's my brother," she reminded her bondmate.

Amid grumbling, smoke, and ash, the dragon retreated about the same time Konstantin came to his senses. Katya didn't expect an apology, and she didn't get one.

He said, "We're leaving," right before the bite of his magic surrounded them.

Katya didn't like the idea of dragon shifters hiding from them. When had her kin become such cowards? Any dragon worth its scales welcomed conflict, lived for it. Was that what had happened here? No opportunity to test their mettle, so they'd left for greener pastures?

She'd find out. It wouldn't take long to hit the remaining sites in this constellation of worlds. Their next stop had air so thin breathing was a challenge. They didn't remain long. The following destination looked more promising. She peered out at a frozen expanse of white, not unlike Antarctica, except there was no ocean. Icy cliffs rose all around them. Snow covered the ground. Katya battled confusion. She'd been to all the worlds in this system, and none had looked like this.

Erin stood close to Johan, gesturing with her hands as she instructed him how to marshal magic to keep himself warm. Katya had planned to do that for him, but there hadn't been time. For the barest instant, jealousy nipped at her, but then she got hold of herself. She didn't own Johan. Far from it. He had an absolute right to sharpen his skills, and—

"And you have a right to him. Dragons were born possessive," her bondmate spoke in take-no-prisoners tones.

"Yes, but he wouldn't understand. He's human."

"Not anymore." Her dragon sounded positively jubilant.

"Katya!" Her brother's tone was pointed, and her head snapped up.

"Yes?" She fanned seeking magic in a rough circle, an automatic response to make certain she wasn't missing anything critical. Breath hissed through her pursed lips.

"Indeed," Konstantin snared. "They were here."

"Who?" Erin asked, looking up from where she was demonstrating a point to Johan.

"The serpents, but its been a while." Katya poured more juice into her spell, willing it to gather information. There were limits, though, to what she could glean from dibs and dabs of magical tracings.

"It might explain what happened to the dragons two worlds back," Johan muttered. Magic glistened around him, and the blue-white cast had left his lips and fingers.

Katya kept her eyes away from the real estate below his waist—this time. She'd helped herself to more than an eyeful before. He had a gorgeous body. On the leanish side but graced by muscle attractively arranged across his shoulders and winding down the length of his arms and legs. Bands of muscle wandered across his abdomen to the thick thatch of dark hair between his legs. Before she recreated his phallus, which was pretty damned impressive, she said, "Dragons would never run from sea-serpents."

Her tone may have been somewhat harsher than normal, but she was doing her level best not to lose sight of the topic at hand. If she didn't watch it, she'd be sunk in lust.

"There is a difference between running and choosing not to fight," Johan replied. Fire jetted from his mouth, and he turned his head to the side to avoid hitting anyone.

Katya resisted rolling her eyes. His dragon was back, and it had taken exception to his offhand remark as well.

Erin bent her head closer and suggested mixing in more air to conserve his magic.

"Thanks. I believe I understand how this one works."

"You did pick it up handily." Erin beamed at him, and another sharp jab of jealousy pricked Katya. It was stupid. Erin was slated to be Konstantin's mate. While the two of them weren't yet joined, they were fond of one another from the looks of things.

Johan and Erin are friends, she told herself firmly. It wasn't exactly a foreign concept to dragonkind, but neither did they glom onto the idea of being surrounded by acquaintances as she'd seen humans do. When you lived forever, most people's company grew stale after enough years passed.

"Not mine," her bondmate reminded her.

"No, dearheart. Never yours."

Erin congratulated Johan once more on his mastery of the magic that warmed him. He hadn't completely grasped the skill, but Katya didn't correct him—or Erin. Anything she said at this point would make her look small, petty. And a know-it-all. Both Johan and Erin were doing surprisingly well shaping their newly acquired magic into something useful. Compliments would serve both of them better than criticism at this juncture.

A muted whirring caught the very edges of her hearing. She angled her head to hear more clearly. Konstantin was kneeling, ear angled toward the ground. Was that where the humming was coming from?

She didn't think so. "We should leave," she told her twin. Uneasiness spiked through her; the dragon felt it too and made a concerted pitch for freedom.

Konstantin shot to his feet. "Dragons, people. Now."

"What is it?" Katya screeched with the last of her human

vocal chords. And then she saw the monsters. Like enormous gray mantises, but with black-feathered wings. Crap. Their wingspan rivaled the albatrosses she'd grown used to in Antarctica. Hinged mantis jaws clacked as the abominations opened and shut them. Their mouths were big enough to sever a human head.

Heat built in her chest, and fire spewed from her mouth even as she changed form. Would dragonfire kill them? Or did they possess magic rendering them immune to it? She'd never seen anything quite like the dozen or so flying atrocities, and she'd run across plenty of monsters.

These looked like a cross between a relatively harmless insect and a raptor with spiky tips on its wings. Except the whole mess was inflated to a hundred times the normal size of either of its components. A sweetish stench with overtones of rot wafted her way. Possibly poison, but she wasn't certain. It lacked the acrid reek she associated with the serpents' venom.

Was this something new? Were they tangled up with the serpents? Seemed unlikely. She started to ask Konstantin, but he was fully engaged immolating everything he could with fire. Beneath him, the frozen landscape hissed and sizzled as chunks of ice cracked away from cliff faces.

Erin was already airborne. Johan seemed to be stuck mid shift. Scales sparkled the length of his body, but his arms were still humanoid, and so was his head.

"Don't fight the transformation." She aimed for a calm note but probably failed abysmally.

One of the mantises swooped perilously close. Johan saw

it and feinted out of its path with seconds to spare. Was his dragon toying with him because it was still pissed about their last go-round?

The whistling, whirring noise intensified. Something about the pitch made her ears ache. It was almost as if they'd picked an amplitude that was destructive on purpose.

Of course, they did. Stupid of her not to recognize ill intent. She flew over Johan, shielding him with her body. *"Hurry!"* She repeated the word out loud in the dragons' language.

A mantis flew close enough to close its nasty jaws over her flank. It burned like mad, and when she wrenched her hip in an effort to get away, the bastard hung on.

Still more heat scored her side. Konstantin was coating the mantis with dragonfire. Much like molten magma, the conflagration would continue to grow hotter and hotter until it exploded, hopefully killing the mantis trapped within its maw. Whether dragonfire was, indeed, a deathblow remained to be seen. Several smoking pyres burned below her, but she sensed life within every single one of them.

The green dragon was corporeal enough to fly. Finally. If she hadn't had problems of her own, she'd have given him the sharp edge of her tongue. Katya edged away, intent on scraping the burning mantis off on a nearby cliff. She directed its body onto wicked-looking rocks. It broke in flaming pieces, accompanied by a geyser of black ichor that smelled so bad, she wanted to gag.

She rose higher in the clear, cold air, shaking her body amid rattling scales. The mantis was gone. Why did the spot still burn? When she angled her head around to look, her whirling eyes spun faster. The thing's head remained, jaws firmly attached to her flank.

How was that even possible?

Between herself and Konstantin, they'd killed it. Dead meant dead, so its insidious teeth should have let go. Growling, snarling, and spitting fire, she took another pass at the cliff. Except now she couldn't get any leverage. There wasn't enough of it left to catch on anything.

Resigned to waiting until she was human again to pluck the remains of the thing out of her flesh, she tried to ignore it, but the pain was worse than when it first bit her. Some treacherous poison, no doubt. She directed a stream of magic, intent on walling that portion of her body off from everything else. She might end up with a big patch of necrotic flesh, but at least she could stem the damage.

A quick scan told her many of the burning mantises were dead. Good. The bastards didn't deserve to live. Erin and Kon had teamed up, wielding the equivalent of a one-two punch. She stopped the mantises in their tracks, and Kon doused them with dragonfire. Johan's green dragon was tossing fire around, opening divots in the ice. When she looked closer, she saw what might have been cocoons. Immature mantises staggered out of them. Small and inept, they stumbled as if they were blind.

The green dragon picked them off easily as he opened one cell after the next. Katya beat back a mixture of horror at the breeding ground this borderworld had turned into and delight Johan had discovered the mantis nests.

"You open. I'll kill," she told him.

He banked in what looked like acquiescence, blasted another hole in the ice, and waited long enough for her to mete death to the young mantises that poked their antenna-waving heads out. Annoyance kindled. The green, a newly bonded dragon, should have absolute trust in her beast. Instead, he was waiting to make certain she killed the hatchlings.

Some arguments were scarcely worth the energy, though. The green dragon only checked her intent once. Satisfied he could trust her, he opened hole after hole, uncovering partially formed mantises for her to dispatch.

They wouldn't stop until they were done. Until every single mantis pupa or larva or whatever the hell they were called, were dead. She dusted mental talons together. One less scourge to plague them. At the rate they were going, though, by the time they returned to Earth, the serpents would have taken over.

They'd no longer be vulnerable in their human forms, and the only reasonable next steps would be to gather up their hoards and leave. The thought of her gold and gemstones pleased her. Only another dragon truly understood the feral possessiveness that attached dragonkind to their hoards. She'd collected every single element in hers over the long years of her life, adding to her treasure as regularly as she could.

She'd been selective, though. Not just any old piece of gold or precious stone would do. The energy had to be just right. Had to complement the items she already had. She and Konstantin had worked out an arrangement. Whoever found a potential hoard item had first dibs. If they didn't want it, they told the other, offering it to them.

Now that there were four of them, she wasn't quite sure how things would work. When fifty of them had shared the same space, everyone's hoard was an intensely private matter. She hadn't been nearly as picky then. Everything she found went into her stash, no matter if the emanations weren't quite correct.

The green dragon was flying in a zigzag pattern, clearly hunting for more nests. She sent magic arcing all around her, trying for efficiency. No reason to squander power unnecessarily.

"We got them all," she told the green dragon.

"I'm not done checking," he informed her with a flick of his long tail.

Konstantin and Erin had settled on a patch of frozen ground and were in the midst of shifting.

Katya regarded Johan's dragon. Would it blow a fuse if she corrected it? Who was in control of their partnership? Had the dragon jerked the reins out of Johan's control again?

"Johan?" She opted for telepathy.

"What?" He sounded beleaguered, but at least he answered her.

"Shall we join Kon and Erin?" She angled a wingtip their way.

Fire splatted from his jaws, followed by a rain of smoky ash. She decided perhaps the best path was nonconfrontational. Johan had enough to deal with without her stoking his dragon's dominance issues.

She banked, intent on circling to land and then shifting and removing the goddess-be-damned jaws that still burned like a bitch in her side. The green dragon wheeled too. At first, Katya assumed her gambit had worked.

The green dragon, no longer having to defend an unpopular decision, would quietly land, and that would be the end of things. They'd move on to the next borderworld in the Fleisher chain, and hopefully locate a dragon or two.

Because she was riding on assumptions, not paying close attention, she didn't absorb that the green dragon was flying right at her until he was only a meter or so away. Shocked, her dragon bugled a challenge. Instead of bugling back, the green dragon closed his jaws over the mantis head, clearly intent on removing it from her side.

His transformation complete, Konstantin leapt to his feet. "Noooooo!" rang from his mouth followed by, "Drop it. Now."

The green dragon was well past her. Hot blood sheeted down her side, staining her scales red, but the wound would heal. Getting rid of the mantis head was an enormous relief. She hadn't realized how badly it hurt until it was finally no longer there.

"Thank you!" she bugled at the green dragon.

He didn't reply. Had he dropped the head like Konstantin ordered? Or was Johan's dragon still into being a "my way or the highway" stubborn ass?

Rather than tracking a straight line, the green dragon

flew erratically. Was it showing off, or was something desperately wrong? Before she came up with an answer, the beast plummeted from the sky and landed with a spat on an expanse of ice.

Konstantin and Erin ran for the dragon, but the expression on Konstantin's face iced her bones. "*What happened?*" she asked her bondmate. It was ancient. Maybe it would know something.

"*Stupid fool. He chewed and swallowed the head.*"

Katya waited, but it made no sense. "*I don't understand,*" she mumbled.

"*These things, they're—*" she rattled off a long name in dragonspeak. "*It's what happened to the dragons here. They got drafted as breeding vessels for the mantises.*"

"*But we're immortal,*" Katya protested, swallowing back disbelief.

"*More or less,*" her beast agreed. "*This was an indirect method of borrowing dragon essence—until naught was left.*"

"*How could we have been so stupid as to let ourselves be trapped?*"

The dragon didn't answer, but she hadn't expected it would.

Katya landed and lumbered next to Johan's dragon. Splayed on the ice, it appeared to be unconscious. Kon chanted furiously, hands placed on the dragon's belly. Erin had opened a channel to her fledgling power, and Kon drew from it as if it were bottomless. She was already panting and swaying on her feet.

"Hurry, Katya." He tossed a glance her way.

"I'm stronger as a dragon," she said in dragonspeak. No need to waste any power at all on telepathy.

She felt him pushing at her magical center and gave him full access. "You've seen these things before?"

"Ask me later," he grunted through clenched teeth.

That he was working as hard as he could told her how precarious the situation was. As if she needed corroboration. The comatose dragon spread before her said it all. She didn't recognize the incantation, but the words were clear enough. Her twin was intent on chasing out the mantis embryos, not letting them gain a toehold.

"Johan!" Katya shouted. "Help us."

"How?" His voice sounded strained but determined.

Thank the fucking gods he's still in there...

"Identify mantis parts and destroy them from within. Your dragon got you into this. He has to help get you out."

Maybe she shouldn't have added that last part, but she was furious enough to throttle Johan's dragon. Arrogance was one thing—if it was based on skill. Arrogance that stemmed from wishful thinking was hazardous.

And stupid.

The green dragon thrashed feebly. A thin thread of fire spilled from its open jaws. Katya took it as a positive sign. Better than the dragon not moving at all. She started to tell him what a sorry excuse he was for a dragon, but her bondmate commanded their vocal chords and vetoed her bid for a voice.

"Not now," her dragon spoke sternly. *"If he recovers, you can excoriate him—right along with me."*

CHAPTER 7

I wasn't even aware my dragon had returned until it took exception to something I said to Katya. I'd been trying to figure things out in this brave new world I was suddenly part of and mentioned that perhaps dragons had chosen not to fight as opposed to running away.

At the time, it seemed diplomatic to me. And an explanation for why there were no dragons on the first borderworld we visited. The one with a plethora of prehistoric beast shifters. I recognized a few dinosaurs, but many were new to me. I've always suspected our methods of reconstructing species that lived tens of thousands of years ago were badly flawed. Today clinched it for me.

Sheesh. Everyone jumped on me for my offhand remark about dragons not hanging about to kick ass in a fight. Katya shot me a look that would have withered crops in a verdant field. And my bondmate forced a stream of fire out of my mouth.

I asked him how long he'd been back, but he didn't answer.

Next I asked if he still had his tail out of joint. I probably could have been more tactful, but he was starting to rub me the wrong way. I'd never leave in a huff if I didn't like the way events were shaping up. My bent is to stay and talk things out, no matter how heated the discussion.

Friends who'd raised children sometimes pointed out their biggest surprise was how different some of their spawn were from themselves. *Not that my bondmate is anything like a child, but we're going to have to find some common ground, or I'm not seeing how this will ever work out.*

I sensed his presence, rolling and writhing within me. He didn't care much for my last set of thoughts, but if he wouldn't talk with me, it was my only way to communicate with him.

We were on our third borderworld. The middle one had a preponderance of carbon monoxide. We didn't remain long. This place might have breathable air, but there was something eerie about it. It looked a lot like Antarctica, minus the Southern Ocean. Everything was crusted over with ice, and it was damnably cold. I couldn't exactly put my finger on what was bothering me, but I felt edgy. Waiting for the other shoe to drop.

Erin was teaching me how to pull heat from the planet's core to warm myself when Kon's sharp command, "Dragons, people. Now," mobilized everyone. I gave it my best shot, visualized my green beast and tried to drop into his form.

The fucker fought me, like he was trying to prove a point or something.

Finally, I shouted, *"I concede. You are stronger than me, but it is not how the shifter bond was conceived."*

Every once in a while, a blind dog wins. The parts of my body that hadn't yet shifted fell into line, and we were airborne. While we'd been at cross purposes, something like a warped science experiment in genesplicing had flown out of everywhere and nowhere. Never mind, it's impossible from a genetic perspective, but the things were a cross between birds and insects.

With maybe some dinosaur mixed it. They were enormous. Dinosaurs share common DNA with birds, so perhaps I'm not so far afield as all that. Katya didn't seem to recognize them, but Konstantin did. He was selectively burning them—and it was working. Because there weren't all that many, he could take his time and make damn sure each atrocity was well and truly doused in dragonfire.

"Look there!" My dragon's voice in my head shocked me, but I resisted the urge to snark something like, *oh, you're talking with me again?*

I peered through our shared vision and saw indentations in the ice. They formed a pattern, not unlike a bees' nest or the cave dwellings in the southwestern United States. Within each cell was a miniature version of the things Konstantin was killing.

"Nests? Those things have nests?"

My dragon didn't reply, just sent a focused jet of fire directly into the heart of one of the depressions. Ice cracked into crystalline shards; two of the insectoid hybrids dragged their way out, using their front legs to grind themselves forward. About the size of a housecat, they didn't appear at all threatening at this stage.

"What are you waiting for?" My dragon's scream deafened me.

Before I could reply, fire shot from our mouth, and the two babies burst into mini-pyres. At least they didn't cry out. Maybe their vocal apparatus hadn't yet formed. I'm not a wimp, neither am I squeamish, but killing helpless children isn't anything I'd ever considered before. These would grow into the twisted monstrosities Kon was still setting fire to, though, which made it slightly more acceptable.

Erin didn't seem to be laboring under my ethical quandary—odd since she was a doctor. Regardless of her reasons, she was helping Konstantin.

Cells stretched as far as I could see. We'd be providing quite the public service ridding this borderworld of the insect-birds, so I set about cracking each cell open and murdering its occupants. After the first few, it didn't bother me quite so much. I stopped labeling them as young and helpless.

In truth, I stopped considering them at all.

I forgot to mention this, but Katya shielded me with her body while my dragon dragged its heels about shifting. One of the winged atrocities bit her when she was protecting me. Made me feel like a total shit, but I was certain if I blamed my bondmate, he'd wiggle out of it by saying she hadn't moved fast enough. Anyway, I thought she sloughed the thing off, but a bit of it still clung to her.

Katya flew next to me, helping me kill the young whatever-they-weres. Maybe she sensed what a hard time I was having with the actual killing, so I ended up opening nests. Once they were exposed, she did away with the not-yet-hatched hybrids. We made an efficient team, and I was grateful for her help. Maybe a way to pay her back would be to pluck the insectoid head from her hide. Even though the rest of the bastard was long gone, those teeth must hurt.

The more I thought about it, the better I liked the idea of aiding her.

"We got them all," Katya said.

"I'm not done checking," my dragon informed her and flicked our tail.

Konstantin and Erin were already on the ground in the midst of shifting. I considered directing my dragon's attention to them and mentioning three out of four of us were in agreement the battle was over.

While I thrashed about for a tactful way to deliver my message, Katya's welcome voice reverberated in my head. *"Johan?"*

"What?"

"Shall we join Kon and Erin?" She angled a wingtip their way.

Fire splatted from my jaws, followed by a rain of smoky ash. I picked my words cautiously and addressed my dragon. *"You did a fantastic job locating those nests."*

"I did, didn't I?"

"Yes. Let's help Katya, since she helped us."

My bondmate understood. No reason for him not to since he was privy to all my thoughts. We angled, flying right next to Katya. Apparently, she wasn't expecting us to be so close because her dragon bugled a challenge. Before I could explain, mine dipped his head and snatched the offending insect head from her flank. Blood flowed from the wound, but dragons healed fast. Absent the chunk of alien protoplasm we'd snatched, the gash should seal right over.

Konstantin leapt to his feet and shouted, "Noooooo!" followed by, "Drop it. Now."

Naturally, my dragon ignored him, reminding me of some dogs. When you gave them the "Out" command, they just chewed faster. Our jaws crunched through whatever we'd extracted from Katya, and we swallowed the sharp fragments.

"Thank you!" Katya's dragon bugled, apparently unaware my dragon had just ignored a direct command from Konstantin.

I wanted to bugle back, but something was wrong. I felt dizzy. Off in a weird way. I was sad Katya's dragon felt the need to protect herself from me, but that couldn't be what was amiss.

"What have you done?" I asked my dragon as I struggled to put Konstantin's warning into perspective.

"I do not know," he replied, not sounding at all like his normal, damn-the-torpedoes-full-speed-ahead self.

In a distant corner of my mind, I felt our shared body

first fall, and then hit an ice sheet hard enough for cracks to radiate out around us.

"Johan!" Katya's worried voice penetrated the haze around my brain. "Help us."

"How?" I thrashed weakly, aware of the cold, slick surface beneath me.

"Identify mantis parts and destroy them from within. Your dragon got you into this. He has to help get you out."

Her words brought everything back in a rush. The insect head. My dragon eating it. Our precipitous fall out of the sky.

A pitiful stream of fire barely left our jaws. When I reached within, hunting for my bondmate, he wasn't exactly standing proud. If I hadn't gotten to know him a little, I might not have recognized his stance as shame for what he'd done, but it was close.

"How do we identify these mantis parts?" I asked my dragon. Katya had intimated he could help us out of this predicament, and now that she'd labeled the insectoid thing as a mantis, I could see the resemblance. I'd missed the connection before because in my world, praying mantises were only a few centimeters long.

Maybe because I'd appealed to the beast's chivalrous side —assuming it had one—it dragged our shared intelligence through its body, stopping here and there. After the first couple of examples, I got the feel of the wrong places.

How could the insect have had such a rapid effect? I might have been lying facedown longer than I imagined, but surely not long enough for the dragon to digest the head it had eaten.

I called a halt to my thoughts. Once again, I was overlaying my old world atop the new one, and the two had very few points of concordance. As consciousness returned, I felt strong magic poking, prodding, and chopping. My dragon wasn't fighting back, though.

My mind was still fuzzy, slow to process that the voice chanting over us belonged to Konstantin. He was the one pushing power into my dragon's body, and my dragon was a whole lot more cooperative than when Konstantin had ordered him not to eat the mantis head.

The spot I stumbled over was why the mantis head was a bad thing, but someone would tell me.

"Brace yourself," Konstantin said, breathing hard. "This will hurt, but it's the last of it."

"I'm sorry," my dragon mumbled just before a wave of pain shot through us. Everything was first hot, then cold, then stabbed by knives. It reminded me of my first shift, minus the broken bones. I hadn't realized I could experience agony in the dragon's form, but it was just as mind-blowingly horrible as when I was human. I'd thought it might be more tolerable—because of knowing we were immortal.

Didn't make a bit of difference.

Except the negatives of immortality raced to the fore. I could be tortured forever. Like Sisyphus and the rock or any other of the gods' punishments. Plucked at by crows, eaten by piranhas, stung by wasps, with my flesh reconstituting itself to experience agony all over again. The dragon gnashed its double rows of teeth until our jaws squealed in protest. To his credit, he didn't yelp.

I would have, but then I'm coming to view male stoicism as badly overrated.

"It is done," Konstantin intoned.

My dragon scrambled to his feet and bowed so low our chin scraped the ice. "Thank you, my liege. But there is one more spot." Still doubled over, my dragon bit a chunk off the side of one of our back feet and spat it on the ice in front of us.

I stared through my layered dragon vision in horror at a cell not unlike the ones we'd destroyed. A cell with a mini-Mantis already starting to develop. Katya sent a jet of magic, and the cell imploded, leaving nothing but an ashy scar. I'd missed her shifting, but she was human again.

I wasn't ashamed to admit I wanted out of my dragon. I needed to be human. Wanted my tongue so I could sort what had happened. Not that I couldn't use dragonspeak and telepathy to accomplish the same thing, but I craved normal. It would take more than a handful of hours to become used to sharing my hide with a bondmate.

The way things had unfolded so far, it was hard not to believe I'd made a mistake. Erin appeared to get along fine with her new sidekick, but dragons had personalities—just like people. Perhaps she was better suited to her bondmate than I was to mine.

Or maybe it was gender-linked. Men have always loved to engage in pissing contests. My dragon had been absorbed in a game of one-upsmanship ever since we bonded.

"Bondmate."

Fearing the worst—because of course the dragon was

tuned in to my thoughts—I said, *"I'm here. Where else would I go?"*

"I truly am sorry. I heard Konstantin and chose to ignore him. I had no idea my actions would produce such far-reaching consequences. I promise I will do better. I nearly caused unfathomable harm to us both."

Konstantin planted himself in front of us. "Give me your foreleg," he ordered.

My dragon squatted and extended a taloned foreleg. Konstantin's form shimmered until his jaws elongated. He didn't fully shift, but he used those dragon jaws—and teeth —to bite hard enough to draw blood, which he sucked and swallowed.

"I am bound by my blood to keep my word," my dragon said, his tone formal as he employed the dragons' language.

"Indeed, you are." Konstantin abandoned his partial transformation.

"Shift," my bondmate suggested. *"I will help."*

Taking a breath, I visualized my human part and fell into it. This time, I remained standing instead of sprawling into an undignified heap. I shook my head from side to side to clear it.

"That thing." I pointed at the ashy place where Katya had destroyed the last bit my dragon excised. "It looked like the nests we destroyed."

"It was," Katya said.

"When your dragon plucked the mantis head from Katya, all would have been well if he'd spit it out. LIKE I TOLD HIM," Konstantin thundered.

"When he ate it, he began the process that would have transformed your body into a breeding ground for the monsters," Erin said, adding, "I know it's foreign and runs counter to everything we understand about genetics and physiology."

"This world has different rules," I mumbled. I was starting to shiver and remembered Erin's instructions about drawing heat upward to warm myself. Once I had the basics of a spell underway, I asked, "All those nests Katya and I destroyed, were they once dragons?"

At Konstantin's terse nod, I asked, "How did they become trapped?"

"I have no idea," the dragon shifter replied, "but I intend to find out. Sea-serpents were here. Whether they were the mastermind behind this unconscionable act remains to be seen. But they're far more intelligent than those creatures we killed."

"What were the things we killed?" Erin asked.

"Don't look at me," Katya replied. "I've never seen them before."

Fire billowed from Konstantin. "It's not so much that these beasts have a name. I've seen conjoined species like these in other places. They are always the work of dark, insidious magic. In this instance, the perfidy did double duty. It borrowed dragon energy to create this particular blend of mantises and raptors. In doing so, it eroded the dragons."

"What would have happened once the rest of them hatched?" I almost didn't want to know, but it was a logical question. Having hundreds of the mantis-bird monsters stuck on this borderworld would only pose a problem for people like us. Ones who had the bad luck to end up here.

"Whoever created them would have moved them to where they were needed," Katya growled.

"If the serpents did this"—Erin chewed her lower lip —"do you suppose the mantis things are part of their master plan to take over Earth?"

"We do not know enough to make such suppositions," I said, aiming to herd the conversation back to what we actually knew rather than what we imagined might be true.

"Come up with an explanation of your own, if you don't care for mine." Erin narrowed her eyes at me.

"For chrissakes, Erin. You are reacting. Understandable, but not useful. We do not even know for certain what the serpents' intentions are."

"Yes, we do," Konstantin broke in. "We overheard them strategizing."

Oops. I winced. I'd forgotten that part, probably because I didn't fancy the idea of an all-out war. For once, my dragon didn't rebuke me. Maybe he was still feeling guilty for almost getting us turned into a brood farm.

"We need to get moving," Kon said. "But first, I must see if those poor dragons encased in the ice can be salvaged. Once that's done, we shall check all the worlds in this group."

"Are there other borderworlds to try if these do not pan out?" I asked.

"Of course, but the farther we travel from Earth, the

longer it will take to return." Katya aimed her words my way. They were a good reminder just how thin a margin we had to work with. Even now, the serpents could have fixed the fault that rendered them vulnerable as humans.

"What was that?" Erin whipped her head around.

I did my best to free up some extra magic—beyond what I was using to stay warm—to search for what had alerted her. It wasn't easy. The strands of my workings kept tangling together until I couldn't tell one spell from the other.

Konstantin ran lightly toward a set of cliffs where most of the ice had chipped away. A ragged looking man emerged from behind a boulder. Rust-colored hair fell past his shoulders. He was unusually tall and quite gaunt, almost emaciated. His eyes shone golden with deep-green centers. A robe fashioned from tawny striped animal skins hung from his shoulders, not doing much beyond providing decoration.

Judging from his eyes, he had to be another dragon shifter, but one who looked as if he'd been hiding out here for years.

"Nikolai!" Konstantin swept the other shifter into a hug and thumped him across the shoulder blades.

Katya waited until her brother let go, and then she embraced Nicolai too.

I hurried toward them with Erin right next to me.

"I shall pay homage to Y Ddraigh Goch for the rest of my days," Nikolai was saying. "You have delivered us."

"Us? How many are you?" Kon asked.

"Eleven, including me."

"Why did you not leave this place?" I asked.

"Because we couldn't give up on the ones who'd been turned into brood mares." He turned his whirling eyes on me. A confused expression marred his craggy face. "Who are you?"

I stuck out a hand. "Johan Petris." Nikolai didn't grasp my hand, so I let it fall to my side.

"Erin Ryan." Having learned from my example, she didn't offer to shake hands.

"But you're both dragon shifters, and I do not know you," Nikolai sputtered. "How is this possible?" He drew back a few paces, confusion yielding to suspicion as his gaze jumped from me to Erin and back again.

"We were human until quite recently," I spoke up, hoping to set him at his ease.

My words had the opposite effect. He raised a hand, and magic scored me from head to toe, as if he were testing me for evil. Or to see if I was real. I shook myself to dispel what had felt like a moderate electrical shock. "Christ, mate. No need to get violent," I said.

Konstantin closed a hand around Nikolai's upper arm. "By the grace of the god, we have two new dragon shifters."

He tried to turn away, but Kon held firm. "What did you find when you scanned Johan?"

"He appears to be like us," Nikolai said in stiff, sullen tones.

"Because he is." Konstantin's voice brooked no possibility of disagreement. "Summon the other dragons. I have a message for all of you."

Nikolai rocked from foot to foot, but he stood tall. "If it truly is you, Konstantin, you will have every right to banish me forever for this request. Nonetheless, I will not put my kinsmen at risk until I'm sure. Shift, so I may see your dragon form."

I'm not sure what I expected, but at the least I assumed Kon would toss fire around, be angry, and order Nikolai to get on with things. Instead, his golden eyes softened.

"Your distrust saddens me, yet I understand its source." Magic glistened, and the black dragon took shape. Its eyes spun as it folded its wings across its back.

Before Nikolai said a word, men and women streamed from the same break in the cliff face he'd appeared from. They threw themselves on their knees in a circle around Konstantin's dragon, murmuring thanks and prayers in dragonspeak.

Their actions moved me. Konstantin was their prince, and they now viewed him as their savior. Somehow, they'd escaped the fate of the other dragons, and now they sought safe harbor.

I waited for him to tell them there was no such thing, that war was upon us, but he gestured them closer and wove magic through the group, healing their wounded spirits and binding them to him. They surrendered to his will, trusted him to make the right choice for them all.

It blew the independent streak I'd always valued right out of the water.

And made me ashamed.

Once men had looked to other men to lead them. Those

days were long gone, and we were worse off for their passing. I'd agreed to become a dragon shifter out of necessity and gratitude to Konstantin and his twin. For the first time, I genuinely welcomed my transformation.

Viewed it as an improvement over who I'd been and the life I'd led. When I looked at Erin, her eyes had sheened with tears. She and I would talk, but I'd have bet nearly anything she felt the same way I did.

Steam puffed from between my jaws. Approval from my bondmate. Would this be a turning point built on something stronger than his guilt? It would if I let it. I turned my voice inward, infusing it with frank gratitude. *"Thank you for taking a chance on me."*

I'd said it before, but this time I meant it with all my heart.

"Thank you for not holding my error against me. You would be justified being angry for centuries."

"We humans have a saying. Let him who is without sin cast the first stone."

More steam puffed through my mouth until soft clouds surrounded me. Olive branch extended and accepted.

I turned my attention to the group around Konstantin. He was human again, and voices rose in a rush as everyone raced to tell him what had happened.

CHAPTER 8

Katya listened as the dragon shifters' stories spewed out. Her heart squeezed in pain for the brave dragons who'd remained on this borderworld. Despite moving well past the point of holding hope for their trapped kin, they kept on trying to rescue them. They hadn't been scrabbling about for a solution for all that long. Not more than two annums or so. Until the first batch of monsters hatched, they hadn't been certain just what was incubating.

And the first hatch was only a few days old.

Good thing. The bastards were just getting the feel of their power. It was why they hadn't fought back in any kind of organized fashion.

"The serpents caught us by surprise, my liege," a woman with flowing silvery hair said. "None of us had seen a sea-serpent in ages."

A lumbering dark-haired man with shorn curls added, "Hell, most of us have never laid eyes on a serpent. The schism betwixt our peoples occurred so long ago, it wasn't much more than a myth."

"Had any of you had dealings with sea-serpents before this borderworld?" Konstantin asked.

"Me, but it was fleeting," Nikolai answered. "I ran across two on a distant world long ago. Once I realized what they were, I left before they noticed me." Fire blasted from his mouth; he batted it away. "My dragon isn't any happier about my decision now than he was at the time it occurred. He wished to stay and fight."

"Is there water here?" Katya asked. "As in large bodies of it?"

Nikolai nodded. He seemed to have moved beyond his misgivings about Johan and Erin. That Kon had readily acquiesced and shifted clearly went a long way to quell his concerns. "Have you not been here before?" he asked.

"Yes, but all this ice wasn't here then," Konstantin replied.

"It wasn't here before the serpents showed up, either," the woman with silver hair said bitterly.

"That was our first clue all was not well," Nikolai clarified. "We sensed others with magic but didn't worry ourselves overmuch about their presence. After all, no one who didn't possess power could show up in a place such as this. But then, it grew colder. Much colder."

"Several of us took our dragon forms and went to

investigate," another woman, this one quite fair with shoulder-length curls, tossed in. "They never returned."

"We tried to reach them with telepathy," Nikolai explained, "but they didn't answer us." A sigh rattled from him, laced with regret and sorrow at the loss to dragonkind.

The silver-haired woman wove an arm around Nikolai's shoulders. "We've been over this ground. You mustn't blame yourself."

"I'm the one who sent my friends, my comrades, on that reconnaissance mission. If it's not my fault, then whose?"

"You had no way of knowing," Konstantin said.

"It does not excuse me. I should have gone to look myself."

"Had you gone as a dragon, you wouldn't have returned," the burly man said.

"Better me than them," Nikolai countered. "I am in charge of our flight, and I performed poorly as your leader."

"Tell us what happened when you went looking for the dragons," Katya urged. Listening to Nikolai flay himself raw hurt her soul.

"We didn't find them right away," he answered her. "We searched for two days before we came across a gaggle of sea-serpents, rolling about on the newly frozen lake. They greeted us like long-lost friends, and when we asked after our kinsmen, they pretended they hadn't seen them."

"Did you test their words with magic?" Konstantin drew his brows together into a thick line.

"Not the first conversation, although I have no idea why I didn't. They must have ensorcelled me. By the time the next meeting rolled around, I warded myself and was far more cautious."

"What had changed?" Johan leaned forward, clearly interested.

"Three things. The dragons were still not back. We couldn't locate them with magic, and our world was many degrees colder."

"Go on," Konstantin urged.

"The second time we approached the serpents, power flowed around them in what appeared to be the beginnings of a teleport spell." Nikolai thinned his lips into a harsh line. "I asked if they'd be returning, and a grayish-black serpent shrugged. Their spell thickened. Before they vanished, another of them said, 'Thank you.' For some reason, the others found it hilarious. I ended up standing there with my thumb up my ass as both laughter and serpents faded from this world."

He spat a mixture of fire and ash on the ground.

"I'll take over," the burly man spoke up. "We searched and searched. By then, we were certain the serpents had something to do with the disappearance of our friends. Months passed, but we didn't give up."

"Nay. We grew more determined," the blonde woman said.

Nikolai held up a hand. "Let me finish the tale. Perhaps because the sea-serpents' spells eroded the longer they were gone, we finally located one of the missing dragons. Loran was buried in ice. As far as we could tell, he'd moved beyond where any of us could reach him—or his dragon.

"Once we found him, it was simple enough to pinpoint the others. All were in a similar state of stasis. They'd been arranged in two rows, as if the serpents had been planting crops. We cut them from the ice with fire, moved them away from the lake, but the next day their bodies were iced back over."

Fire mingled with his last words. His dragon must have been frantic about the others. Desperate dragons were dangerous dragons. The more agitated they became, the harder to control. Katya would have complimented the shifters on not ending up with renegade bondmates, but she didn't want to pour fuel on the dragons' discontent.

They had every right to be disconsolate. The loss of six dragons was perhaps the worst defeat dragonkind had ever suffered.

"At least your companions are no longer trapped." Konstantin's observation carried a tiny flicker of hope.

"Yes," the dark-haired shifter concurred. "We thank you for delivering them from the wickedness draining their magical essence."

"Did you ever reach within the dragons to do away with the larvae siphoning their power?" Katya asked.

Nikolai shook his head. "As you discovered, each dragon contained many larvae. We weren't certain of the exact number. Nor were we clear what would happen if we bombarded our friends with lethal power."

Katya looked away. They should have at least tried. Six dragons lay encased in sorcery-laden ice. They could have experimented on one of them... A thin tongue of guilt stabbed her. She'd always been too judgmental for her own good. If it had been her friends in the ice, could she have chosen a sacrificial sheep?

Probably not.

Easy to cast blame. Harder to put herself in someone else's position.

"I can answer the how-many question," Johan said. "Twenty-four cells per dragon. Those serpents are organized fuckers. Although at the time, I had no idea the cells I was destroying were embedded in dragon bodies." He angled a look Kayta's way. "Did you?"

She nodded. "Not until my dragon pointed it out, though." She carefully avoided questioning why Johan's dragon didn't figure things out. Or maybe he had but was so intent on being a rebel, the significance of frozen dragons buried in layers of magic didn't compute.

"That dragon needs a stern talking to," her bondmate muttered. Ashy smoke puffed from Katya's mouth.

"Later." Katya put steel behind her command. *"We have more important things to attend to."*

Her twin's form took on a liquid aspect, and she understood he was shifting. She intuited what he wanted to try and opened the channels within herself to shift back to her dragon form. She'd be tired when this endless day drew to a close, weary to her bones, but it couldn't be helped.

More dragons rose into the silver sky streaked with teal and violet. For the first time, she noticed an oblong sun hanging low on a distant horizon. Nikolai was golden like her, except his scales shaded more copper in spots. Erin's red was airborne.

"*What are we doing?*" Johan asked, followed by, "*Do you need me?*"

"*Kon is going to attempt to revive the dragons. Absent the parasites that were sucking the very spirit from them, we may meet with success.*"

"*Is that even possible?*" Johan's question brimmed with hope and excitement. Her annoyance at his dragon fell away.

"*He saved you, didn't he? To answer your other question. You needn't shift. Regain your strength so you can help with the spell breaking once we've moved the dragons away from the ice.*"

"*I hope I didn't hurt them. I wasn't being careful.*"

"*Neither was I.*" Katya clamped her jaws tightly together. It was tempting to blame her dragon for not telling her they were blasting destruction into other dragons until the deeds were done, but they were in uncharted territory. Dragons were ancient beings with extensive memories. Perhaps her bondmate had taken a while to understand what the embryos were embedded in.

That it hadn't reacted with horror spoke well for it. Her dragon could just as easily have turned into a rage-ridden beast ripping up the skies with fire.

None of this was anyone's fault, and she focused all her energy on helping her twin. If they could only rescue one dragon, it would be a victory. Better to keep her goals modest to avoid soul-crushing disappointment. Fire shot from dragon jaws as everyone worked together to finish cutting the dragons' bodies from their icy crypts.

The remaining ice broke up far more easily than she would have expected, but they shot the equivalent of a hundred blowtorches at its uneven surface. Plus, the top layer had already been shattered when they killed the hatchlings. Eight dragons, including her and Konstantin, worked fast. Soon, the half dozen buried dragons lay atop the ice. Their wounds from removing the hatchings smote her. Blood welled, staining the snow-streaked ground.

Her twin swooped low enough to grab a red dragon with his powerful hind legs. He carried it to a spot near where Nikolai and his flight had emerged from the cliffs. Katya's jaws parted in approval. The flight probably had a dwelling carved out of the inside of the crags. Dragon magic would be strong there, and it was just the thing to coax their kin back from whatever dark places they wandered.

She snatched up a dragon—careful not to make its injuries any worse—and flew after her brother. After placing the comatose wyrm gently next to the red, she summoned her next shift. Shapeshifters were never meant to execute so many transformations in a short time. She was panting and wheezing by the time she was human again.

All six dragons lay next to the bottom of the cliff. Ice was chipping off the rocks and clattering onto scales. Between killing the hatchlings and freeing the dragons, she assumed the last of the sea-serpent sorcery had departed. At least this borderworld would thaw out.

Konstantin, Erin, Nikolai, and the rest of his flight formed a half circle around the fallen dragons. Everyone else had reclaimed their human body. Nikolai speared

Konstantin with a gaze like burning coals, if coals were ever golden. He bowed his head slightly. "Guide us, my liege. We cannot afford to make a mistake."

"Your confidence in me is appreciated." Konstantin's words held a formal note. "Much of magic is intuitive. You knew these dragons far better than I do, so you must take the lead. You will recognize their energy and can fine-tune your magic to encourage it to return."

"Once we settle on a spell," the silver-haired woman said, "we will each focus it on the dragon we knew best." A tear formed in one eye and clattered to the ground as a shiny, violet gemstone. "I will do my best to coax Loran back."

Sadness slammed into Katya. "By the goddess. He was your mate."

The woman nodded, tears still welling from her eyes. "I am Auta. Loran will always be my mate."

"We will mix the drawing spell with a cleansing incantation," Konstantin said. "Before you begin, though, you must be aware it is possible the serpents poisoned these dragons beyond redemption." He blew out a strained breath. "They did not fight back. It means they were either snared so deeply, they knew nothing, or that they became willing participants."

A chorus of hisses and snarls rose, punctuated by fire, ash, and smoke. "Not possible" was overlaid with "You're mistaken."

Kon held his hands up, palms outward. "You may not fancy my message, but you must attend to it. If at any time, you—or your dragon—senses the shifter you are working on has been corrupted, call me."

"What will you do?" Auta asked.

"Call on Y Ddraigh Goch to destroy them." Pain streamed from her twin in gray sheets. She wanted to ease his torment but couldn't offer anything. Except maybe killing them herself, and she wasn't at all certain she knew how to accomplish that. The six shifters were deep in stasis, but dragons were still immortal. She had no idea how to smash their comas and edge them into permanent nothingness.

"We cannot leave them like this," Konstantin went on. "Surely, you understand why we must act. The serpents will realize their pets have been destroyed. They'll return and start the same process all over again so long as their breeding vessels are intact."

"We understand," issued from many mouths. It sounded like a dirge and broke Katya's heart.

Johan edged next to her, not touching but offering silent support. The shifters formed small groups around each fallen dragon. Auta was by herself next to her mate. The other five dragons had two shifters crouching next to them. Kon placed himself a little bit apart and gestured to her, Erin, and Johan to join him.

The characteristic smells of dragon castings—sunbaked clay and herbs—wafted through the air, growing thicker by the moment. Katya wanted to ask her brother what their odds were, but someone might hear his answer and lose heart. She didn't see how this could meet with success. The dragons had been checked out for too long... Understanding washed through her. Konstantin didn't believe this would work any more than she did, but it was kinder than simply calling in Y Ddraigh Goch and having him do away with the fallen dragons.

"Do not give up hope." Her dragon's voice was stern. *"It is all that remains. Once it departs, we shall have no chance at all."*

She extended her hands to the sides, clasping her brother's and Johan's. Erin grasped Kon's hand. When they were joined, she sent positive energy spiraling outward, hoping to augment and strengthen the dragon shifters' efforts as they fought to call the others back from dark corridors.

Strong magic flickered at the edges of her vision. She blinked to bring it into focus and wasn't surprised when the dragon god formed out of motes of brilliance. He rarely came when summoned, but Kon's message must have broken through. Nothing like six dragons trapped in the maw of wickedness to attract Y Ddraigh Goch. Particularly when these dragons had been snatched by sea-serpents. Beings banished by the dragon god for treachery.

Hope jabbed her below her breastbone. If anyone could salvage these dragons, it would be the dragon god. She cautioned herself to temper her expectations. He was fully justified to be furious his children had allowed themselves to be trapped in the first place. Y Ddraigh Goch was capable of compassion, but he also had high expectations of his dragons.

He would expect better of them than to be snared in serpent chicanery.

A golden dragon with two shifters chanting over it stirred, bugling weakly. "That's it, Leona," one urged.

"Return to us," a russet-haired man leaning over the fallen dragon commanded.

Katya took a step closer. Konstantin closed a hand around her arm, warning her not to get in the way. "But she's waking up," Katya protested.

Kon shook his head and angled his chin at the dragon god who'd trudged to Leona's thrashing form. He laid a taloned foreleg on her head, chanting low. Power flared blue-white around all the dragons in that group.

Y Ddraigh Goch lifted his foreleg. Angling a talon, he drew it down Leona's scaled forehead, leaving a shiny, scarlet track. "Fly," he shouted.

Leona shook herself, spread her wings, and made her wobbly way into the air. Her flight path stabilized after a short time, and she bugled. Joy, delight, and thanks rang through her trumpeting.

Katya was grinning like a fool, but she couldn't rein in her happiness. Somewhere a million years ago, she'd told herself if they could save one dragon, it would be a victory.

One dragon had been saved.

Over the next half hour, four more took to the skies. Sven, a blue-gold combo, took longer than the others to get his aerial balance back, but after a couple of false starts, he winged his way through skies that were growing dark with the other newly-resurrected dragons amid a riot of bugles, trumpets, steam, and smoke.

Even the dour dragon god looked pleased with himself.

Only Loran remained with Auta keening over him. "Help me." She angled a glance at Konstantin and the dragon god. "Please. I feel Loran. He's close, but then he slips away."

Y Ddraigh Goch focused his spinning eyes on Auta. "Move over, Daughter. I will see what I can do."

"Do I have to let go of him?" she cried. "I just got him back. He is my mate, and—"

"Do you wish my help or no?" the god thundered.

Auta looked away and moved back from her mate. A steady stream of tears formed precious gems as they fell around her.

Konstantin must have sensed something because he flanked the god, hands raised and power arcing between them.

Y Ddraigh Goch raised his forelegs. A multihued shroud formed around Loran. It pulsed and vibrated as if something wanted out, but Katya couldn't see through its opaque surface. At least whatever lay within was moving.

The other dragon shifters had moved before they reanimated. Surely, it was a good sign.

A quick look at Y Ddraigh Goch disabused her of that notion. The god's visage had darkened into a thundercloud. He was chanting faster, and magic whirled around Loran in a black vortex.

Her brother might be a black dragon, but it wasn't ever one of the power colors used by dragon shifters.

The next part happened so fast, she didn't trust the sequence of events. A foreleg punched through the shroud, followed by a sharp wingtip. Loran bellowed. Y Ddraigh Goch bellowed back.

The shrouding sheeted away, followed by the vortex spinning itself out. Auta shrieked, "My love. You're whole again." She started to race toward her mate, but Y Ddraigh Goch held her in place with magic.

"He is corrupt. You must not go to him."

She twisted and barred her teeth at the god. "Everyone else was fine. My mate is too. You are mistaken."

Katya swallowed shock at her impertinence. Auta might be distraught, but it didn't excuse her insolence.

"I will release my hold on you," the god went on. "If you go to Loran, you will be lost along with him."

"What will you do?" Maybe his words had penetrated. At least Auta had stopped snarling long enough to ask a question.

"What must be done. He has been corrupted by the serpents. I cannot allow him to live." The god's words were implacable, yet not unkind. A magical being taking on a distasteful task out of necessity.

"Nooooo!" Auta wailed, a long keening tone, and lurched toward where Loran stood, fire streaming from his open jaws.

Magic flared around Auta, gold, silver, and russet. Her dragon rose from her body. Wings spread, it hovered off to one side. Katya bit back alarm. The god had broken the bond. Could this get any worse? Would he punish the dragon as well?

"Fly free, Daughter," he told the beast. Return to your world and heal."

"Thank you for sparing me," she bugled in dragonspeak. More power flashed around her, and she vanished.

Auta flung herself against Loran's scaled chest, sobbing in earnest except her tears no longer formed gemstones. Y Ddraigh Goch barked a word that hurt Katya's ears. And her heart. And her dragon's soul.

When she opened eyes she didn't realize she'd clamped shut, Loran and Auta were gone. Where they'd stood was a blackened splotch standing vigil against the rocky cliffs.

Nikolai fell to his knees in front of the god. "Thank you for purging my flight."

Y Ddraigh Goch replied, "Thank you for recognizing the necessity of my actions," just before he vanished in a blaze of blue-white illumination.

Johan wrapped an arm around Katya's shoulders. Not saying anything, but there for her if she needed him. She reminded herself of the five dragons they'd saved, but it didn't make up for Loran.

Dragon justice was swift. Cruel. Necessary.

"To me," Kon bellowed. "Today was an unexpected accomplishment, but we can't rest on our laurels. We have a war to plan." He waited while the five who were flying about landed and shifted into their human bodies.

Katya blew out a weary breath. A war. The fucking war. It

was why they were here, but she was heartily sick of bloodshed. And the war hadn't even begun.

"We are DRAGONS!" her bondmate reminded her.

Something inside Katya snapped. She didn't bother with telepathy. So what if everyone heard and it shamed her dragon? "Stuff it. You abandoned me. For years. Do not tell me what it means to be a dragon. Not until you've figured it out for yourself."

Damn. Damn. Damn.

That was the problem with anger. It felt so good to give in to it. And so crappy afterward. When she sent a tentative tongue of magic inward, seeking her dragon, she wasn't surprised to find it gone.

"Fine. Be that way," she shouted after it. The beast probably wouldn't hear, but this was one instance where Katya wanted the last word.

CHAPTER 9

I heard Katya talking. At first, I figured her words were aimed at me since I was right next to her, but when I recognized the anguish laced into what came after *stuff it*, I knew she was upbraiding her dragon. What had passed between them? I started to ask—until I got a look at the closed-off expression on her face.

It was a tender subject, and I'd only find out if she wanted to confide in me. I'm far from an expert on women, but even I know when not to pick scabs off wounds.

I trotted to the circle of shifters around Konstantin. Katya followed, but not right away. Today's events had turned out reasonably well, all in all. Despite Loran's defection—or whatever had happened to him—and Auta's inability to lead with her head, we'd gained fifteen dragon shifters who should willingly sign on to fight the sea-serpents. They'd be grateful to Konstantin for his intervention, and they should be furious with the serpents for tricking them into giving up their independence and becoming breeding farms for evil.

My assessment was right on the money. Everyone was promising aid. Kon looked pleased, but stern. Would fifteen plus the four of us be enough? Or was our search to build our ranks not done yet? I smothered a wry smile. Erin and I were scarcely substitutes for fully vetted dragon shifters. Between the two of us, we might count for one.

Maybe.

"What happened to the dragon shifters on the dinosaurs' world?" Katya asked. She wasn't standing next to me, or anyone else. I tried not to stare at her, but she looked unyielding, reminding me of a latter-day Joan of Arc. Determined to power through, no matter what it cost her on a personal level.

What the hell had happened between her and her dragon? I'd just made peace with mine—at least I hoped I had. Maybe it was more temporary than I imagined it to be.

"We moved here," Nikolai answered her question.

"A very long time ago," a silver-haired woman added.

"Are there other dragons in the Fleisher system?" Konstantin asked.

Several shifters nodded. "We split up when we left the first world," Nikolai clarified. "Most of us came here, but about ten are on the sixth world. We haven't heard from them, but we have no reason to assume they aren't doing fine."

"Did you try to raise them to help with the six ensorcelled dragons?" Katya asked.

Nikolai shook his head. "I was ashamed. I'd failed, and—"

"Enough of that," Konstantin boomed. "We move forward from today." He tossed his hair back over his shoulders. "I will go to the sixth world."

"Damn! I'll be a dragon's uncle," Nikolai muttered. "Once we understood our comrades had fallen under sea-serpent sorcery, the sixth world should have been our first stop."

Solemn nods ran through the assembled shifters. "If the serpents could locate us here, they had the means to find our fellows," a russet-haired female growled. Fire blatted from her open jaws.

I was certain she was one we'd rescued. She appeared to be making a solid recovery.

"I'll go with you," Erin offered.

Konstantin angled his head to one side. "All right. But this is not the place to experiment with your fledgling magic. After what we discovered here, I have little faith in what we'll find there."

The smile on Erin's face faded. "I don't have to come."

She didn't have to say anything else for me to know what she was thinking. In the world we knew, both of us were considered more than competent. We sat at the top of the ladder in our respective disciplines. It was quite a tumble to go from top dog to greenest of the green neophyte.

The air around Konstantin developed a liquid aspect, and I recognized teleport magic. "If you're coming," he told Erin, "move close to me."

I watched her, not worried she'd think me rude for

staring. Would she stand on ceremony? Let her hurt feelings trip her up? Or would she embrace this new life of ours, even if it meant following orders from the man who might well become her mate?

Women had deferred to men—at least on the surface—for almost as long as humankind existed. Not that it was right, but it was accepted until the last couple of generations when females demanded—and grudgingly received—equal treatment. At least on paper. Most of them still didn't earn as much as men in equivalent jobs.

Smoke puffed from my jaws, reminding me how far removed I was from a place where equal wages for equal work even mattered.

After a hesitation, while Kon's spell gathered momentum, Erin hurried to his side. The next moment, the place they'd stood was empty.

"Do you think the other dragons will aid us?" Katya asked.

"I have no idea," Nikolai replied. "We were of two minds about remaining with the other shifters. The dinosaurs and their ilk. We weren't getting along all that well. The primary world in this system is big, but not large enough to constantly be at odds with others living there."

"It took quite a while before we agreed leaving was the only logical solution," another dragon spoke up.

"Are there no humans in this borderworld system?" I asked.

"Yes, but they're on the fifth and eighth worlds," the blonde shifter replied.

"Could you please tell me your names?" I looked around the group. "Katya knows all of you, but I do not."

"You know who I am," Nikolai said. "Moving to my left you have..." he rattled off fourteen names. I learned the blonde was Teena and the silver-haired woman, Melara. The burly dark-haired man was Boris...

Other than Nikolai, everyone else was naked. I was getting used to it. Europe is full of nude beaches, but I never had the time or inclination to frequent them. If I had, the transition might have been easier.

Nicolai paced in a rough circle, hands clasped behind him. The robe—open down the front—fluttered in a breeze that had blown up. Channels were opening in the ice, and the sound of running water was one familiar element in an otherwise alien landscape. It reminded me of lying in the chromium dig site for some reason, although listening to water run down the wall there had been torture since I was thirsty and unable to do anything about it.

"I should follow our prince to the sixth world," Nikolai said.

"Give him more time than this to return," Melara countered.

"Yes, if he's not back in one turn of the glass, then several of us can offer our assistance," Boris growled. The barrel-chested dragon shifter turned to one of the resurrected dragons. "How is it you did not reply to our many efforts to reach you? Did you not hear us? Or were you constrained in some way and unable to respond?"

The five dragon shifters who'd been buried in ice moved

until they stood close to one another. "A better question to ask"—the russet-haired female—Daria—raised a perfect brow—"would be what happened to Loran?"

"All right." Nikolai planted himself in front of the group of five. "Did you know he'd been tainted beyond redemption?"

"We weren't sure," Piotr, a gangly, silver-haired shifter replied in a thoughtful tone. "The day we were snared, Loran located the serpents first. By the time the rest of us arrived, he was settled on an ice floe chatting it up with them as if they were old acquaintances."

I edged nearer the dragon, not wanting to miss any of his story. I had a lot of questions, like why Loran had been so trusting, given the serpents' history, but I was the new kid on the block. Better to listen than to pepper the dragons with interminable questions.

Katya sidled next to me and tapped my arm. When I looked at her, she said, *"This has the feel of a setup to me."*

It took me a moment to connect the dots. *"Are you suggesting Loran had been in contact with the serpents before they showed up here?"*

Every head swiveled to face me.

Katya grimaced. "No more telepathy for you until you learn to direct it to a particular person."

I mumbled, "Sorry," except I wasn't. Not really.

I pressed my shoulders back. I had no excuses, nor did I offer any. "I was human until just a couple of days ago," I reminded the group. "It will take me a long while to learn enough about how magic works to avoid making rookie mistakes. My ineptitude is not the point here, though. If Loran—who presumably understood what traitors the serpents were—was treating them like friends, my guess is he had already been recruited."

"But what inducement could they have offered?" Piotr sounded confused. "Loran ended up just as trapped as we were."

"Yes, but what if they made promises and welched on them?" Katya asked. "It's very like something a serpent would do."

Fire shot from many mouths, mine included.

"We have a potential explanation for Loran's perfidy," Nikolai said sadly. "I cannot believe his dragon would have agreed with such a plan, yet Y Ddraigh Goch didn't offer clemency to his beast, either."

"How could he have?" Katya demanded. "Dragon and human become more and more alike as years pass. Had the dragon been worth his scales, he'd have severed the bond, or petitioned the god to. Were the dragons as mired in the sleeping spell as their bondmates?"

"Yes," Daria answered. "I clung to consciousness, but I'd have given anything to be asleep—or dead. To be aware I was helpless, that I had no power to do anything except lie buried in ice while parasites sucked the marrow from my bones was the worst torture imaginable."

She inhaled raggedly and blew out smoke and ash before going on. "Sometimes my dragon would almost break through. Almost. Sometimes I would, but I could never claw my way through the last of the barrier. It was as if those horrible things feeding from me knew their meal ticket was potentially on her way out. They upped the ante, fed more darkness into the binding spell. I'd sink, screaming my defeat—except no sound came out—and fall forever."

"We never hit bottom," Piotr broke in. "I urged my dragon to leave, to return to the dragons' world for help, but he was just as trapped as I was."

"Even if Y Ddraigh Goch had killed us all," Daria growled, "it would have been an improvement over where we wandered."

"Your dragons?" Nikolai asked. "They all seemed well, but—"

One by one the five shifters weighed in. Mercifully, the dragons hadn't been harmed. The net result of their lengthy imprisonment was fury.

"I am missing an elemental bit in the sequence of events," I said. "The five of you came across Loran chatting it up with the serpents. How did you end up snared?"

"I asked myself the same question many times," Melara focused her golden eyes dead on me. "Loran encouraged us to land. The moment my hind feet connected with the ice, I was doomed. Consciousness deserted me. When I woke—if you can characterize any part of my imprisonment as being totally awake—I was sheathed in ice. I couldn't move. At first, I thought it was a mistake. An accident. Until I cast every spell at my disposal, most of which I had a hell of a hard time remembering, and none of them made any difference at all."

"Cursed ice." Daria shook a fist skyward.

"It is, indeed, unnatural ice that has been cursed," Boris agreed.

I realized I'd slacked off on drawing heat upward from this world's core to warm myself, yet the temperature wasn't intolerable. Not like it had been when we first arrived.

I looked from one dragon to the next, hoping for an answer. "This world is warmer than it was. Is it because the serpents' magic was defused?"

"I'm not sure it's the serpents," Nikolai said, adding, "Feel free to disagree with me, any of you. My sense is that this world is outraged at being shanghaied in the pursuit of wicked magic. When it formed ice sheets and became cold, it was trying to create an environment so uninhabitable, the serpents would give up and leave."

"They did the same thing when they showed up in Antarctic waters," I murmured.

"Where is that?" Piotr glanced my way.

"The extreme southern end of Earth," Katya replied. "At the time, I thought the serpents were creating the ice, but Nikolai might be onto something. Power is vested in the land. It's what makes my twin a prince among us."

"Has he established the same connection with Earth that he had with Mu?" Nikolai asked.

"I don't believe so," Katya replied. "Or if he has, he's kept it to himself. When most of the dragons in our flight left in search of more habitable lands, he took their departure personally. He's only just now starting to recover."

"Understandable." Nikolai nodded. "Knowing your twin, he selected that particular spot because he believed it would be good for dragonkind. To have many dragons decide otherwise must have angered him."

"No. It made him doubt the wisdom of his choice," Katya said. "And whether he still deserved a leadership role among our people."

I leaned closer, wanting to understand. I'd wondered why she didn't appear to share his status. If dragon royalty was blood linked, she should hold an equal rank to her twin's.

As if Katya intuited my confusion, she went on, "Dragon shifters were linked to Mu's magic. Kon was in sync with that world. It was when we realized he was our prince. It was also how he understood we had to leave because Mu was dying. The land confided in him, trusted him. Konstantin opened channels on Mu. Using them, we could augment our magic by joining with the land. On a much more modest scale, it's why we can draw warmth upward from whatever world we're on, and why we're impervious to the elements."

"Worlds welcome our presence"—Piotr offered a small, sad smile—"because they understand we will treat them with respect. It was a great boon when Konstantin resurrected our age-old tradition of joining with the land."

"Who was prince before him?" I asked.

"Inmar," Katya answered. "But many centuries came and went between when he chose to fly with Y Ddraigh Goch and when Konstantin learned the land link hadn't faded with Inmar's leave-taking."

"I don't understand. You—er, we're—immortal. Why would this Inmar fellow abandon you?"

Nikolai trained his golden gaze on me. For a bare moment, I looked into his soul and saw world-weariness that was an eye-opener.

"Abandon is not the right word," he corrected me. "Inmar left because he could no longer bear the weight of his life. Our god offers...options. The dragon shifter may fly forever in the golden one's realm. Or the bond may be severed. In that case, the dragon returns to the beasts' special world, and the human eventually withers and dies."

I had a feeling both options were permanent. As in dragon shifters didn't get do overs if their brand-new existence wasn't everything they'd hoped for.

"Do not leave before I return," Katya told Nikolai. Next, she angled a pointed glance my way, said "Walk with me," and set off across the cracking ice.

I followed her without question. But then, I'd have followed her damn near anywhere. I don't care if it makes me appear weak. Many Dutch men pride themselves on running their households with an iron hand. I was never one of them, perhaps because I never had a home that was more than a spot to eat and sleep while I was in Leiden.

Katya stopped about fifty meters from the rest of the dragon shifters on a newly melted-out patch of muddy earth. She turned to face me and folded her arms beneath her breasts. "How are you doing with all this?"

It was a fair question, so I didn't gloss over it with a pro forma answer like, *I'm fine.* "I am absorbing everything I can, but I look forward to some uninterrupted time with the books and scrolls."

"What if you don't get that *uninterrupted time*?"

I shrugged. "I will keep going, gathering information and adding it to what I have learned so far. It is a slow process, but no matter how I approach things, it will take a long while. At least now I understand why you are not second in line for the crown."

"Think about it," she challenged me. "If blood were the deciding factor, how could we choose our leaders? All dragons are related in some fashion if you go back far enough. Besides, we live forever. It would never work to have some crown prince lurking on the sidelines plotting ways to make the current prince so miserable he opted to leave the same way Inmar did."

I did think about it. The living forever part was the stumbling block that would take the most getting used to, but it was one of the cornerstones of what it meant to be a dragon shifter.

"Kon and I had lived over a millennium in Earth years when I began to suspect there was something special about him," she went on. "I'm who encouraged him to talk with the land. He thought it was ridiculous. So much tripe."

"What would have happened if you said nothing?" I asked.

"His destiny would have found him sooner or later." She dropped her arms to her sides. "Destinies are like that."

A corner of my mouth twisted upward but stopped well short of a smile. "You can run, but you cannot hide," I murmured.

"Something like that." She nodded. "Anyway, it's why he's

a prince, and I'm just a dragon shifter. I wouldn't want the mantle of responsibility. It's a heavy weight, and about to grow far more onerous."

Katya gripped my forearms. "We are in full on preparation for a major war. One we have no certainty of winning. The universe is a big place. If we fail and Earth falls to the serpents, there are many other worlds."

A string of protests bubbled up, but they were swept away in a haze of fire and smoke, courtesy of my dragon.

"Earth is far more important to you and Erin than it is to the rest of us. Our fight is against the serpents. Earth is secondary. We would push forward with this battle no matter where it was." She took a measured breath. "It may seem we stumbled onto the sea-serpents' hatching grounds by sheer, blind happenstance, but it might not be as random as all that."

"Not random, as in someone sent us here?"

"Nothing that organized, no."

"Are you worried we will find other dragon shifters similarly encumbered?" I considered the ramifications and came up lacking. I had no idea how many worlds existed. Should we be out there searching every single one?

It was impossible. By the time we'd covered even a small portion of them, the serpents would have snatched up Earth and made it theirs.

She tightened her hold on me. Where she touched me, heat traveled up my arms. An urgent, alluring tingling that shot straight to my groin. This time when I wished for clothes, it wasn't for warmth but to conceal my unruly appendage.

"I share your concerns about the serpents and how wide their reach extends," Katya said, her tone solemn. "And yes, I've been tracking your thoughts. After today, Y Ddraigh Goch and his minions will travel far and wide, searching for serpent contamination and setting things to rights."

"How can you be certain?"

"Because I trust our god. For him to sever a bond as he did between Auta and her dragon told me how horrified he was by what occurred here. He will not leave even a single spot where dragon shifters reside to chance."

"Did he know what Auta would choose?"

Katya trained her gaze on me and nodded. "It's the only conceivable reason he would have freed her dragon. It was bad enough he condemned Loran's to death."

Katya believed her assessment, so I tried to lay my concerns aside—at least about that problem. "Do you suppose the dragon god knew Loran was a mole?"

Her forehead crinkled. "Moles are creatures with poor eyesight who live beneath the ground."

"They are also spies, turncoats, and double-agents." I wrapped my arms around her and breathed in her scent. Her hair tickled my nose, and she molded her body to mine. I could have held her in my arms forever, but I let go and stepped back a pace. My cock jutted from my body. Nothing I could do about it. Desire for her swept through me in a sweet, slow tide of longing.

I needed information more than I needed sex, though. At

least, I told myself that was the case. "Describe this link to the land? What exactly is it, and how does it work?"

Katya raked her appraising gaze from my head to my feet and back again. "If he chooses, Konstantin can speak with the land, urge it to take certain measures. Worlds are living entities that wish to survive just as any of the rest of us do. They have innate knowledge that recognizes both good and evil, but they move slowly. One of the reasons we took such good care of the blind fish was to curry favor from Earth. When our crops failed—due to incompatible soil and no direct sunlight—Konstantin could have appealed to Earth."

"Why didn't he?"

"By then, the remainder of our flight was intent on leaving. Kon was outraged, but neither would he beg them to remain. We are a free people, and we do not force our will on anyone."

"This group of dragon shifters were quick to call him liege," I pointed out.

"Because they went seriously astray on their own." She shifted to telepathy, ostensibly not to hurt anyone's feelings. Probably wise since Nikolai had already flayed himself raw.

I didn't dare risk a reply in mind speech since I'd already demonstrated my clumsiness.

Katya's head snapped up. "Konstantin is returning."

"Is anyone with him?"

I felt the flicker of Katya's magic swirling around her. Baked clay, musk, cloves, and vanilla filled my nostrils, enticing and calming by turns. "Yes, but not dragons."

Before I could mine for more details, she took off at a

brisk trot for where the other shifters had broken into small groups, chatting amongst themselves. As we approached, the conversations halted abruptly and everyone stared upward, scanning the cloud-filled skies.

Katya hadn't exactly answered my questions about the finer points of being linked to various worlds. It appeared it took a long time before the land trusted a person enough to open up to them, but I was thinking in human terms. It was the only frame of reference I had.

Brilliance flashed so starkly, I shut my eyes. When I opened them, Konstantin and several unfamiliar people were passing through a gateway not unlike the one Surek had opened to the serpents' world, except this one didn't feel menacing. Unlike the dragons, this batch of folk wore clothing, mostly made from leather and animal skins. And high, lace-up boots that encased their lower legs and reminded me of medieval footwear.

"No dragons on the sixth world," Konstantin said, "but these bird shifters volunteered for our cause."

Cheers rang out interspersed with "thank-yous."

Was I the only one who wondered if they were truly bird shifters or some kind of insidious serpent trap? Did Konstantin know them? Had he asked them to shift the same way Nikolai had challenged him?

Could I even ask any of those questions without pissing him off?

Erin had edged off to one side. I tried to make eye contact, but she either didn't notice or was avoiding me.

Katya made a point of hugging her brother. I felt power

flare between them. Was she checking to make certain nothing had happened to him on the other world?

Maybe so because she smiled at the eight men and women who'd journeyed with her twin and said. "Please don't take my request amiss, but some of you are strangers to me. If you could be so kind, shift. Let me see your birds."

My eyes widened, but I cloaked my surprise fast. Along with her words came a compulsion spell. Thick as molten lava, it flowed around the newcomers, capturing them in its folds.

"Perhaps we shall rethink our generosity," a short, brown-haired man mumbled.

Around him, the others stripped off their clothing. The air surrounding them flickered, glistened, and sparkled. Feathers in a plethora of colors rained down as eagles, crows, and two cormorants took to the air. Apparently, they were immune to Katya's spell. Or maybe it wasn't aimed at them.

The only one left was the brown-haired man. Katya's shimmery net, visible to my third eye, tightened around him until I saw the serpent nestled within his illusion. Black-edged magic hovered around him but couldn't punch through thanks to Katya's casting.

"Do not let him leave," I shouted.

"We have no intention of doing so," Konstantin snarled.

Something about his words told me he'd known about the traitor all along but had lured him here with a purpose in mind. I glanced at the birds circling overhead. One by one, they landed on their erstwhile companion and began pecking at him, grabbing bits of flesh and swallowing them whole.

The old Hitchcock movie, *The Birds*, flashed through my mind. Maybe Alfred knew more than we gave the old guy credit for.

CHAPTER 10

a Few Moments Before

Katya sensed her twin returning, but without a single dragon in tow. Granted their circumstances were desperate, but dragon shifters stuck together. For Kon to be bringing someone other than their own kind along meant something had gone sideways. She craved more time with Johan—a lot more. He'd actually held her close. Not for very long, but being in his arms had felt incredible.

She imagined the feel of his mouth on hers. The touch of his hands running the length of her body. Longing filled her. Johan was an extraordinary man, and she yearned for him with a singlemindedness only another dragon could comprehend.

Maybe one of these days, she'd throw caution to the goddess's four winds and kiss him. He wouldn't shove her away. She was certain of it. Today, though, wasn't the time for such pursuits. He'd been right to step away from her and refocus both of them on all the things he needed to learn.

He shared her longing—at least in the lust department. The hot length of him pressing against her belly had provided ample proof of his arousal.

Konstantin was nearly back. She shelved her sensual imagery of Johan's cock and hurried to the other dragon shifters, ready for damn near anything. Before the newcomers were fully through the gateway, she scanned them with magic to verify their identity. Bird shifters, if she was any judge. She made a show of hugging Konstantin. Touch opened an absolutely private communication channel between them. He said enough in those few seconds to galvanize her into action.

They had a serpent in their midst. If they managed him properly, maybe they could learn something. He'd never talk without prodding, but pain could produce surprising results. Adopting what she hoped was a disarming smile, she asked the birds to shift. A reasonable request given the problems they'd dealt with.

Katya held her power ready. As soon as the real shifters summoned their birds, she launched an immobilization spell at the one remaining man. His disguise was exceptional. Best use of illusion she'd ever run across. If she hadn't known to pick it apart, she'd have been convinced he was an eagle shifter just like two of the other birds.

That he couldn't extend the illusion to shifting would be his undoing. She wove power around him, magic that would keep him from teleporting out of there—or summoning any of his kin.

Apparently, the Fleisher group of worlds was riddled with sea-serpent contamination. Had they gotten to the prehistoric beasts? Threatened them with goddess only knew what if they revealed the serpents' presence.

According to Konstantin, the birds hadn't realized their companion wasn't one of them. Fury streamed from them as they plummeted out of the sky and settled on the serpent, plunging their beaks into his flesh. He remained on his feet, shielding his face with his hands. The birds kept right on pecking. Soon, bone showed through shredded flesh.

No way out for the serpent. They'd bind him with magic that would hold him until the end of time. His only choice would be to talk with them. If he did—and told the truth— they'd imprison him on a distant borderworld. A place he'd never leave, but a far more merciful alternative than what the serpents had done to the dragons.

If he opted for silence, he was deader than dead. She, personally, would take the time to torture him. Drag his death out to make up for the misery the dragons encased in ice had suffered. Not that anything she could do to him would make a dent in that particular debt, but she'd give it her absolute best shot.

Fire blew from her mouth. Interesting. She hadn't noticed her bondmate's return. The beast must have snuck back quietly. Katya avoided making a snarky comment to her beast. She'd expected the stubborn creature to be gone for at least a few days after their last argument. Maybe her dragon had a run in with Y Ddraigh Goch. The dragon god wasn't in a mood to tolerate prima donna anythings.

Not with serpents riding roughshod over his dragons and using them as breeding boxes for evil.

The dragon shifters surged forward, battering the serpent with bolts of magic. Blue. White. Amber. Golden. Taking care to avoid the birds, they hit the serpent—still in his human form, thanks to her binding spell—again and again until blood flowed, staining the snowy ground. Johan was right in there slugging with the rest of them. It pleased her. He'd disabuse himself of his misplaced sensibilities soon. She'd sensed his initial distaste at murdering the hatchlings, but he'd gotten over it.

"Do not kill him," Konstantin roared to make himself heard.

"He's immortal," Nikolai yelled back.

"Not in his human body, he's not," Kon corrected him.

Nikolai's golden eyes widened. "What happened?"

"I don't know," Konstantin answered. "I'm sure their lack of invincibility isn't a fact they want bandied about. If we hadn't overheard them talking, we'd never have known about it."

"Ha! A mortal weakness," Melara crowed. "I love it."

The birds were still pecking merrily away, cawing and squawking as they fed from the serpent. Konstantin barked a few words in the dragons' tongue. They continued to ignore him. Katya wasn't surprised when a focused tongue of flames licked at the birds' taloned feet.

Amid a chorus of outraged squawks, they let go and took

to the air, circling like the pack of vultures they were. "Shift!" Kon shouted skyward. "You'll get ample chance to torture our prisoner."

The dragons had formed a circle around the faux bird shifter. As the seven birds found first their bodies, and then their garments, the circle pressed closer. Everyone was waiting until the birds joined them.

The serpent remained immobile, head bent, hands still shielding his face. One of the bird shifters pushed through the line of dragons, followed by the others. "We allowed you and your family sanctuary." A barrel-chested brown-haired man with crystalline green eyes shook a fist at the serpent.

Katya's ears perked up. Family, eh? "How many arrived with him?" she asked.

"Three," another bird shifter answered.

"Shit!" Johan muttered.

"Indeed," Erin cut in. "The others are long gone. Off to warn their serpent buddies."

"Not necessarily," Konstantin corrected her and angled his gaze at Katya.

She understood his unspoken question. "My spell was absolute," she told her twin. "No way he could have communicated through it. Or shifted. Or done anything except stand where he is."

"My guess," Konstantin went on, "is this bastard thought to gather information and volunteered to come along. He must have known about the breeding project here, and—"

"What breeding project?" The thick-chested bird shifter unfisted his hand and twisted to look at Kon.

He didn't flinch beneath the man's intense scrutiny. "I purposefully didn't tell you everything. I sensed right away something was amiss with this one"—he jabbed a finger at the serpent—"and crafted my words in such a way to entice him to come with us. If I'd revealed we'd blown up the breeding pool for evil, he'd like as not have waited for you to leave and run to tell his companions. Wherever they might be stationed."

"Yes, but what were they breeding?" another bird shifter, this one female with cropped straight blonde hair and dark eyes pressed.

"In a nutshell, the serpents immobilized half a dozen dragons, buried them in ice, and were using their magical essence to nurture a clutch of hybrid monsters bred with dark magic," Katya replied.

Hisses, snarls, smoke, and ash were joined by disgruntled bird caws.

"Be angry later." Konstantin was back in charge. He elbowed his way until he stood squarely in front of the serpent. "Lower your hands," he commanded. The serpent didn't have a choice, not in the face of her twin's magic.

Slowly and jerkily, he dropped his bleeding, broken hands to his sides. His face was unremarkable, but perhaps that was by design. It wasn't a face that would be easy to remember. The only feature that stood out were his eyes, and they were so black iris and pupil merged into one.

"You will give us information." Konstantin still employed compulsion.

The serpent just stared at him like a sleepwalker.

"If you fail to provide anything useful—or worse, lie to us —we will ensure you spend the rest of forever in misery. Do you understand me?"

The serpent still didn't move.

Katya scanned him with magic, just to make certain she hadn't broken something inadvertently with her casting. She hadn't been particularly careful. No reason to be. Her assessment yielded a living creature, though. A shudder ran through her. It was unnerving how similar serpents were to dragons, and she didn't like it.

They were monsters. Born of night and darkness and evil, they shouldn't be anything like her.

She dug deeper and found the serpent's sharp intelligence coiled and waiting. "Konstantin."

He didn't turn toward her, but said, "Yes?"

"Reach inward. Establish communication with the serpent. It's there. The human part has checked out."

"You must be mistaken," Nikolai said. "They're like us— or they used to be. When they wear their human skins, both serpent and man must be within."

Katya shook her head. "Check for yourself."

A long, low, sibilant hiss emerged from the serpent's mouth. Katya tightened her spell. Had acknowledging the serpent empowered it? She wasn't willing to take that chance.

"We should go back," the burly bird shifter said.

"Noooo," several shouted, followed by variations of, "We want retribution. They lied to us. Used us. If they're mortal, all of them must die."

The hissing grew in volume. Someone, maybe Boris, or perhaps Nikolai, shot a tongue of flame down the serpent's body, close enough his clothing began to smoke and smolder.

Katya gestured to Johan. "Help me hold him."

"Tell me what to do," Johan said as he worked his way to her side through the line of dragons and birds.

She extended a hand. "Your dragon will understand. Open your power to me, but watch what I'm doing. In case you need to use this same working on your own someday."

Johan's grip was warm and sure. It would have been easy to fall right back into longing and possessiveness for the man by her side. Instead, she made certain he followed the circular steps that kept her spell alive and the serpent trapped within it.

Kon and the birds were engaged in a debate, peppered with people speaking over one another.

"Enough!" the broad-shouldered bird shifter boomed. "I, Gustaf, am your leader. We shall return to the sixth world. Assuming the other three who arrived with our prisoner are still there, we will kill them. Pair up. Two of us against one of them. Use destructive magic set to the highest level. I will oversee each execution and provide additional magic if such is required."

Katya glanced up from her spellcasting. "What if this one won't talk? Is it wise to knock off the others? Surely with four of them, there's bound to be a weak link."

An ominous rattling added to the sounds issuing from the serpent's mouth. His bottomless dark eyes were impossible to read, but fury was stamped into his nondescript features. Katya felt him pushing, testing the boundaries of her control.

"What exactly do you wish to know?" Gustaf asked.

"Everything," Konstantin snapped. "How many serpents have left the worlds Y Ddraigh Goch consigned them to. Where they are now. The bones of their plans."

Katya shook her head. "We'll never get all that. We'll be lucky to find out if any serpents remain where our god put them. My assumption is they all broke free."

"So if we had a rough idea where all of them were, it would be useful?" Gustaf said.

"It would," Konstantin concurred.

"If we can get anything out of them before they die, we will." Gustaf sounded grim and resolute. Power bubbled around him, and he drew the other six bird shifters off to one side. When the air cleared, they were gone.

"I am not sure how it is happening," Johan muttered in a strained-sounding voice, "but the serpent is growing stronger."

Nikolai ran close and added a blast of his own magic to their mix. His golden eyes developed a harsh cast. "I'll say. Either that, or he was cloaking his ability before."

"No," Johan said. "He is definitely stronger."

Katya picked her way around the perimeter of her spell and groaned. "That slimy fucker. He's tapping power from my spell. Once Johan's magic kicked in, he hid behind it to conceal what he was doing."

She barely got her words out before the world turned

into a confusing jumble of madness. Konstantin bugling. Other dragons roaring. Johan shouting curses. Dragonfire flared around her, bright and reassuring, until a burning, clawing sensation tore at her midsection, flattening her.

She fell to her knees, unsure what had unbalanced her. Something was wrong with her vision. The scene in front of her wavered, undulating in waves. Her hearing was truncated, as if sounds came from the bottom of a very deep well.

Johan's voice ebbed and flowed. So did Konstantin's.

Nikolai grabbed her shoulders where she knelt and shook her. She opened her mouth to protest, but no sound came out. Her body had escaped her control, and she had no idea why. Fear gripped her, but she couldn't give in to it. Nikolai lifted her—or maybe it was Konstantin—but the moment they let go, she fell back down. Her teeth began to chatter.

When she reached for her bondmate, the dragon was behind some kind of barrier. She sensed the beast but couldn't reach it.

What's happening to me? The words repeated again and again but never made it out of her mouth.

"Do not let the serpent in!" Her twin's voice rolled through her foggy brain. *"Fight him, goddammit. Shift. You're stronger as a dragon."*

Was that what had happened? Interested in more than subverting her spell, the serpent's plans included commandeering her body? She'd never heard of magic like that. Her twin must be mistaken.

"He's overreacting, right?" she asked her bondmate, and then remembered it was lost to her. Or it may as well be. Still, something soothing emanated from somewhere. Everything would be fine. If she'd just let go and trust to the future.

Muted and from a distance, she heard Johan shouting in Dutch. "Take me, instead."

The panic she'd been holding in check bloomed into full-blown terror. What in the fuck was wrong with her? Konstantin's assessment must have been spot on, just like all his appraisals. How could she have doubted her twin? Johan had just bade evil to join with him. Shifters weren't like vampires. They didn't require an invitation, but it made things so much easier with a willing victim.

She struggled against whatever had gained a toehold over her sanity, her will. It was uphill every step of the way. Steep. Rocky. Icy. She slid back several metaphorical steps for every one she managed. Meanwhile, had the serpent jumped ship? Was Johan's invitation too appealing to turn down?

"Come on, you bastard. Stick with me," she exhorted.

At the edges of her peripheral vision, Konstantin's black dragon blasted into view. Around her, the other dragons were forming. At least she thought they were. Her ability to see anything was still truncated, wavering. Crap. If this was how serpents viewed the world, how did they ever get anything done?

The burning, tearing sensation amped into agony so searing it took center stage. She reached for her chest, wanting to do something, anything to make it stop. Images of water pounded through her. Water would fix everything. Water cooled burns. Water was life. Hope.

She would have crawled toward melting puddles of snow, but she was surrounded by dragons and Johan, still in his human body. He crouched next to her, put his face right up next to hers. "I love you, Katya. You have to fight through this. Kon says he can't save you if the serpent completes the transformation."

Johan grabbed her shoulders and shook her. "Did you hear me?"

She tried to nod, may have managed it, but probably not because his next words were, "Blink once if you heard me."

She shut her eyes. It was a hell of a struggle to open them again.

"Katya!" He sounded panic stricken, but then her ears stopped cooperating.

I am stronger than this.

She repeated the words, turning them into a mantra with no beginning and no end. Her dragon could read thoughts. *We're in this together,* she reminded her bondmate. *If I am lost, you are too. We must shift. Break through before the enchantment pushes us beyond salvation.*

No wonder she felt compelled to find water. Sea-serpents shifted in water. It wasn't life or hope for her. Water would seal her doom. Her muddled thoughts cleared slightly.

The pain raking her might have lessened a little. It was still so pervasive, she couldn't be certain. Except now she recognized it. The goddess be damned serpent was trying to shift, using her body as a conduit out of its trapped one. She could not allow that to happen.

Gathering her will in tiny bits and shards and pieces, she cobbled it together, ignoring the inner humming meant to soothe her into insensibility. If she'd noticed that insidious droning earlier, she wouldn't be stuck in her current predicament.

Anger flared. It helped beat back pain and hopelessness. When she reached for her dragon this time, she punched through the barrier. Furious bugling burst from her mouth, the first sound she'd made since this entire odyssey began. Katya plowed through layers of slime. Of muck. Of shit standing between her and her shift magic.

Power shot into her. Johan and Konstantin. Doing their damnedest to help. *"We can do this,"* she told her bondmate. Katya wanted to crow. She had a voice again.

"Yes," the dragon answered. *"We can."*

Ripping, stretching, tearing exchanged the pain she'd been living with for something far more familiar. Shifting hadn't hurt since she was a very young girl, but it hurt like a bitch now. Gave her a whole new appreciation for what Johan and Erin had gone through.

Still frightened to her soul hers and her dragon's combined efforts wouldn't be enough, she ran wide open. Or as wide open as she could. She saw the serpent now. Felt its malevolent presence and booted it out of her body. One mighty heave, and she was free.

Free and flying. She'd never shifted so fast, nor been so relieved to see her beast's golden scales. Below her,

Konstantin and Nikolai closed on the serpent and hammered his human body with lethal force. The man who had housed the serpent formed a conical pyre, burning like only dragonfire could. Heat blasted upward.

"What happened to us?" her bondmate asked, sounding very subdued and not dragonlike at all.

"We were tricked," Katya bugled in dragonspeak. "It will never happen again."

She flew in tight circles, watching the serpent burn to a pile of blackened cinders. Once it was well and truly gone, she landed and summoned shift magic. Having her power back within her control felt damned good. She'd never take it for granted again.

Kon and the others hurried to her. As soon as she could talk, she asked, "Why didn't you kill it before?"

Her twin nailed her with his gaze. "We couldn't have while it was partially within you. Your immortality protected it."

Shame gutted her. She'd misjudged. Because of her, they'd lost their chance to grill the serpent and maybe learn something. "I'm sorry. I never dreamed it had the kind of power to take over my body."

Nikolai thinned his mouth into a grimace. "They might not be dragons anymore, but we underestimate them at our peril."

"No kidding," she muttered.

Johan ran to her. "Thank Christ, you are unharmed."

Konstantin turned his whirling eyes, still dragon's eyes,

on Johan. "You will never invite wickedness into yourself again."

"Got it. You already said as much. I do not require a reminder."

"Just making certain I was clear," Konstantin growled.

Johan's earlier words returned in a rush. He'd said he loved her. Had he truly meant it? Or was he so distraught about the serpent, he was pulling out every trick in the book to draw her back from disaster?

"He is ours," her dragon spoke up and puffed steam in Johan's direction.

Katya hoped her bondmate was right. More than hoped. Her dragon nature needed to hold him to his word. Except humans didn't operate like that, and Johan was still more human than dragon.

She wrenched her thoughts back from the man who'd been willing to trade his freedom for her own and stood tall. "Again. I am sorry I wasn't more vigilant. Do we wait for the birds to return? Or do we all travel to the sixth world to make damned good and certain none of his"—she angled her chin at the still-smoking cinders—"relatives survived the birds' attack?"

CHAPTER 11

Short Time Earlier

When I understood the serpent was trying to seize Katya's body to escape the hold we had on its own, I felt helpless. Incensed such a thing could have happened, and ill-prepared to fight back. I could have left it to the other dragon shifters—the ones who actually understood how to wield their power—but I didn't have it in me to walk away.

Katya knelt on the ground, head down as if she were praying. Her hair fell around her in a cascade of copper curls, the golden highlights pronounced in the soft light of this world. I may have danced around my feelings before, but in that moment I understood I'd fallen in love with her. Maybe my dragon had something to do with it, but I'd been attracted to her from the moment I laid eyes on her.

A man would have to be dead to not be smitten by her charms, yet my feelings extended far beyond her curves and hair and eyes. I'd fallen in love with her spirit, the bedrock of what made Katya who she was. Determined. Sure of herself.

Because I was still linked to her magic, I felt the moment when the serpent made the leap and tapped into her. My dragon shut off our magical flow damned fast, before I even thought it might be the wisest move.

"That was selfish," I told my bondmate. *"Now we cannot help her. Not as easily as we might have."*

"We would do no good at all if the serpent nabbed us along with her," he retorted.

His words gave me the idea to offer myself. I'd wait until the situation was truly desperate, of course. But surely one dragon shifter was as good as the next for the serpent's purposes.

All around me, dragons were shifting and bugling. Some took to the skies, but Konstantin and Nikolai remained on the ground. Kon tried to pick Katya up, but the moment he released her, she collapsed in a nerveless heap. It was as if she'd been drained of the ability to do anything. Not so much as an eyelid quivered.

It may have been ill-advised, but I shouted at the goddamned, fucking serpent to take me instead. My dragon gave me nine kinds of grief. I waited for Armageddon to fall on my head, but nothing happened. Apparently, I wasn't as appealing a vessel as Katya.

Kon was chanting over her. Nikolai picked up the refrain. They seemed to have whatever magic they'd selected well in hand, so I knelt next to her. I blurted that I loved her and told her what I'd gleaned from her twin, which was that once the serpent fully had its claws into her, we wouldn't be able to pull her back from its clutches. Not easily, anyway. The difference with the dragons we'd found in the ice was there were no serpents physically here guarding them, merely remnants of sea-serpent magic.

Even those remnants had given us a merry chase as we defused them.

Kon had also chastised me soundly for offering myself in Katya's place, but she didn't need to know that part.

Katya didn't respond at all to anything I said. Finally, in desperation, I told her to blink if she'd heard me. She did, but it took her forever to close and then open her eyes. Surely, that level of inertia didn't bode well. I shook her. Told her to try harder, but then Konstantin pushed me aside and pretty much did the same thing.

Except he shook her far harder than I had.

Erin pulled me to my feet. She didn't say anything, but her presence provided a small bit of comfort. "Believe in her," she said.

I was trying, but the shell of a person kneeling in front of me didn't feel like Katya anymore. If I'd been more vigilant, more savvy about magic, maybe I'd have noticed what was happening sooner than I did. The fucking serpent had been trying for stealth, but once Katya voiced her suspicions about what it was up to, it had jettisoned stealth in favor of expediency.

"You should shift," Erin told me. "I'm going to. We're all stronger as dragons."

"Thank you for caring about her, but I shall remain as I am. For now."

Erin nodded that she understood and moved back a few meters. When I next glanced toward her, the red dragon was spreading its wings. Kon and Nikolai were still chanting like madmen. The serpent's human body wasn't standing anymore. It's posture mirrored Katya's, and the similarity gave me the creeps. I had the oddest feeling it would crumple to dust, like a discarded prop, once the serpent severed its connection.

I wanted to be closer to Katya, but Nikolai and Konstantin blocked my way. Nikolai was gold, like Katya but with more copper shadings. I missed her, ached for her in a way that left a hole in my soul.

Erin had told me I had to believe Katya was resourceful enough to find her way back from wherever she wandered, but the six brood-farm dragons hadn't been able to break free from serpent ensorcellment.

Not on their own.

I told myself to think positive. I knew the drill. Imagine what I wanted to happen. Visualize it, and make it so. But this wasn't a metallurgical project. This was the woman I loved.

"Not so different, after all," my bondmate said. *"Imagine the outcome you want. Focus all our energy on it. You're spinning your scales picturing the worst possible result."*

I glommed onto my dragon's words. Carved them across my forehead as I imagined Katya breaking through the serpent's hold on her. "Come on," I urged. "You can do this." I'm certain she didn't hear me. Not with two dragons bugling over her, but I repeated my command several times.

I sensed a not-so-subtle shift in the magic flowing around me. I took it as a good sign. Between two breaths, Katya's body exploded. At first, I feared all was lost. The serpent had destroyed her in a fit of pique. But then, I saw golden scales and copper wings and Katya flapping to gain altitude.

I whooped and cheered and fist-pumped the air. Dragons shifted back to humans all around me.

Some combination of our efforts had worked, but I bet Katya had a whole lot to do with her freedom. She wheeled above us, banking and flying in figure-eights. The second she broke free, Kon and Nikolai set upon the serpent and killed it by dousing it in dragonfire.

I was still whooping and doing a victory dance when she landed. Suddenly shy about blurting out how I felt, I merely told her I was grateful as hell she'd survived. I wasn't expecting her to fall into my arms, and she didn't. She apologized to everyone—something I should do too, at some point—and asked what would happen next.

Maybe she wouldn't even acknowledge what I'd told her. Perhaps she hadn't heard, which might be better for everyone concerned, now that I thought about it.

"We could go to the sixth world," Konstantin answered her question about what our next moves would be, "but I'm not at all certain we'll find any remnants of either the bird shifters or the serpents."

"They offered their help to us," Erin pointed out. "The least we can do is show up on their world."

"Erin." Kon angled a pointed look her way. "The likeliest scenario is the serpents killed the birds and left."

"We have to go," I spoke up. "Erin is right. We owe them."

Nikolai raked curved fingers through his messy hair. "You have a lot to learn about shifter hierarchy. We owe nothing to those below us."

"Why are they below us?" Erin asked. She had a mulish expression I recognized from our days aboard the *Darya*. It meant something was important enough, she wasn't about to back down.

"Their magic is inferior," Boris answered.

"All the more reason to help them," Katya insisted. "At the time we agreed they should return, we had no idea how sly the serpents were." She stopped to blow out a tight breath. "It's entirely possible while I was engaged in mortal combat with the monster, he was able to communicate telepathically. I underestimated him. And overestimated myself."

Katya turned to me. "I feel terrible for involving you. How did you know to disengage?"

I winced. "It was not me, but my bondmate."

"Well, thank the dragon god for your beast's common sense." She strode to her twin. "Come on. The sooner we take a look at the sixth world, the sooner we can figure out what to do next."

"We were already there," Erin reminded Kon, although I was certain he hadn't forgotten. "There were hundreds of bird shifters, and a few other varieties too. We can't just walk off and leave them to the sea-serpents' whims."

Konstantin let his gaze rest on each shifter briefly. "The sixth world it is. Any who don't wish to accompany us, remain here. We'll come back for you before we move on."

In the end, everyone opted to join us. Guess they felt ashamed withholding aid. Our journey to the sixth world only took a few minutes. This place reminded me of eastern Colorado. Rolling and barren. Blue skies held a few fluffy clouds. Nowhere in Europe looks like this. It's peppered with towns, hamlets, and villages sitting nearly on top of one another. Not much in the way of wide-open spaces until you get to the northern reaches of Scandinavia.

The various spells that transported us here frittered away. "We were in a different spot last time," Erin noted.

"Of course, we were," Kon replied. "No reason to bring us out in the middle of a battle. Or a field of dead shifters. Ward yourselves. Another small jump about two klicks due east, and we'll be in the bird shifters' primary village."

"Ready yourselves to kill," Nikolai warned.

"The illusion shielding that serpent was sophisticated," Katya said. "Be damn sure your target isn't a shifter."

"Easy enough," Kon cut in. "We tell everyone to shift."

"There were long minutes when I couldn't have," his twin noted bitterly.

"Point taken. Let's get this over with." Konstantin dropped a transport spell over us. When it cleared, I was glad the women had insisted we come. Fighting raged around us. There might only be three serpents, but each was ringed by at least a dozen shifters.

And they were barely holding their own.

The air ran thick with power. The sickly sweet rot of sea-serpent contamination mingled with the clean earthbound smells of shifter magic. I hustled to the farthest group, along with Nikolai, Melara, Boris, and Teena. Nikolai shifted, but the rest of us opened our mouths and let our dragons douse the serpent pinned in by the other shifters with dragonfire.

Once Nikolai was airborne, he hit the serpent from the air, coating it with still more flames. I've always been a bit of a pacifist. Not that there have been any wars I could have signed up for, but even if there had been, I doubt I would have volunteered without someone planting their boot in my behind.

This newfound bloodlust, where I welcomed opportunities to kick some serious ass, amused me on the one hand. And surprised me on the other. The transformation had truly changed me, and I liked the new me better than I had liked the old one.

He's more primal. More tuned in to what's truly important. And right now, ridding every world of sea-serpents had blasted to the very top of my list. The craven, sly fuckers didn't deserve to waste the air they breathed.

Our serpent was reduced to an ash heap in short order. Nikolai clunked down heavily and shimmered back to being human. "I'm going to need a break," he announced. "Food. Rest. All this shifting burns through magic like nothing else."

When I glanced at the rest of the field, two more pyres crackled merrily. I dusted my hands together. End of this batch of serpents. Or was it? I eyed the group of shifters ranged around me.

"Do all of you know one another?"

A lissome young woman—although for all I knew she could be hundreds of years old—glided toward me. Red hair fell to knee level, and her eyes were an arresting shade of hazel. Like the other bird shifters, she wore formfitting leather breeches and a tunic that reached to hip level. "Yes. Beyond the four newcomers, the rest of us have been here since the dawn of time." She laughed, lyrical and sweet, and moved nearer still.

"Thank you for saving us," she went on. "We were holding our own, but our magic was fading."

"Because the serpents were hogging it up," another bird shifter cut in bitterly. "Every time I turned around, the bastard had nabbed a little bit more from me."

I wasn't quite ready to let the topic of unwanted possession go. "Everyone here may look familiar, but the serpents have made an art form out of taking over other shifters' bodies."

Nikolai nodded brusquely and clapped his hands. "Indeed. Everyone here shift. At least far enough I can see your animal form."

To their credit, no one grumbled or said it was unnecessary and a waste of time. Clothing hit the ground in piles, and a variety of birds glistened into being. Along with two coyotes, a wolf, and two deer. The red-haired beauty who'd spoken with me turned out to be a wolf.

She was gorgeous in that form too, with a thick black-and-gray pelt and the same eyes I'd noted when she was human. She brushed up against me, and I couldn't resist burying my fingers in her fur.

"All right. Thank you for obeying my order," Nikolai said. "Shift back. I have a feeling Konstantin will want to talk with all of us."

I loved the earthy scents of shifter magic. They reminded me of rain-wet greenery and the smell of mossy rocks, or the ocean on a sunny day when the briny smells were strongest.

The wolf was human now, and very naked, just half a meter away. She smiled knowingly and walked near enough her pert breasts were nearly touching my chest. My cock, faithless dog that it was, started to thicken. Before it embarrassed me, I turned away, intent on locating Konstantin and Katya.

She loped up from my other side and stopped dead, looking from me to the wolf and back. I'm sure she noticed my partial erection, or smelled sex or some such thing. The wolf growled. Katya shot smoke and ash all over her. The wolf bared her teeth and batted the smoke aside.

I felt like a sap. I hadn't given Missy Wolf even one shred of encouragement. Yet it appeared she didn't require any to have staked a claim to me.

The wolf snarled. Katya started toward her but then shook herself. "We're all meeting over there." She pointed to a spot behind her.

It was time to do something other than stand around while the wolf and Katya squared off. I hooked an arm beneath Katya's. "Let's go. Shall we?"

She cast a coolly appraising glance my way. "Unless you'd rather remain here."

Before I could come up with a tactful reply since I was still mired in twenty-first century manners, the wolf said, "But you two are not mates."

Katya twisted out from under my grip and bared her teeth at the wolf. "No, but he is mine, and you would do well to remember that."

The wolf dropped her head and looked away, probably the equivalent of showing her tummy to an enemy and requesting clemency. "Apologies, dragon. I didn't know."

Katya whirled and took off at a lope across the rolling plain dotted with scrub grass and sagebrush. I ran to catch up. Her announcement about me being hers had both shocked and pleased me, but I needed to double check I hadn't misunderstood. Perhaps I was only hers because she'd helped me through my first shift, and there was nothing romantic about her statement.

"Wait a moment," I called after her fleeing form.

She kept right on running. I sped up, loving the augmentation in my physical abilities, courtesy of my bondmate. We were nearly to the assembled group of shifters when I was close enough to grab her arm.

"I'm sorry," I told her.

She raked me with that same assessing glance she'd

employed a few moments before. "What do you have to be sorry for?"

I grinned sheepishly. "Nothing. Except him." I batted my cock. "He has a mind of his own. Means nothing." Before I lost my nerve, I plowed on. "What did you mean about me being yours?"

"It's clear enough, but I misspoke," she said. "You and I have no claim on one another."

I laid aside a lifetime of emotional isolation and dove off the high board, the one that's always terrified me because I was never certain I could keep up my end of the bargain. "I want us to, though."

She angled her body until she faced me. God she was so gorgeous. When I thought how close I'd come to losing her, it froze my heart into icicles. "Want us to what?"

Was she being purposely obtuse? Or had I truly misunderstood? No time to play games. Kon clapped his hands, wanting order so he could begin talking. I bent close to her ear. "I meant what I said when you were in the serpent's gunsights. I love you. I want you as my wife, or mate, or however dragon shifters do such things."

It felt like several lifetimes passed before her generous mouth curved into a soft smile. "I accept. And that will have to be good enough for now. We shall be betrothed, although Y Ddraig Goch only knows when we will come up with time to solemnize our commitment."

"Quiet, everyone. Come closer," Kon's words were threaded with command.

I wanted to cheer and shout to everyone that Katya had

just agreed to marry me, but it would be disrespectful to Konstantin. Besides, he might still be furious with me for offering myself to the serpent. Maybe he wouldn't think I was good enough for his sister. What would we do if he didn't offer his blessing? Did dragons elope absent approval from their nearest relatives?

Beneath everything, I recognized I was focused on fluff because I was more-or-less the same commitment-phobe I'd always been. If Katya and I married, would I be able to keep my side of the covenant?

I wasn't worried about my unruly appendage. Remaining faithful had never been an issue, but I had a straying spirit. Adventure had always trumped romance. Maybe being a dragon shifter would, indeed, change all that. The ability to shift forms and fly whenever I wanted added a whole new dimension to things.

Katya gripped my hand and kissed me once, sweet, quick, and full of promise. Our tongues tangled for a few seconds, and then she stepped away. With a great deal of difficulty, I focused on Konstantin. Nikolai had joined him, and the two of them were gathering data from the assembled shifters. They admitted they'd heard rumors that the next world over, the seventh, contained at least a few serpents. Not wanting to court trouble, they hadn't gone to look for themselves.

"We were a bunch of fucking cowards," Gustaf cursed. "Given what I know now, the seventh world is probably the serpents' command post within this group of borderworlds."

Privately, I agreed with him, but it didn't make our next

steps any clearer. Should we take them on and risk the serpents on Earth becoming too strong to vanquish? Or should we remain here long enough to cleanse these borderworlds and make them safe for habitation once more?

"Can you ask Y Ddraigh Goch for help?" I shouted from my spot near the back of the crowd. The dragon god would speed things up. It might be wrong of me, but I was still driven by an illogical need to ensure Earth's safety.

"We have our own gods as well." A shifter turned to look at me. "We have already put out the call."

"Why was I not informed?" Konstantin's tone was deceptively mild.

"Because we don't report to you," the shifter who'd spoken to me replied. He was medium height with short black hair, and I remembered him turning into a hawk.

"This is war." Kon's tone was decidedly less neutral. "War requires leaders, and we must all pull in the same direction. What that means is I must know everything, no matter how inconsequential you deem it."

"Understood," the man murmured. "My apologies, dragon prince."

"Accepted." Kon nodded. "We move forward. I require a small team of spies to visit the seventh world and report back."

"I'll go," Katya called.

"Not without me," I told her.

She grinned, but it held savage edges. "Excellent. Kon will get two of us for the price of one, so long as he agrees."

CHAPTER 12

The last thing Katya wanted to do was spy and fight, but her self-discipline took over, rose to the fore. Just because she and Johan had pledged their troth didn't mean they'd find time to tumble into one another's arms.

No matter how much she longed for him.

She wouldn't have been so brazen about her feelings, but when the hussy wolf made her intentions clear, with pheromones streaming from her, something in Katya had snapped. Her dragon possessiveness snatched away common sense, and she would have battled the wolf to establish her claim to Johan. Fortunately, the wolf backed down.

Smart of it. Teeth were no match for fire.

"Told you he was ours," her bondmate gloated. *"We must fly and formalize the bond."*

"Not before he understands how permanent it is."

Katya winced. There was that part. Johan had to understand once they made love in either form, they would be bound together forever. No divorce in dragon-land.

"Are you certain you've recovered your full strength?" Konstantin asked.

Katya wasn't certain he was speaking to her; she dragged her full and complete attention back to the task at hand and tried for a confident demeanor. "Probably not, but all I have to do is ward myself."

"That ward has to be totally invisible," her twin reminded her. "And invincible. The serpents will be on the lookout for anything out of the ordinary."

"They'll know about their dead kinsmen, won't they?" Gustaf furled both brows.

Konstantin nodded. "They will, indeed. What they may not know is the manner of their deaths. By now, I'm certain they also know their little hybrid breeding project is no more."

"What were they going to use those mantis-bird things for?" Erin asked.

"To augment their ranks," Nikolai answered her. "What better way to create an army than to build one from the ground up. No need to train your troops. No worries about their commitment to your cause since part of their programming is absolute loyalty."

Katya did a quick count of the cells they'd destroyed. 144 hybrids, twelve of which had hatched just prior to their arrival. When the dragon vessels were once again available, she had no doubt the serpents would have filled them with more of the hybrids. Perhaps a different variety. Soldiers specialized to do something other than fly around snapping off heads with their insectoid jaws.

"Question for the shifters living here on the sixth world." She raised her voice to be heard over the din of burgeoning side conversations. "How long ago did the four serpents show up?"

"Not long," Gustaf replied. "Perhaps a couple of months. Hardly long enough for us to get to know them. Why are you asking?"

Katya shuffled back into battle mode, having left dreams of a romantic interlude far behind. She trotted to the front of the group and faced them. "We ran into sea-serpents a short while ago at the extreme southern end of Earth. They'd fled a world they decimated and were searching for a new home. At the time, Kon assumed they were plotting evil. A conversation we overheard clinched it, but Earth is a big place."

"Hence the need for an army?" Gustaf nodded grimly.

"Are you thinking the group on the seventh world showed up about the same time as the batch on Earth?" Konstantin asked.

"Perhaps a little earlier," she replied, "but I can't believe the two clusters are unrelated. Like us, they communicate telepathically. This group of borderworlds is closest to Earth. It's probably not coincidental there are serpents here."

"How did you discover the serpents on the seventh world?" Konstantin asked.

A willowy woman with masses of black hair walked closer to where Konstantin stood. "In the worst possible way. My mate and his two brothers traveled to the seventh world to gather a particular type of grain that only grows there. They make the same trip every annum."

She spread her arms to the sides. "You may have noticed how dry it is here. Not the best for crops. There are advantages to not living in the midst of a rain forest, though, which is why we never considered moving."

"What happened?" Kon's voice was as gentle as he ever made it.

"They never returned," the woman said. Sorrow had hollowed circles beneath her eyes. "I heard his pain—and his death—through our mate bond. Not too long afterward, the four serpents showed up. They said they were from the first world, but that the dinosaurs had chased them off."

"We believed them," Gustaf picked up the tale, "because our prehistoric kin can be crusty and are particularly harsh on strangers." He shook his head. "I blame myself. I meant to check out their story, but I never carved out time to teleport to the first world. If I had, perhaps we'd have had a different outcome."

"Hard to say what it would have been," Konstantin said. "When we arrived, you were holding your own against three of them, but barely."

"You're right of course," another bird shifter spoke up. "We outnumbered them, but they clearly had reinforcements nearby. By the grace of the gods, more serpents never showed up."

Katya latched onto his words. Damn it! Had the three serpents put out a disaster call before the dragons arrived and killed them? What about the one intent on occupying her body? Surely, between all of them, they'd managed to launch a single cry for help.

Why wasn't the sixth world crawling with serpents who would have harkened to their companions' summons?

"Do you supposed Y Ddraigh Goch got to them first?" she asked.

"All the gods know one another," Nikolai said. "The shifters here called upon their own gods. Perhaps they converged on the seventh world, and—"

"I'm going to go look," Konstantin cut him off. "Katya. You're coming with me."

Johan hurried forward. "Then I am coming too."

"No, you are not," Kon said.

Johan stood tall and faced her twin. "Either you take me, or I shall teleport there on my own."

Oh-oh. Katya made a grab for her brother's arm before he advanced on Johan and pulled serious rank.

"I want to come too," Erin announced brightly. "Johan and I will stay out of the way."

Konstantin looked from one brand-new dragon shifter to the other. "Fine," he said through clenched teeth and motioned to Nikolai, who nodded tersely.

Red-tinged magic boiled around her twin. He was so angry, he wasn't trusting himself to speak. She understood why. Both Erin and Johan had challenged his leadership—to his face. It may not have carried ill intent. In truth, she was certain it didn't, but Kon would feel he'd lost status in front of the other shifters. Not a good place to be on the leading edge of planning a war.

Johan's announcement he'd show up on the seventh world one way or another was tantamount to challenging Konstantin to an aerial duel. She had to educate him—and damned fast.

The teleport spell swept them up and spit them out nearly as quickly. Where the other world was arid, desert like, this one was so damp water dripped off greenery. Her feet sank into warm mud, and tepid rain dribbled from a cloud-filled sky. Sludge sucked at her feet. No wonder the shifters didn't want to live here. She doubted the waterlogged ground could support any type of structures.

"Remain here." Kon's words shot through her head like a cannon. He and Nikolai vanished into the thick mist.

Katya located a tangle of gnarled, slime-coated roots that formed a natural cave. She tested the warding around the three of them and added another few layers of protection before herding them deep into the roots. Damp sand beneath her hands and knees was pleasantly warm.

"This is a good place to wait." She kept her voice very low.

"Why is he so angry?" Erin whispered back.

"He is mad at me for offering myself to that serpent," Johan explained.

Katya shook her head. "Not it at all." She hesitated. Where to begin?

"What then?" Erin pressed. "Help me understand. He

wants me as his mate. I was almost ready to accept, but it's like he's turned into a different man since we left Earth." She closed her teeth over her lower lip. "He's so abrupt. It's hard to find anything approachable about him anymore."

"Dragon culture is very different from human," Katya replied. "It's based on hierarchies and obeying the dragons above you in the pecking order without question. I'm sure it seems terribly medieval to you, but it's how we've operated since the first dragon shifter was formed with Y Ddraigh Goch's blessings.

"When both of you challenged Kon in front of all those other shifters—"

"But we didn't," Erin protested.

"Yes, you did. It was for him to select whom he wanted to send to this world. You were free to indicate you wished to be chosen, but the actual choosing was for him to do."

"So when I announced I was going regardless, it was rather like a big fuck you?" Johan asked.

Katya nodded. "A very big one because it was public. The other shifters would be within their rights to assume Konstantin lacks control over his people."

"That's the reason he was so angry he almost couldn't speak?" Erin blew out a sad little breath.

"Why did he not simply tell us to stay put?" Johan cocked his head to one side. Dark strands of hair fell across his face.

"Don't you see?" Katya spread her fingers in front of her. "He was in an impossible situation. You'd already announced you were going no matter what. Had he forced his will onto you—made it impossible for you to leave—the other shifters would have grilled you, wondering if a rebellion were brewing."

"We would have said no," Johan replied. "End of story."

"Not really," Katya said. "They'd have assumed it was a secret rebellion." She beat back half a smile. "Shifters are grand at cloak and dagger theories. Regardless, the net impact would have been they'd like as not have decided as a group not to follow us dragon shifters into battle. Presenting a united front is critical."

"Even if it's false?" Erin asked.

"Is it?" Katya pressed. "It isn't that you were truly challenging Kon. You were merely forwarding an opinion. It's a very human way of interacting. You didn't see any reason to muffle your desire to be included." She stopped to collect her thoughts and drew two partially overlapping boxes in the sand. "If one of these is how things really are, and the other is how people perceive them to be, you see there is some overlay, but large areas remain that are full of potential misunderstandings."

Erin nodded. "I'm beginning to at least have a frame of reference. I spent six months in Japan several years ago. I was working in a hospital, and it was very different from the surgical practice I was used to. I missed a whole lot of social cues, and I was certain my Japanese hosts were laughing at me behind my back, but I never caught them at it."

Johan snickered. "They were. Trust me."

"I finally decided you almost had to be born Japanese to live in that culture without mishap," Erin went on. "It wasn't so much unpleasant as I always felt like an outsider."

"They consider us inferior," Johan muttered. "Gaijin. I played dumb when I was there, but given my facility with languages, I got the gist of most of their taunts."

"What could they possibly have made fun of you for?" Erin asked.

"Not me *per se*, but how I look. I'm much larger than the average Japanese, and they likened me to a gorilla." Johan shrugged. "Apes are very smart, so I took it as a back-handed compliment.

"Circling back to dragons," Katya said. "Dragon shifters are at the top of the heap. The other shifters owe us allegiance whether they wish it or not."

"We have military examples of the same type of thing," Johan explained. "They all operate as hierarchies with severe penalties for failing to follow protocol."

"They used to shag unpopular officers during the Vietnam war." Erin shot a look Johan's way.

"What does that mean?" Katya asked.

"Bad officers met with untimely deaths in the jungle," Johan told her.

"But that's terrible." Katya's voice had risen, and she lowered it. "Were those responsible punished?"

"Only if they were caught." Erin leaned forward. "Humans don't have magic. We lack foolproof ways of sorting out the truth. Good liars can get away with a whole lot. Including murder."

Katya's bondmate thrashed within her. The dragon was outraged. Underlings did not plot to kill their masters. For them to do so and not suffer consequences was unconscionable.

"My dragon is pitching a fit," Johan said.

"Mine too." Erin frowned.

"They're incensed by what you described. It violates precepts at the very heart of what it means to be a shifter." Katya placed a hand on Johan's thigh and her other on Erin's. "You are dragons now. You must learn and accept new ways. This will not be like your experiences in a foreign country. We consider you equal to any other dragon shifter—except Konstantin.

"He is your prince. Mine too. It means you respect him and defer to his guidance."

"Do you ever think he's made a mistake?" Erin asked carefully.

"Oh my, yes." Katya rolled her eyes.

"What do you do then?" Erin's forehead scrunched into a web of tiny lines.

"I share my concerns, but ultimately, the decision lies with him."

Erin pushed her hair back over her shoulders. "So I can have an opinion. That's a relief."

"You can have lots of them"—Katya withdrew her hand —"so long as those opinions don't challenge his authority in a public setting."

Breath whistled softly from between Johan's teeth. "I will do my best. Thank you for the explanation. I recently established what I hope is a permanent détente with my bondmate, but my job is far from done. I see now that we are only free so long as what we wish to do does not fly in the face of Konstantin's will."

Something about the stiffness and formality of his words told Katya he wasn't pleased with his newfound knowledge. She started to apologize but decided against it. Being a dragon shifter was a great honor. That a dragon wished to share its heart and soul with Johan outweighed any petty inconvenience he might find in the arrangement.

This is all very new to them, she reminded herself. It would take more than a few hours for him and Erin to fully embrace their bondmates and their new lives.

"Come now." Konstantin's voice rattled through her head. *"There is much you must see."*

A glance at her two companions told her neither had heard her twin, which meant his communication had been for her alone. Yet, she couldn't leave Johan and Erin by themselves. They weren't quite defenseless, but almost. Katya cleared her throat. Perhaps she wasn't as obedient to her twin as all that, despite her recent pep talk.

"Kon just summoned us," she said and began the process of crawling out of the tangle of roots.

"So, of course we must go," Johan mumbled under his breath.

Katya wanted to shake him. Had he not heard any part of what she'd said this past half hour or so? She remembered the discussion they'd had about freedom before he'd chosen to try to transform himself.

Katya filed it away. She'd remind him if she had to, but it

wouldn't do to rub his face in what he'd said about not truly being free within his human world, either.

"He'll come around," her bondmate spoke up.

Katya didn't answer. She wasn't as certain as her dragon they'd made the wisest choice. But they didn't have to consummate their troth anytime soon. By the time they got around to even talking about the permanence of the dragon shifter mating ceremony, she'd have more information.

"Which is precisely why we have remained mateless," the dragon snarked. *"You've found something wrong with every single dragon shifter who wanted you."*

Katya cringed. What her beast said was true—to a point—but now wasn't the time for that conversation.

She straightened and bit the end of one finger. A few globules of blood bobbed before her. Erin and Johan had crawled out of the roots. Once they stood nearby, she instructed the blood vectors to take them to her brother.

She smelled the battlefield before she saw it. Blood, spilled entrails, and the smoke from at least two dozen fires seared her nostrils. Her dragon bugled merrily. It lived for shit like this.

Kon and Nikolai were in dragon form. They stood next to Y Ddraigh Goch and two other dragons she didn't immediately recognize. A dark-red one and a brilliant-blue monster who stood even taller than the dragon god.

She wove through the killing field, jumping over the odd serpent foot or tail or severed head. Apparently, the fires were an afterthought, not the primary means of destruction. When she reached the other dragons, she bowed low.

Following her lead, Erin and Johan did the same. Thank the goddess they understood to pay obeisance to the god. Katya bet the two she didn't know were his minions.

Nikolai blew fire skyward and trumpeted, pawing the blood-soaked ground.

"Thanks to our god, we won a great victory today," Kon said in dragonspeak, his words mingling with flames.

"May I ask what happened?" Johan's head was still bowed.

"Why is it important for you to know?" Y Ddraigh Goch asked in his deep, rumbly manner.

"It is more than curiosity," Johan answered. "I wish to know how many serpents were here and if you discovered anything that shed light on their plans for Earth."

Both the red and blue dragons had focused their spinning gazes on Johan, but he'd have no way of knowing since his eyes remained downcast. Katya handed him points for courage. Generally, if Y Ddraigh Goch wanted you to know something, he told you. Although, she'd broken a few rules when she'd rebuked him for dragging her from Johan's side in the space between worlds.

Perhaps many of their rules were anachronisms, but she wasn't about to probe that particular rabbit hole.

"We have other constellations of worlds to attend to, sire," the red dragon said in a deferential tone, one that offered the god leeway to demur. Power flashed between Y Ddraigh Goch and his minions.

"Before you go," Kon spoke up, "we stand ready to examine the other worlds in this group."

"See that you do so," the god said. The power flare grew infinitely brighter. Katya shut her eyes against its brilliance. When she opened them, the god and his fellows were gone.

A secondary flash, and Kon shifted back to human.

"Did you find it like this?" Katya asked.

"No. When we arrived, Y Ddraigh Goch and the other two were ripping serpents in pieces and tossing them every which way. Along with a few of the other shifter gods. I recognized Anubis and Thoth. They left once it was obvious the battle was won."

"I thought serpents were immortal." Johan picked up part of a serpent head and chucked it a few meters away.

"Our god still holds dominion over them," Nikolai said. He was back in his body as well, although Katya hadn't noticed him shifting.

"There were twenty or thirty serpents here," Konstantin went on. "A few were still alive when we arrived."

"Not for long." Nikolai's gaunt face split into a satisfied smile.

"Who were the two with Y Ddraigh Goch?" Erin asked.

"Dragons who had tired of immortality and wished to serve," Katya answered.

"I didn't recognize them," Konstantin said, "but they were damned handy at meting out destruction."

"Must be why he picked them," Nikolai said.

"Any evidence of the serpents' plans for Earth?" Johan asked and looked from Kon to Nikolai.

"What were you thinking we might find?" Konstantin countered.

Johan shrugged. "Notes. Journals. Tablets, although I do not imagine the electronic age has had much impact on dragons."

"None of the above," Nikolai said. "Any plans the sea-serpents had are locked in their dead little heads."

"We need to get back," Konstantin said. "We have seven more worlds to examine and ensure they remain habitable."

"Five," Nikolai corrected him. "Eleven and twelve lack breathable air. The fifth and eighth are primarily inhabited by humans, so they shouldn't take long."

"Even easier." Kon smiled.

"From the sound of things, the dragon god is on a search and destroy mission," Johan murmured.

Konstantin nodded. "He is, indeed. He blames himself for this chaos and believes he should have destroyed every sea-serpent eons ago. Pity stayed his hand then. No more."

"How can you know?" Erin asked.

He draped an arm around her shoulders. "Because he told me."

Johan repositioned himself until he faced Konstantin. "Katya explained a few things, and I wish to apologize. I was not defying your authority back on the sixth world. Not on purpose, anyway. I will take care to watch what I say from now on."

"Apology accepted. I must appear very heavy-handed, but until the serpents are fully dispatched, we are engaged in war. My leadership must remain undisputed, or it will dilute our efforts to eradicate our enemy."

Erin leaned into his embrace. Katya hoped it was a good

sign. Her brother loved Erin, but she had to accept him for what he was, or the mating would never work.

Her dragon bugled. At first, she didn't understand what had gotten its attention, but then its meaning hit her broadside. She was really grand at dishing out advice for her twin. But the selfsame guidance went for her too. Johan was who he was, not someone for her to make over into someone more to her liking.

"I love you," she told her beast.

Steam puffed through her open jaws. The creature's way of loving her back.

The mantle of Kon's transport spell snared her and the others. She rode it back to the sixth world. Their next task—after checking the other worlds in the Fleisher system for serpent contamination—would be ensuring every shifter in the Fleisher borderworld group joined them on Earth to fight the serpents.

Even the dinosaurs.

She chuckled. If the war ever left Antarctica, and it well might, what would humans think about seeing beasts they'd thought extinct for tens of thousands of years?

Guess I'm about to find out.

CHAPTER 13

*J*can be a stiff-necked bastard. I'm Dutch. It's in the blood. But after Katya's explanation about some of the ins and outs of dragondom sank in, I felt I owed Konstantin an apology. I'd been laboring under the illusion I could do as I pleased. I have no inkling why I clung to that idea.

Maybe it was a way of doing my damnedest to hang onto what used to be familiar. Seeing that smoldering field filled with dead, dismembered serpents was a hell of a wakeup call. Nothing familiar is left, and the faster I build new habits from the ground up, the smoother things will go.

I wished I'd arrived early enough to see Y Ddraigh Goch and the other shifter gods in action. My newfound taste for gore surely boded well for my future as a dragon shifter.

We dropped onto the same rolling plain we'd left. It

appeared even more shifters had assembled, so I guess the word had gone out.

Konstantin loped to the place he'd recently vacated and faced groups of men and women, all shimmering with what I'd come to recognize as shifter enchantment.

"Thank you for heeding Gustaf's request." Kon must have projected his voice with magic because it boomed all around me.

"What happened?" rang from every corner of the field, voices echoing and repeating themselves.

A man standing next to me leaned close. "Did you find serpents?"

I pointed toward Konstantin, determined not to steal any of the attention or dilute his message.

"When we arrived," Konstantin said, "Y Ddraigh Goch was already there, along with two other dragons and four of your shifter gods. They were fully engaged in killing serpents. I counted twenty-seven, but I could be off by one or two. Not much for us to do but light pyres to burn the remains and cleanse the land."

"Was it frozen?" Melara called from a spot off to one side.

Her question brought me up short. Perhaps Nikolai had been onto something when he'd theorized the ice came from an outraged land and wasn't the serpents' doing at all. But why wouldn't the seventh world have mobilized to defend itself?

"No, it wasn't," Kon replied. "I would have liked to ask our dragon god about that, but I never had a chance. I did sink my consciousness into the land, though."

All around me, shifters moved nearer. Konstantin's link to the land must be something all shifters understood and revered. It was certainly something I wanted to know more about. If we ever returned to the library deep beneath the Antarctic land mass, it was the first thing I'd look up.

"The seventh world is slow, sluggish," Konstantin went on. "But she was willing to talk with me. She was working up to crafting a defense, but the simplest route for it was adding more water to the already porous earth, creating quicksand."

"I'd have liked to have seen that," the dark-haired woman who'd lost her mate said. "Those unholy bastards thrashing around up to their scaled heads in slime."

"They'd still have had access to magic to break free," Konstantin reminded her, "but they'd have had no choice but to leave. I understand why you've chosen not to live there."

"We tried to establish an outpost," Gustaf said, "but everything we constructed eventually sank. Wood rots in all that damp, and stones drift into the mud."

"The most important part is all the serpents on the seventh world are dead," Konstantin went on.

Cheers erupted all around—along with hoots and howls and bird noises. He waited for them to die down before continuing.

"Our current task is ensuring the remainder of the worlds in this system are free from serpent taint. My small group will return to the first world. The remaining worlds are the fourth, fifth, eighth, ninth, and tenth."

"Five and eight will go fast," someone shouted. "Mostly humans."

"Make sure no serpents are hiding in their midst," Konstantin cautioned. "Although serpents are much like dragons in that we prefer living in groups. It would be very unusual to find a single serpent anywhere."

He ran his whirling golden gaze over the crowd. "Volunteers? I seek ten shifters to visit the worlds I listed."

"Ten for each world?" Gustaf asked.

"No. Two apiece."

The broad-shouldered shifter moved quickly, light on his feet for such a big man, and tapped a shoulder here and another there.

"Consider yourselves forward guards," Konstantin said. "If you locate serpents, do not engage them. Return here as quietly as possible. We will send a much larger crew, including dragons, to deal with any serpents you might find. Do any of those worlds contain shifters?"

"A few," Nikolai replied.

"Bring them back here with you," Kon instructed. "Assuming things go well, we will leave sometime tomorrow for Earth."

"How long will we be gone?" someone asked.

"I wish I could tell you," Kon answered.

"Must we all accompany you?" Gustaf asked, adding hurriedly, "Not that we won't if you require such, my liege, but our crops sit at a precarious juncture. If no one is here to water them, we will have no grain during the cold season."

"Pick a hundred of your strongest," Konstantin said. "The rest may remain."

Gustaf bowed his head. "Thank you."

I wondered what Konstantin had in mind returning to the dinosaurs' world, but I'd find out soon enough. He hurried away from his spot facing the assemblage and motioned to Katya, Erin, and me.

Nikolai and Boris joined us. Kon nodded once, sharply. "We will shift to our dragon forms as soon as we arrive on the first world. The dinosaur shifters consider themselves the First People, so they have never paid homage to dragons."

"Why are we bothering with them if they pose potential problems?" I asked. Probably should have kept my mouth shut, but I was in a hurry to return to Earth. I still considered it my home, and I cared about it far more than this constellation of worlds. It wasn't rational. Earth wasn't any better or worse than any other spot, but I had friends there. Family. People I'd known for years.

Ja. And will probably never see again.

I couldn't quite envision myself stopping in for tea at Aunt Margaret's house. What would I say to her lovingly crafted queries about what I'd been doing of late? Or why I hadn't visited her in months? The same held true of everyone else too.

The corners of Konstantin's mouth twitched downward. "We are approaching them because I believe it's the proper course of action."

Maybe he was testing me, seeing if I'd keep my word

about not publicly challenging him. Ignoring any hidden intent on his part—since I couldn't figure it out, anyway—I nodded and said, "Full show of force, eh?"

Konstantin nodded. "Dragons have wished to form an alliance with the dinosaurs for a very long while. We've approached them many times, but they always rebuff us. They are powerful in a way we are not. Where we destroy with fire, they use their bulk and impenetrable hides. Like us, many of them can fly."

"They used to live many other places," Katya said.

I'd been surreptitiously glancing her way. She'd seemed cooler toward me since her mini-lecture about dragon culture, but it might be my imagination. Maybe she labored under some of the same problems I had. As I thought about it, I decided I was mistaken.

I'd remained unattached because I valued my freedom. None of the dragon shifters I'd met appeared to be mated, so perhaps that was one more cultural difference. Humans were expected to pair up, form family groups of one type or another. Shifters lived forever, so they could afford to take as much time as they wanted before settling down.

"They did, indeed," Nikolai was saying. It took me a moment to reconstruct what he was responding to. The dinosaurs and their domiciles.

"They're still quite widespread," Kon said, "but our focus is the ones here. If we are successful, it will forge a path for future partnerships."

The mantle of a transport spell hovered around us. My beast linked us into it. As the sixth world ceded to darkness,

I smiled to myself. Konstantin had answered my question about why we were bothering with the dinosaurs, but he'd done it in his own way. Indirectly. I could live with that. It might teach me patience, a perennial weak area.

I sensed my dragon within me and realized I was growing used to its presence. Something about it was fast becoming a part of me. A welcome part, not the yoke I'd first imagined it to be.

"Not easy for me, either," it muttered, proving it was paying close attention to my thoughts.

"You are working to get to know me, aren't you?"

"Would you expect any less of me? How shall we work together, live together, if we are constantly at cross purposes?"

Gratitude rolled through me. Appreciation for the beast I shared my skin with. He'd taken quite a chance on me.

"Good you realize it," my dragon pointed out quite unnecessarily, but I didn't snark back.

The darkness of the transport spell grayed around the edges. I felt my dragon's anticipation. He knew we'd shift to his form as soon as we arrived, and I could practically feel him spreading his wings.

Soon enough, we were dipping and twirling, flying above the jungle and fissures below. The dinosaurs sensed our presence and lumbered out of caves and burrows. The winged ones joined our flight, above and below. Apparently, we were not completely unwelcome.

So long as we didn't ask anything of them.

After an aerial display that would have done the Blue Angels proud, Konstantin set a flight path for an open spot atop a large mesa. Vegetation didn't grow as thickly there. My dragon wasn't keen to land, but he joined the other five.

Kon shimmered into his human form. My beast groaned but ceded our shared body. Half a dozen dinosaurs, including two who'd been flying with us, took on a glistening aspect. Soon they, too, were human. One was the silver-haired man from our first visit. The others didn't look familiar.

Like us, they eschewed clothing. It was warm here, but didn't seem quite as humid as it had the last time. Maybe it was a comparison thing. Almost anywhere would seem on the dry side after the seventh world.

"Why have you returned?" One of the men asked. Dark hair fell past his shoulders in many small braids. His silver eyes looked even stranger to me than the dragons' golden ones.

"For your assistance, why else?" Konstantin leveled his gaze at the man who'd spoken.

"We already refused." The man's nostrils flared, making his broad, flat nose appear wider still.

"I know, but I haven't given up."

"Dragons always were a stubborn lot," the silver-haired man muttered.

"Ha! You should talk," Nikolai skewered the man with his whirling gaze.

Kon shook his head at Nikolai before returning his attention to the other shifter. "When we were here last, did you know the Fleisher worlds had been invaded by sea-serpents?"

"Of course, we knew. Anyone with magic would have to be incompetent not to sense their foul sorcery."

"So you lied to us when you refused aid on the basis the serpents might invade your world next," Konstantin growled.

"Yes. Anything to send you on your way," the man with silver hair confirmed, a defiant note in his voice.

"Did they truly show up here like they claimed?" Katya asked.

The man with many braids nodded. "We never let on we knew what they were, but we made things uncomfortable enough, they left on their own."

Once again, I was having a hell of a hard time keeping my mouth shut. I wanted to ask why they hadn't warned the other shifters, like the birds on the sixth world, about the scourge.

"From here, they went to other worlds within this system." Konstantin's tone was mild, as if he were recounting a shopping list. "They set up a brood farm for wicked hybrid creations, using dragons to grow their spawn. That was on the third world. They created a de facto headquarters on the seventh world. From there, they dispatched spies masquerading as shifters to the sixth world."

I was watching the dinosaur shifters' faces carefully as the story of our last couple of days unfolded. They did their best to remain stoic, but here and there grimaces surfaced.

"We took care of the breeding farm," Kon continued with more animation in his recitation than before. "We salvaged five out of six dragons who'd been trapped in ice, and we killed all the hatchlings. Meanwhile, I traveled to the sixth world. A handful of bird shifters returned to the third world with me. One was a serpent, masquerading as a shifter.

"I recognized his perfidy but played along with him until we were back on the third world. Despite my caution to corral him, he very nearly took over my sister's body."

"How did you fight him off?" braid-man asked.

"With a great deal of help," Katya replied crisply.

"I'll spare you most of the details"—Konstantin let his gaze settle on each dinosaur shifter in turn—"but with the help of Y Ddraigh Goch, some of his underlings, and a few other shifter gods, we destroyed all the serpents on the seventh world. Other shifters are checking each world in this system to ensure we missed no one."

"You provided a great boon for this group of borderworlds," the silver-haired man murmured.

"And now they are here expecting a quid pro quo." Braid-man sounded bitter, but resigned. Or maybe I was reading in the resigned part because I presumed it had to be there.

"Something like that." Kon nodded. "You know as well as I do that eventually the serpents would have overrun every world in the Fleisher system. Because it's how they operate. Sooner or later, they would have returned here, and you would have had to fight them." He paused, perhaps for emphasis before adding, "Except by then, they'd have become ever so much stronger."

"We would have lost." Braid-man stated it as fact.

"Yes, you would have."

"It would be hard for us to refuse you at this point," the

silver-haired man growled, "but you knew that when you showed up here."

"I did," Konstantin admitted.

Somewhere during the exchange, my respect for his statesmanship took a great leap forward. He'd understood full well this group of shifters would be beholden to the dragons, and that their debt would leave them little choice. They could refuse, send us away, but word would spread. Other shifters would know dinosaurs didn't treat fairly with other shifters.

Idly, I wondered where this group sat in the shifter pecking order.

"Just beneath us." My dragon's quick answer told me he'd been following the proceedings right along with me. *"Unless they told Konstantin to leave again. Then they'd slip quite a few notches."*

Someone, maybe Kon, maybe Katya, had said my dragon would be a tremendous resource. I was coming to appreciate that.

"Give us a few minutes to talk with our people," the man with braids said.

"Of course. We'll wait here, unless you'd prefer we selected another location," Konstantin told him.

"Here is fine. How many of us were you hoping for?"

I waited for Konstantin to tell him we needed everyone. Instead, he replied, "At least twenty-five. Our first stop will be Earth's southern pole. You will not find the climate to your liking, but we should be able to deploy you to a more temperate location quite soon."

"Any particular type of dinosaur?" the silver-haired man asked.

"I am building an army. I need warriors."

"Understood." Braid-man beckoned to his fellows. They turned as a unit and stepped off the edge of the mesa. The air swallowed them immediately.

Katya strode to the lip of the mesa. "Neat trick. They teleported without a burst of magic to cue me what they were up to."

"Nicely done," Erin told Kon.

"Why thank you. Did you doubt me?"

"Never."

I left them to coo at one another and hustled to Katya's side, but when I got there I wasn't sure what to say. Apparently, she wasn't either. We stood next to one another as an awkward silence grew.

"Are you angry with me?" I asked.

She hesitated before shaking her head. "No. I was, but no longer." She turned to face me. "My dragon is certain you'll adapt to our ways given more time."

"But you are not as sure?"

She raked a hand through her unruly hair before she looked me square in the eyes. "This is as much about me as you."

I waited to see if she'd say more. Like I've mentioned, I'm no expert on women, but it didn't seem to me that a flood of questions would hurry things up on her end.

"I've been alone a long time. You as well. From what I've read, it's uncommon for humans to remain unmated.

Dragons, however, can choose many different paths. Some mate when very young. Others never mate at all. Some of us tell ourselves we'll settle in with a mate eventually, but eventually stretches further and further out."

She scrunched her forehead into thoughtful lines. "My beast reminded me a little bit ago about how I've sidestepped mating. She's lonely. She longs for a dragon to fly with, but there are things I've neglected to tell you."

Katya's words were flowing faster now, almost as if she was afraid she'd lose her nerve, although the Katya I knew was fearless. "Much like the bond with your dragon is permanent, dragon matings are as well. Once we've consummated our relationship—in either form—we will be bound to one another as mates forever."

My eyes widened. Not that I planned to dally with Katya and then abandon her, but I'd never anticipated not having a choice in the matter.

"No divorce?"

She shook her head. "It's one reason I never mated. I was unsure I'd be able to sustain that level of commitment to anyone except my bondmate."

My vow not to ask questions foundered. "What is different with me? Or is it more that you did not want the wolf to move into your territory?"

She shrugged sheepishly. "I admit, it was a wee bit of a driving factor, but I'd never have chased her away if I weren't seriously intrigued by you."

She'd said intrigued, not that she was in love with me. The two were very different. I threaded an arm around her shoulders, treasuring the silk of her skin and hair beneath my fingers. She didn't pull away.

"I meant what I said before. I do love you, with all the messy, emotional bits that go along with loving someone. I love you enough to drop the wall I have always hidden behind and take a chance on what our future could hold."

My beast bugled and puffed steam. It settled around us in a cloud.

Katya nestled into my embrace. "I was certain once I told you there was no escape, you'd find a million excuses to…"

"To what?" I murmured. "Run away? I am not the running type, particularly once I have made a commitment. Before, I never got as far as the commitment stage, but I am well past it with you."

Kon and Erin and Nikolai and Boris had faded to background noise. My entire focus was on the woman in my arms.

"What about you?" I asked.

"What are you wanting to know?" She tilted her head and looked at me.

"Do you love me?" Breath snagged in my dry throat. It might not be a fair question, but I needed to understand where she stood. She'd agreed to marry me, but she'd never said a single word about love.

Steam puffed from her mouth, mingling with the steam from my bondmate. Her dragon approved of me, and of our match, but I needed to hear from Katya.

She twisted until she stood in front of me, arms wrapped around me and head tucked into the hollow between my neck and collarbones. "I'm not sure I fully comprehend what love is. I love my beast, but that's different. She is part of me. I love my twin, but we have been together since we shared space in our mother's womb.

"I respect you. I admire you. My heart yearns for you, and I cannot imagine my life if you weren't part of it, which surprises me since we've not known one another long. I'm who noticed you and Erin first. Something about your energy drew me, and it still does."

She hadn't said *I love you*, not exactly. But what she'd told me was deeper, had more substance. It gave us grist for our relationship to grow.

I cradled the back of her head in one hand and kissed her. She kissed me back, and the passion that had smoldered between us burst into flames as hot as any dragonfire.

Katya broke the kiss before it got totally out of control. "Not here," she murmured.

"Ja. Not here."

"Hey, you two lovebirds," Erin called from the other edge of the mesa. Apparently, everyone had retreated there to offer us privacy.

"The dinosaurs are returning," Kon added, "but if we ever get to the far side of all this, I'll be the first to throw fire around during your mating flight."

"Another custom you failed to mention?" I grinned at Katya.

"One of many." She grinned back.

Fingers laced together, we walked to where the others

stood. Sure enough, the other shifters were taking shape from thin air.

"You've come to a decision?" Konstantin asked after they were fully corporeal.

"Yes, dragon, we have," braid-man replied.

CHAPTER 14

Katya still felt the press of Johan's lips against hers. His scent eddied around her, deliciously male and thick enough to coat the inside of her nose. She inhaled hungrily, wishing for more.

The dinosaurs were back wearing grave expressions. Her twin had done a masterful job maneuvering the other shifters into a corner. It would force them to cooperate, but she didn't totally trust any capitulation that came under these circumstances.

If she was in their position, she'd resent the fuck out of Konstantin. It didn't make for trustworthy allies, but if this was the best they could do, it wasn't for her to tell the dinosaurs to buck up or go home. Kon was convinced they needed help. She agreed, but she'd have stopped with the shifters on the sixth world.

The willing ones.

"We shall provide thirty shifters." The man with his black hair braided in what looked like a Celtic warrior pattern said. "Tell me when and where you require them, and they will be there."

"Thank you." Konstantin's tone was formal. "I have wished for a closer working relationship between our people for a long while now. It is my hope today's alliance will forge a new path."

"We are not looking beyond the battle with the serpents," another of the dinosaurs spoke firmly.

Katya clamped her teeth together. There it was. Proof the dinosaurs had been backed into a corner. They didn't like it, but they'd do the right thing. On a one-time basis.

"I appreciate your candor." Kon nodded. "As you desire, we shall proceed one event at a time. Worlds are failing. We always lost the occasional one, but ever since Mu shattered, my observation is that far more realms have followed suit. Either they copy Mu's dramatic path and explode, or something changes in such a way they can no longer support life."

"Your point, dragon?" one of the dinosaurs asked. This one was a little shorter than the others, but shared their copper-toned skin, straight black hair, and silver eyes. Katya wondered how the one with silver hair came to be. He must be far older than he appeared. The delegation was all male. Were there no women in leadership roles?

Konstantin narrowed his eyes. "My point, my *friend*"— he stressed the word, friend—"is times are changing around us. Nothing remains the same, and we must be nimble enough to adjust as the need arises. Shifters have a long history of sticking with their own kind, to the exclusion of all else. My sense is that era is coming to a rather rocky close."

"What are you basing your conclusion on?" Braid-man leaned a bit closer.

"I can talk with the land," Konstantin replied. "Doesn't matter which land. Most of them respond to me, given enough time and effort. I am why dragon shifters escaped Mu before it burst into fragments and scattered through the universe. The land came to me. Warned me."

Katya took a few steps forward and inclined her head. When she straightened, she addressed the dinosaurs. "I, too, offer my thanks for your assistance. Once I was a seer for my people, but I have been remiss in scrying the future. I will pick up the banner soon and will share anything the god chooses to show me."

Kon sent a pointed look winging her way. If she read it right, it was a rebuke for not doing more. She stared right back. "I already said I'm sorry. While we were moldering away beneath Antarctica, I didn't see the need to push it when so many of my attempts to bring our future into focus failed."

The silver-haired dinosaur trotted forward. "You say you used to possess seer magic, but that it has weakened?"

Katya closed her teeth over her lower lip. "Not exactly. Without spending a whole lot of time on this, my dragon left for years. I had a difficult time caring about much of anything during her absence, and my few efforts to look into my glass weren't fruitful. I haven't attempted to scry anything since my beast returned."

"Your dragon left?" Shock lined braid-man's question.

"It's a long story," Katya said. "One I'm not going to discuss."

"I am shaman for our tribe," the man with silvery hair cut in smoothly. "Yle is my name. I use water to call up my visions, but they have been unclear for many years. When first the serpents and then you showed up on our world, I tried harder to see the path before us but with the same paltry results."

"Do you suppose this has something to do with worlds failing?" Katya asked her twin.

"Probably, Sister, but we will worry about it once we have the serpents on the run." He directed his next words at the group of dinosaurs. "Send your selected warriors to the sixth world as soon as possible. Once everyone is acquainted and we've determined how to maximize all the different magics, we will leave for Earth."

"Thank you for not turning us away," Nikolai said. Boris murmured much the same.

The dinosaurs were savvy enough not to mention Konstantin hadn't given them much of a choice.

Katya glommed onto her twin's transport spell, and in a trice everyone was back on the sixth world. Melara and Gustaf ran forward. "Trouble on the ninth world," Gustaf shouted. "I've been waiting for you to get back."

"If you hadn't shown up when you did, we were on the verge of going after you," Melara cut in.

"Serpents?" Nikolai spat the word like the poison it was.

"No, but they were using that world as a storage dump for abominations like the insect-bird hybrids." He shook his head. "We didn't do a thorough tally, but we saw over a thousand...oddities."

"Hungry bastards." Melara made a sour face. "And smart. I kept changing up my ward, but they'd find a way to drill through it."

"We counted poison, brute force, and rather weak magic among their arsenal," Gustaf muttered.

"Are you certain serpents weren't present watching over their pets?" Katya asked. Killing hybrids was simple, but not if a serpent or two crawled out of a cave with blood in their eyes.

"We scanned with magic, probably more than we should have used," Melara replied. "Neither of us sensed serpents, but if they were hiding their essence as thoroughly as the one that nearly nabbed Katya, we might have missed something."

"Is anything else living on the ninth world?" Nikolai asked.

"We don't think so," Gustaf said.

Katya wondered what had happened to them. None of the habitable worlds in this system had been empty. Before she could pose a question, her brother said, "This will provide a splendid opportunity for us to learn to work together. A select group of dinosaurs will—"

"Dinosaurs?" Gustaf thundered. "How in Thoth's name did you get them to agree?"

Konstantin made a noise midway between a snort and a grunt. "Guilt. Works almost every time. Once they show up, we'll split into battalions and head for the ninth world."

"We already started herding folk into groups that would maximize their magic," Melara told him.

"Good!" Konstantin took off running as he angled toward bands of shifters blending their power into synergistic volleys.

"What did the hybrids look like?" Nikolai asked Gustaf.

The big, dark-haired man rolled his green eyes. "If you combined all the nightmares that ever were into one and plopped them onto the ninth world, you wouldn't come close to capturing how bad it was."

"The worst were the winged ones, though," Melara said. "They'd attack out of nowhere. And all the ones I saw had teeth. Long, sharp teeth. Not birdlike at all. Different kinds of wings. Bird wings. Bat wings. Webbed wings like dinosaurs have. Not so many with feathers. Mostly scaly hides or patchy fur."

"Don't forget the smell." Gustaf made a face as if he'd bitten into something rotten. "Melara and I changed clothes as soon as we returned."

"The others are soaking," Melara agreed, "but I'm not adverse to burning them if we can't get the stink out. It was like hundreds of decomposing scraps of garbage raised to the twentieth power. My stomach is still complaining."

"Beyond winged hybrids, what else?" Johan asked.

"The whole thing was such an affront to nature, it's hard to drag my mind back there," Gustaf muttered. "Wolf bodies with reptile heads. Horses, but with sharp hoofs and short necks. Furred monsters that stood upright on two legs with enormous heads. Trolls." He blew out a tired breath. "You'll see them soon enough."

"Did you kill any?" Katya wanted to know how easy it would be to mow through them. If they died as obligingly as the mantis-bird horrors had, this shouldn't take all that long.

"We did," Melara said. "In self-defense. They seem to be able to communicate telepathically. We showed up in a clearing with a handful of skunk-like animals, except they were as big as lions. It didn't take long before animals were streaming toward us from every direction imaginable. Including above."

"We had to fight our way out of there," Gustaf added. "It's why our scans for serpents were perfunctory."

"They didn't penetrate your warding, did they?" Boris ran his sharp gaze over the two shifters.

"No." Melara sounded fierce. "But if we'd been there much longer, they would have. It might be their intelligence is additive in some way, but they seemed to learn something from failure. Like I said, I had to alter the weave of my warding a couple of times before we finally teleported back here. I had hell's own time keeping my dragon from breaking through. Her bloodlust was kindled."

"They did not follow you," Johan noted, "so perhaps that type of magic is beyond them."

"It isn't beyond the serpents' ability," Katya growled.

Thumps shook the ground, followed by shouts of, "Welcome."

She turned, not surprised to see dinosaurs. Damn they took up a lot of space in their animal forms with their huge, scaled bulks. They were beautiful, though, in their own right. Some had long, majestic soaring necks, not unlike her own in her beast's body. Others were solid with interlocking plated scales covering them from stem to stern. The birds had incredible wingspans and wicked looking beaks.

"We should join the others," she said and hurried to center field, threading her way around the newcomers.

Johan flanked her. "I could have done without this delay, yet perhaps it is a necessary evil."

"What do you mean?" She glanced his way.

"Armies need to practice working together. Dealing with the hybrids will provide a timely opportunity." He lowered his voice. "Has your brother ever led troops into battle before?"

She had to think about it. "Not exactly. Dragons don't have wars like humankind. And most magical creatures live forever. Not much point in waging war."

"Until now. Something has happened. It prodded the serpents into secretly crafting magic to build up their forces."

She thought about it. If Johan was correct, and the serpents knew something that had galvanized them into action, she needed to get moving with her scrying tool.

"You and Johan go with Nikolai's group," Kon yelled, followed by still more deployments until everyone was part of a mixed company of various types of shifters. Their troop contained three dragon shifters, two dinosaurs, four birds, two wolves, and a deer.

Depending on how well each troop worked together, Kon would make needed adjustments. Johan had asked about her twin's experience in a military leadership role. She'd hedged. The bare truth was her brother had never commanded more than a couple of dragons.

Until now.

She said a hasty prayer to Y Ddraigh Goch that Kon's quick temper, coupled with his lack of proficiency, didn't create unanticipated issues. Like mini-rebellions within their ranks. He'd done a decent job finessing the dinosaur problem, so perhaps she was selling him short.

Dragons weren't the most diplomatic creatures. Much like their bondmates, they expected immediate cooperation once they made their will known.

Nikolai herded them into a rough circle. Other than the dinosaurs, everyone was in their human body. "We teleport as a group. From the sound of things, we will take our animal forms before we leave. We've been assigned two types of hybrid."

He knelt and sketched in the dirt. Something lion-like took shape along with a weasel-esque creature. "Both of these are quite large," he warned. "We kill any that cross our path."

"What if other types attack us?" a wolf asked. Red-gold hair fell straight as a stick to her shoulders, and her eyes were a brilliant blue.

"I say we kill anything that comes within range," Johan snarled.

Nikolai nodded agreement. "Our other task while we're there is to see if we can locate the breeding farms. Kon's orders are to blow them sky high so they can never be used again."

"I wonder whom they leached magic from when dragons weren't available?" Katya set her mouth in a harsh line. Within, her dragon tugged hard at its invisible leash. It wanted to shift and be gone. Yesterday.

"Leave as you will." Kon's voice rose over everyone else's.

"Before we shift and leave," Nikolai said, "we're a team. We have each other's backs. Part of our job is killing hybrids. The other part is ensuring our own safety. It includes protecting ourselves and each other from dark power jumping ship and taking over our bodies.

"You may deem such an event unlikely, but it happens in the blink of an eye. One moment, things are as they always were. The next, you're trapped beneath sea-serpent sorcery."

Nods ran around the group. Clothing hit the ground as shifters reached for their bondmates' bodies. Katya's dragon was more than ready. It adored killing. To be on the leading edge of a mission where it could kill as much and as many as it wished was second only to Nirvana.

Johan's green beast took shape next to her. Eyes whirling, nostrils flaring, he looked as excited as her bondmate. Nikolai's copper-gold dragon formed next. As soon as they were ready, he wove a transport spell that linked them all together.

She hadn't thought to ask what this world looked like. Maybe because of what it had been turned into, she assumed it would be an ice-shrouded hellhole, but when it bloomed around them, it was beautiful.

Above her, a violet sky showcased twin suns. Pastel shades spread in every direction from blue and green dirt to orange rocks. Scrubby grass was a charming seashell pink. The temperature was mild, and a bubbling brook cascaded down multihued rocks and over a small cliff not far from where they emerged. Who had lived here before the serpents polluted it? More importantly, were they still here, or had the hybrids killed them all?

Why hadn't the land reacted to whatever transpired here? It should be layered in snow and ice.

Nikolai bugled. The dinosaurs roared. Her dragon spread its wings, flapping to gain altitude fast. Kon had planned for each constellation of troops to come out in vastly different locations. That way, they wouldn't have to worry about inadvertently hitting one another.

It made sense in some respects, but it also forced each group to rely on themselves. So far, the foul odors Melara had described weren't present, but neither were any hybrids. She and Johan overflew the area, but all she saw was more bucolic scenery. She wouldn't have been surprised by a herd of goats or cows, but the hybrids had probably eaten them.

"See anything?" Nikolai asked.

"No."

"Return to me. We'll employ magic to draw them out."

Johan's dragon bugled and took off at top speed for goddess only knew where.

"Come back!" she shouted after him. A similar command from Nikolai came a split second after hers.

Johan kept right on flying. What in the unholy hell? Katya hovered, unsure what to do. She should obey Nikolai, but someone needed to go after Johan. What if he was in the clutches of magic she couldn't sense?

He bugled again and wheeled sharply, beating a path back to her. She angled her gaze downward and understood. Johan's dragon must have sensed evil. Hybrid horrors were streaming out of holes in the perfect ground. Out of cliff faces. Out of places she couldn't make out.

"They're coming," she shouted in dragonspeak. Fire streamed from her mouth, obliterating her next words.

Johan blasted them with fire and ash. A few burst into flaming pyres, but more abominations formed from thin air as best she could judge. Assigning each group specific hybrids had been stupid. They'd kill what was in front of them.

The birds from their group leapt skyward, fanning the air with their wings. On the ground, the dinosaurs mowed through clumps of hybrids. Insect combinations seemed primary, but the insects were a hundred times normal size. A spider body glued to four legs was particularly loathsome. She could smell the acrid stench of its poison from her aerial perch.

There were more of the mantis-bird things, but so far, they'd been easy to shoot out of the air. The variety of twisted genetic experiments was dizzying. It was as if a serpent mad-scientist had taken bins of DNA and cobbled them together in as many permutations and variations as he could. Some of the fuckers could barely walk. Others tried to fly but fell out of the air.

She wasted a few moments feeling sorry for the misshapen ones who had no chance at all, but then she got her priorities straight. Just because the wolf limping below her had a tentacle where it should have had a leg didn't make it any less her enemy.

A dinosaur stomped a path through a hundred hybrids, crushing the life out of them as it went. Another dinosaur joined the group in the air. It wasn't overly efficient, but the birds worked as a team chivvying a small batch of hybrids away from the others. Once they had them separated, they drove their sharp beaks into eyes and carotids and jugulars.

The smell of blood grew thick and cloying. Between her and Johan, they had so many fires burning, the others drove hybrids into them. One of the wolves first barked, and then howled.

Katya peered through the smoke below trying to see what had happened. The wolf howled again, mournful and desperate. Katya said to hell with it and dove toward the sound determined to pulverize whatever had hurt the wolf.

Johan swooped below her and let out a bellow.

Katya narrowed her eyes to slits. She was finally low enough to make out not a wolf, but the deer. A troll-like hybrid held the deer suspended high in the air. It kicked with sharp hoofs, but couldn't reach the troll's body.

Not that it would have done it any good. Last she checked, trolls were made of stone. One of the few substances impervious to fire. The troll had taken a chunk out of the deer's shoulder. Blood sluiced across its pale fur, sheeting downward.

"Shift!" Katya screamed at it.

"I can't."

No time to ask why. She aimed to fly close and put out the thing's eyes with her talons, but Johan beat her to it. He charged in front of her and drove the spiked ends of his fingers into the troll's eyes.

It was slow to react. Trolls are stupid, and it had to process the fact it couldn't clap its hands over its eyes while still holding the deer. She flapped closer, shooting a stream of fire at his ruined eye sockets, but Katya had another goal in mind.

Catching the deer once he dropped it.

Johan trumpeted. This pass, he grabbed handfuls of the mossy crap that passed for troll hair and dragged it out by the roots. Between this latest indignity, her fire, and being blind, the troll bellowed. The deer piece he'd been chewing shot from his mouth.

He let go of the deer.

Finally.

Katya grabbed onto it, knowing she was hurting its injured shoulder, but it would hurt a whole lot worse if it hit the ground from three meters up. Behind her, the troll fell into a jumbled heap that disintegrated into a pile of dusty rocks.

Interesting. Very interesting. It meant something, but Katya couldn't figure out what it was.

"Sorry," she told her passenger as she ferried her to the ground.

"It's all right. At least I have my magic back. That thing. It blocked me from my power. No matter what I did, I couldn't break through."

The wolves formed a protective circle around the deer. One had retrieved the chunk of shoulder. Good. It could be reattached with magic. Quicker and easier than the deer using her power to grow a whole new body part.

"Take her back to the sixth world," Nikolai ordered in the dragons' tongue.

"I can go on my own," the deer said. Snatching up her detached body part in her mouth, magic flickered around her, and she was gone.

Johan landed next to Katya. "Nice work."

"Someone had to catch her," Katya replied. She turned in a circle, surveying the area around them. Impossibly, hybrids kept right on coming. They'd killed hundreds. Maybe thousands, and hadn't made a dent.

"We need a different strategy," Nikolai said and gathered the eleven of them close. "This one isn't working fast enough."

Sudden insight rocked her. "Serpents are here," she told everyone. "One was piloting the troll. It was never more than illusion cobbled together with dark magic. It's why he turned to stone after we destroyed his eyes."

"Ha! Of course! Wonder if we rendered the serpent blind as well?" Nikolai shot a jet of fire skyward.

"Probably not," Katya told him.

"What about the rest of these?" a dinosaur asked and stomped on one of the poison spider things.

"Yeah," another boomed. "We've got to go for the source. Or they'll never stop coming."

"Exactly, but how?" Nikolai snapped off the words. More fire blasted from his open jaws. The latest batch of weasels did an abrupt about-face, leaving flaming contrails as they ran. "Ideas, people. Now!"

Almost as an afterthought, I killed something that had sunk its teeth into me, adding to the slime and muck beneath my huge back feet. "If these are not really hybrids," I said, "but illusion built of dirt and rocks and whatever else the serpents have patched together, can we attack the flow of magic?"

"Some of them are flesh and blood, but you might be onto something, Johan." A triceratops lashed its head back and forth. "If we locate the source of magic and follow it, we should find the serpents."

Excitement built within me. My dragon loved the idea. Almost as much as it adored killing. "We need more dragons if we are going after the serpents," I said.

"*We do not.*" My bondmate made his position abundantly clear.

Fortunately, I was the only one listening to him.

"And more dinosaurs," a pterodactyl cawed.

"We can't be the only ones who are just now figuring this out," Katya said.

Two of the wolves pounced on an unrecognizable hybrid with a long, bloated body and a reptilian head. It burst, showering us with poison that stung like a bitch even through my scales.

The dinosaur was right about not all of them being made of dirt. I considered Katya's premise about the troll being remotely controlled. The concept of piloted horrors wasn't new to me since drones and model planes had been around for a long while.

My bondmate spread our wings, intent on flight, but I held him back. *"We lack a cohesive plan. Until we have one, we aren't flying anywhere,"* I told him.

Ash blatted from my mouth. I turned my head so it did some good, coating the nearest of the ungainly poison bags with their alligator heads. At least twenty stubby legs propelled them forward.

Roaring filled my ears. Beneath me, the ground bucked and heaved as if in the throes of an earthquake. Katya bugled. She'd done a nice piece of work ferrying the deer to safety. I was proud of her fearlessness and her spirit.

Nikolai trumpeted. The wolves howled. The dinosaurs kicked up an unbelievable racket. I expected the quake to play itself out. They never lasted long, but this one kept right on rolling. It might have been my imagination—I wasn't the one linked to the land, after all—but I could have sworn I heard the earth squealing in outrage beneath my feet.

Katya prodded me with a shoulder and jerked her jaws at a hazy spot a few meters away. I'd figured it was dust from the earthquake, but it didn't act like blowing dirt. It hung in the air, puffing in and out of view almost as if it was alive.

"What is that?" I asked.

"A gateway," multiple voices answered me.

Great. Everyone but me recognized magic at work. I was certain my dragon had known as well. No one posited a theory about where the gateway led. My hunch was it went straight to a bunch of serpents. But how many? They hadn't kept any on the world where dragons incubated their hatchlings, so my guess was there wouldn't be many here.

It didn't matter. Even one would stretch our resources. Unless the dinosaurs possessed some tricks I wasn't aware of.

Crackling and an odd whistling behind us brought me around fast. Konstantin and four other dragons stepped through a shimmery spot rimmed with fire. That was the fizzing noise. The whistling intensified until a different spot punched through. Half a dozen dinosaurs plodded into view.

The earthquake intensified until keeping my balance required attention. I turned back toward the hazy spot, except it had changed. No longer blurry, a full-on gateway hung a meter off the ground. A weird kind of vine, black with red leaves, wove around the portal. I couldn't tell if it was holding the thing open or had been tacked on as an afterthought.

"Your call." Nikolai deferred to Konstantin.

I wondered how he'd known to show up, but probably either Katya or Nikolai had summoned him. The dinosaurs must have done something similar. We all edged toward the gateway. Something hypnotic pulsed from it that challenged my beast.

"Wait!" Kon trumpeted. "No one enters. It is a trap, but one seeded with dragon magic."

"Not possible," my dragon announced. *"None of us would join with evil."* It took a step toward the inviting portal, now flowing in a rainbow of colors that soaked into the pastel-shaded earth and then circled around again.

Before I could stop my beast, he bugled a challenge at Konstantin.

The black dragon glided next to us, displacing Katya, and I stared into Kon's whirling eyes. *"Sorry,"* I told Kon. *"I will do a better job controlling my bondmate."*

"See that you do," he thundered. "We have bigger problems than a dragon who didn't care for my assessment." He edged so close to the portal, the stream of color washed over his black hide, turning it rainbow-esque. The roaring noise, which had lessened, deepened until my ears ached. Cracks formed in the restless earth, falling away into deep fissures in spots.

Maybe this world was just now waking up to the evil attacking its bones. Or perhaps Kon had enlisted its aid. I'd assumed the earthquake was the serpents' doing, but I might have been wrong.

Fire formed a circle around Kon, burning bright white.

"Purification spell." Katya was next to me again.

Meanwhile, the flow of hybrids had finally slowed. We still killed them, but the dead weren't automatically replaced by ten more. Gateways popped open all around us, and more shifters emerged.

"We heard Konstantin's summons," many said.

It sank in that my group had accidentally been assigned the location housing the epicenter of evil on the ninth world.

The magic around Konstantin thickened. I moved nearer him with all the other dragons, and we added our power to his working. I seemed to have control over my beast again, but I remained vigilant. Just in case.

With zero warning, three dragons shot through the portal. Two reds and a blue. All male. Somehow, they evaded Kon's spell and winged above us, bugling defiantly.

Serpents weren't the enemy here. Dragons were. I blinked stupidly at the three flying above us, assimilating their treachery. I'd assumed Loran was the only traitor. I'd been wrong.

My beast proved I wasn't truly in control of anything because he slipped his leash and we leapt skyward. But the other dragons were right there with us, flying, bugling, shooting fire at the three traitors. They shot flames right back at us.

My bondmate's fury was like a live thing, coiled within us. No wonder my will hadn't been sufficient to contain him. *"Who are they?"* I asked.

"Loran's brothers. Disloyal scum."

Christ! Had there been a conspiracy to erode dragonkind? I wanted to dig until I got to the bottom, but right now, we had dragons to kill. Except they were immortal. Last time, we'd had the dragon god to help us. This time, all we had was ourselves.

The three dragons, who'd apparently been responsible for turning the ninth world into a macabre breeding ground for evil, blanketed the skies with fire and smoke. Magically stronger than serpents, they'd had access to an enhanced range of ability. No wonder the land hadn't tried to drive them out. It had assumed—wrongly—that all dragons were a force for good.

Kon, Katya, Nikolai, and all the other dragons were incensed. And ashamed. To be betrayed by their own—twice—was beyond comprehension. I bet something like this had never happened before.

The bunch of us shot fire, dodged fire, and did it again. My beast was having a grand time, but he wasn't a tactician. I understood soon enough no one could win this fight. Konstantin knew it too. He flew above one of Loran's brothers and laid his body across the red dragon, pushing him out of the sky.

"This way," two of the dinosaurs yelled. "We have a plan."

Below us, the dinosaurs apparently stood ready, but what could they do besides crush the dragon, who would use magic to bounce right back.

Unfamiliar magic built around the dinosaurs. Wind soughed, increasing until it was strong enough to whip rocks around. I copied Konstantin's actions and flattened my body across the other red dragon. He fought me, tried to twist and turn beneath my beast's bulk, but I moved fast, holding him in place.

My beast was good at anticipating his moves and stymieing them.

I felt the renegade dragon trying to push into my mind. Keeping him out was paramount. Whatever he had to say, whatever inducements he had to offer, I didn't wish to hear them.

Next to me, Katya had tackled the other dragon. Maybe because her beast was smaller, she was struggling. The blue dragon kept escaping from beneath her and blasting her in the face with fire. Incensed, she bugled her outrage and tried to get her body above his again.

So far, he was evading her, but I had my hands full. I couldn't help her and make sure my captive didn't twist out from beneath me. A flurry of copper wings told me Nikolai was on his way to aid Katya. It should be me, but she'd want me to finish what I began.

Because my attention had shifted momentarily, the red dragon beneath me broke through my mental shielding. *"Join us,"* it exhorted.

"Never!" My bondmate spoke for us. *"I knew you long ago. You're a disgrace to all dragons."*

"You'll be sorry you refused. We will win." The red dragon sounded certain, and I wanted to know more.

"Why do you think so?" I cut in. So long as it was talking with me, I may as well find out as much as I could.

Below us, Kon drove his captive into the midst of a circle of dinosaurs. I'd figured they'd use brute force, but instead a web of magic closed over the red dragon, wrapping tendrils around it. He writhed, thrashed, bugled. He bit at the amorphous bonds tucked around him, but they grew thicker despite all his efforts.

The dragon trapped beneath me upped the ante on his struggles. Twisting, he scored the front of my chest with fire. I thought scales were supposed to be impervious to burning, but pain ratcheted through me. The stench of burning flesh thickened in my nostrils.

At first, I didn't understand it was mine.

My beast reacted by sinking its teeth into the red's neck. Scales and bones crunched, and we pushed the red lower still until I felt the pull of whatever the hell the dinosaurs were doing.

"Let go!" I screeched at my dragon, but he wouldn't release the red. Dragon anger flashed through my mind, scorching fury that knew no bounds. The burnt meat smell was stronger, and smoke stung my eyes. God only knows how, but I was on fire. How the hell had the red dragon managed to burn through my scales?

Hot blood spilled down my chest. There had to be a way to fix it with magic, but not as long as we held onto the renegade dragon. It took all my will—and Konstantin, who flew next to us shouting curses in dragonspeak—before my bondmate finally released the red. He plummeted downward, landing on top of his brother.

I was panting, and I tasted blood. Had my lungs been punctured? How could that be? Katya and Nikolai were still fighting the blue dragon. Somehow, he'd escaped both of them and zipped this way and that, bugling his disdain.

Intent on bringing him down—I assumed my injuries

would fix themselves—I pushed my wings to perform, but they were sluggish. A wave of dizziness unbalanced me.

"Land!" Konstantin ordered.

"No!" my dragon trumpeted back. "We must help Katya."

"If you do not land, you'll never help anyone again." Kon's words were grim enough, they got through my beast's thick skull. Mine too.

I crashed more than landed, thudding into the ground and missing one of the newly formed fissures by centimeters. It was big enough, we'd have fallen a long way. Blood gushed down my front, a shocking amount. What had happened to our magic? Why wasn't it healing us?

"Do something," I exhorted my bondmate.

"I'm trying." His reply was appallingly weak.

Kon plopped down next to me. "This will hurt, but I must move quickly."

"What happened to me?"

"Later."

He angled his head until it lay alongside mine. Dragon magic burned as it augured into me. More than burned. Indescribable agony started in my head and raced to the tips of my hind legs. I bellowed. I screamed. It hurt too much for me to be ashamed I'd fallen headfirst off the stoic pedestal.

Something ripped from between my chest and stomach and hovered in front of me. Dark and slimy and putrid-smelling, it mocked me and kept trying to dive back into the hole it had made in my middle when Kon dragged it out. He blasted it with dragonfire, but it didn't catch right away. For long moments, it just pulsed as if it were laughing at us.

"Die!" Kon exhorted in a language I'd never heard before, but I understood his meaning well enough.

The black blob finally exploded, the bits burning as they scattered around us.

As harsh as the pain had been, it lessened to a dull throb. Blood still dribbled from the gash down my sternum, but it wasn't draining my life away. I felt the bite of Konstantin's magic as he examined me. He must have been satisfied with what he found because he said, "Remain here."

He didn't explain himself, but then he didn't have to. He leapt skyward, fury streaming from him as he aimed straight for the blue dragon still laughing his head off at our inability to corral him.

He took Katya's place, and she touched down next to me. "By all the dragon gods who ever walked, I'm so grateful you're not dead. I didn't know what to do. I saw what was happening, but Nikolai and I were all that was keeping the blue from teleporting out of here."

"Dead? How could I have been dead? Are we not immortal?"

Her eyes spun faster. "These dragons, they figured out how to merge serpent magic in with their own. It's made them more powerful than we are. The one you were trying to push out of the sky managed to introduce insidious magic inside you. It was eating you up from within. Fighting the good parts of dragon power with its serpent-dragon mix of evil."

I shuttled my horror aside. "How?"

"It's a very good question, and one we will need to find

an answer—and an antidote—for before we take on the serpents back on Earth."

"They were not stronger than you," I reminded her.

"Not then. But we found four corrupt dragons in this system of borderworlds alone. Four of them. It doesn't bode well."

I supposed not. I hadn't known how close I'd come to dying. I hated to admit I'd talked with the dragon, but I had to know if I'd inadvertently given the bastard some kind of access. "I made an attempt to talk with him—" I began

"Not important." She pointed upward.

I followed her talon and saw Kon and the blue facing off against each other. Fire lit the skies. Nikolai swooped in from one side, running into the blue dragon and knocking him sideways. It looked like a coordinated attack because Kon dove onto the blue's back. Nikolai added his weight.

Between the two of them, they herded the last of Loran's brothers into the dinosaurs' net.

"How are they holding them?" I asked Katya.

"Another thing I don't know," she said. "Seemingly, they possess magic that can immobilize dragons. Who would have guessed?"

Who would have guessed, indeed? Would Kon have been so eager to partner with them if he'd known how dangerous they were to dragonkind?

"We are healing," my bondmate informed me. *"I apologize. He should never have penetrated my warding. That he did says I must be more careful during future engagements."*

"We are still here. It is all that matters."

Steam puffed from my jaws. Dragon apologies.

I took a deep breath, gratified my lungs were working and only a slight residual soreness remained down my midline. When I glanced around, the gateway was gone. The infernal roaring had ceased quite a while back as had the earthquake.

Not a hybrid in sight, but I wasn't convinced there weren't hatchlings somewhere. I wanted to be done on the ninth world, but a few tasks remained.

I motioned to Katya and lumbered over to the circle of dinosaurs. "Impressive work. How long will your enchantment contain them?" I used the dragons' tongue since it allowed me to talk out loud in my current form.

"We were just discussing that," a brontosaurus mumbled. It seemed odd to hear modern words from a prehistoric monster, but no more unusual than dragons talking.

"If Konstantin can harness the land's power, we believe we can create a spell that will hold them in perpetuity." A pterodactyl clacked its jaws together, sounding satisfied.

"What if serpents arrive?" I asked.

"They can't undo our magic." A triceratops snorted laughter. "Now, if it was your spell, yes, but our magic has a different source."

"I heard my name and your request." Konstantin trudged next to the pit holding the three dragons. It was slowly hollowing out a large hole in the ground. "Let me see what I can do."

Power burned a pure bright white around him. I'd have given a lot to hear his conversation with the land because the hole sank deeper, taking the dragons with it. Within the span of a very few minutes, dirt and stones whisked in from the surrounding area until the pit was filled in.

No sign of the dragons remained.

"It is done." Konstantin sounded weary, but vindicated. "The land didn't require much dinosaur magic, and it has promised to hold the dragons captive forever."

"Did it know what it was being used for?" the pterodactyl asked.

"Not until I told it," Konstantin replied.

"What about the hatchlings?" Katya nudged her twin.

"That part is taken care of," he told her. "When I arrived, I opened a line of communication with the land. At first, I was afraid it wouldn't talk with me. It seemed as if it had been drugged, but I persevered and broke through."

He blew out a fire-tinged breath. "Once I did, it helped me locate a brood farm so extensive it shocked me. It must have covered 200 hectares. I offered to annihilate it with dragonfire, but the land helped. Between us, nothing remains."

"Good," Katya said. "I shouldn't admit this, but I felt sorry for some of those misshapen animals. Whoever formed them didn't take any care at all."

"You're too softhearted, Sister." Kon angled an indulgent glance her way and then turned to the dinosaurs, still arranged in a circle around where the dragons had sunk beneath the ground. "Thank you for your skill and ability. Without your aid, this day would have had a far grimmer outcome."

"You are welcome." A tyrannosaurus bobbed his large, ungainly head. "I had my doubts, but I can see now that you truly need us."

"We do," rang from many shifter mouths.

"Are you fit to travel?" Konstantin's gaze fell on me.

"Thanks to you, I am mostly recovered."

His jaws lolled in the dragon approximation of a grin. "I had to save you. Katya would have had my hide if I'd let you die."

She hissed steam at her twin. He puffed more back her way.

"We will return to the sixth world and discuss what occurred here." Konstantin projected his voice so it carried to every shifter.

I'd been in a godawful hurry to return to Earth, but even I was smart enough to know I needed food and rest to finish healing and replenish my magic.

Enchantment rose all around us, its many iterations reminding me I'd signed on not just for dragon shifterdom, but as part of a brotherhood of magic wielders. I, the lone wolf scientist, was part of something bigger than I was, and I wasn't fighting it. Surprisingly, it felt right.

"Come on," Katya bugled. "I'll manage the spell."

"*I do not need you to.*" I winced at my damned Dutch pride surging to the fore.

"I know." If she'd been human, the sounds rippling from her might have been laughter. "But I want to take care of you." Her whirling gaze bored into me. "And what dragons want, dragons get."

I joined her laughter and let her spell spirit us away. An uphill road lay ahead, but I'd be damned if I wouldn't savor the moment. Katya loved me. She may not have said it in so many words, but caring shone from her and wrapped me in tenderness.

"The mating flight, mating flight," my dragon chanted from the sidelines, cock rising to curve against our scaled belly.

"I heard that." Katya snugged her spell closer around me.

Heat spilled through me, desire sweet as thick honey. *"Dragons are wise. Perhaps we should take his advice under consideration."*

"No divorce," she reminded me.

"None needed. You are stuck with me, Madame Dragon, until the end of time."

"Maybe we're stuck with each other, but I can think of far worse fates."

The sixth world took shape around us. For once my bondmate didn't grumble when I made a bid for my human form. Katya and I shifted, and she wrapped her arms around me. Her eyes were still dragon's eyes as she covered my mouth with her own.

CHAPTER 16

*D*riven by a heady combination of lust, love, and relief, Katya crushed her mouth over Johan's and clasped him as close as she could. Fingers splayed across his richly muscled back, she kept reminding herself he was still here. It wasn't productive to focus on how close she'd come to losing him.

WHEN SHE'D LISTENED to her dragon, a creature steeped in overconfidence, she'd assumed they'd have no trouble chivvying one of Loran's brothers out of the sky. Ha! It had turned into a horrible pitched battle. She never got close to pushing the dragon-traitor out of the air. Best she could do was to punt and parry with magic that barely, barely kept him from teleporting his sorry hide far away from the ninth world.

Konstantin was still busy with another of Loran's brothers. Nikolai had noticed her plight and joined her, but even the two of them together didn't make much progress. It was easier to keep the slimewad dragon from leaving, though. While they wrestled with the blue dragon, she kept an eye on Johan. Things weren't going well with the red dragon he'd corralled.

At first, she thought he was managing, but she felt an unpleasant shock as the dragon beneath Johan twisted and pushed something so wicked inside him, it made her scales shudder.

Her attention, which should have been on the blue dragon, wavered dangerously. What had the other dragon done to Johan? His dragon had closed its jaws around the red's throat. She heard bones and scales crunch, but Johan's ability to remain airborne flagged. His wings flapped slower and slower, and still his dragon wouldn't let the other one go.

"Our mate is hurt," her bondmate shrieked. *"We must go to him."*

"Katya! Pay attention! We're losing," Nikolai trumpeted.

Torn, desperate, she dithered between frantic desire to help her almost-mate and knowing if she abandoned Nikolai, the blue would escape. Dragons were never *hurt.* That Johan was reacting so strongly to whatever the red dragon did to him scared the hell out of her.

Konstantin rose from where he'd pushed his captive dragon into the dinosaurs' waiting clutches. Once she understood he was headed for Johan, she focused all her power on aiding Nikolai. The blue just laughed at them. It knew they couldn't touch it.

It also probably knew eventually they'd burn through enough magic, they'd have to release their hold on it. "I give up." She kept her words conversational. "How'd you get so strong?"

"State secret," the blue chortled merrily. "But you could join us. Then you'd learn how to weave serpent power in with yours."

"Serpents? You parlay with serpents? How could you?" Her dragon's rebuke was punctuated with fire.

"Hush!" she told her beast. *"Trying to learn something here."*

"No lessons from traitors," her bondmate said firmly amid smoky grumbling.

Meanwhile, below them, Kon had forced Johan to land. She felt an intense blast of magic when her twin extracted a black blob reeking of pure evil—a charnel pit stench of putrefaction and rot she recalled from much earlier times. Relief coursed through her. She wasn't certain Johan would recover, but the odds had just shot up by a pretty big percentage.

Kon leapt skyward, heading right toward them. Her twin was livid, so angry the very air glowed red around his black hide. He bugled his death battle cry, and she and Nikolai moved aside.

"Go ahead," Nikolai spoke into her mind. *"Between Kon and I, we've got this."*

~

Katya halted the replay of earlier today. Tightening her hold on Johan, she willed herself to focus on now, not on the horrors of nearly losing him. He kissed her with increasing urgency. Between them, his cock swelled to fullness. Her nipples peaked, and need slicked her sex and her thighs.

She opened her mouth to his tongue, lashing it with her own. Little biting kisses traded turns with suckling and deep kisses that stole her breath and her wits. He ran his mouth over to her ear and trailed his lips down her neck, stringing kisses along the way. Every spot he touched ignited into mini-explosions of desire.

Her hips surged forward, thrusting rhythmically against his cock sandwiched between them. She wriggled until he was between her labia. He made a delicious male sound and moved a hand between them to cup one of her breasts. His touch as he rubbed her taut nipple made her moan with hunger.

Johan's breath came fast as he lifted his mouth away from where he'd been kissing her neck. "Can we move somewhere more private?"

She nodded. Shifters had no body modesty. Not after spending much of their lives naked, but they didn't engage in public displays of sex.

"Attention!" Kon's command cut through the lusty haze that filled her brain.

She groaned in earnest, but couldn't bring herself to move her body away from where it was plastered across

Johan's. His cock twitched, and he pushed his hips into her belly, rotating his shaft from side to side. Its heat seared her swollen lips, and she pressed her clit harder against him.

"Take him," her bondmate urged, oblivious to everything except cementing the mate bond. Once that was done, the mating flight she longed for was sure to follow.

Johan's hands had travelled to her ass where he gripped her tight against him. "I do not suppose we can ignore your brother," he murmured but made no move to let go of her.

"Probably not." She licked the hollow between his neck and collarbones. When she glanced about, they weren't exactly by themselves, but everyone had given them as much space as possible. Johan's close brush with death had probably rattled everyone, and no one would begrudge them time in each other's arms.

"Take half an hour," Kon was saying. "Eat. Rest. Come back ready to strategize. The mixture of serpent and dragon magic is troubling. We can't simply target dragon power because it will impact us too."

Katya's brain edged back into partial awareness. She shouldn't have allowed her bondmate to sidetrack her when she was trying to dredge information out of the blue dragon, but that opportunity was lost.

If it had ever existed in the first place.

Konstantin had said half an hour. They could retreat somewhere private and make love, but then they wouldn't have time to eat or regroup. Johan, especially, needed to recharge his magic. Dark power had come unnervingly close to killing him.

Her brain stuttered over the idea. Dragons were immortal. Up until now, nothing could kill them. Except Y Ddraigh Goch, and even the god was loathe to destroy dragonkind. He preferred exile as a punishment.

"What is it, Liebchen?" Johan let go of her ass and cradled the side of her face.

"You need sustenance," she began.

"You are my sustenance." He smiled, and his tenderness melted her heart.

"Magic doesn't work that way. It can't survive on sunshine and rainbows." Reluctantly, she untangled her arms from around his body. "Besides, what I have in mind for us will take far more than the half hour my twin has allotted."

"I bet we can manage a little of everything." Johan winked and took off running for a nearby stand of scrubby trees.

Katya hustled after him. When she ducked into the grove, he'd piled prairie grass into a soft oblong. Drawing her onto it, he picked up where he'd left off, except this time he ran his mouth lower, kissing breasts and ribs and stomach on the way to her aching, distended nub.

Twisting beneath his embrace, she captured the hard, hot length of him in a hand and fastened her mouth over the velvety head. She started with little licks and gentle strokes until he began sucking on her clit. He ran his tongue around her nub, across it and then sucked again. Fingers slid inside her body, and he worked her between his mouth and hand.

There was nothing elegant about the climax that pulsed through her. Hot and heady it kindled every nerve ending. She urged him to join her, pressing against the sensitive spot at the base of his balls and adding a shot of magic to the mix as she stroked his shaft, laving it with her tongue every stroke.

A second orgasm washed through her as semen pumped into her mouth. The bitter-salt taste of him made her hot all over again, but twice was enough—for now.

They lay, gasping and panting, before he rolled until his face was level with hers. When he kissed her, she tasted her arousal on his tongue. What they'd done wasn't enough, but she suspected no matter how often they made love, it would never be enough for her. Not with this man.

"You did not complete the mating ritual." Her dragon sounded unhappy.

"We will," she reassured her bondmate before it could launch into another lecture about its disappointment—and its fears Katya would remain forever unattached. Betrothed wasn't the same as mated.

"There! Did not take so long as all that." Johan flowed to a sit, drew her to her knees beside him, and patted his still erect cock. "At least now I can think again. Of something other than loving you."

"Are you sure about that?" She batted her lashes his way, miming a coquette.

"No, but I can try."

"Good enough for me. Let's find something to eat, and then we'll join the strategy session." She scrambled upright and waited for him to join her. Together they walked toward the rich smells of roasting meat.

The shifters who lived on this world had been busy pulling an impromptu feast together. Many of the dinosaurs were engaged in eating the plain down to dirt as they inhaled grass and sagebrush. Others had clearly gone hunting and were chewing on a variety of game animals.

"We could have hunted as dragons," Katya told him as they closed on stacks of cooked meat, "but this will be faster."

Every shifter they talked with told Johan how happy they were he'd escaped the red dragon's enchantment. His pleasure that they cared shone from him, and made Katya glad.

"Come here." Her twin beckoned from a few meters away. A respectable pile of picked-clean bones sat between him and Erin.

"Yes?" She walked near enough to talk, munching on a piece of tender sage grouse.

"Any chance you could attempt to look into the future?" Konstantin asked.

She hadn't anticipated his question, but did a quick internal survey of her magic. Her tanks were reasonably full. "I don't see why not," she answered. "I don't have a mirror, but perhaps I could find a still pool."

"I located something I think might work." Kon rose to his feet.

"Should I accompany you?" Johan asked. "Or is this more individual magic?"

Grateful to him for understanding enough to pose the question, she replied, "Out of all spells, this is one that only works when I'm by myself. If it works at all, it will be reasonably quick, though."

Konstantin jerked his chin her way, and Katya fell into step next to him. It was the first time she'd had alone with him since setting foot in this borderworld system. "You're worried," she said.

"You bet I am." He kept his voice pitched low, only for her. "What happened to Johan was unprecedented. I was flying blind. I knew something was very wrong, but I had no idea what it was."

"You saved his life," Katya murmured, shaken by her brother's admission.

"I got lucky." Bitterness lined his voice. "And I had nothing to lose. Johan was dying, along with his dragon. If they'd lost much more blood or magic..."

He took a ragged breath and started over. "What if I'm leading this group of shifters, men and women who are willingly offering their aid, into a massacre? What if many die? I'm not sure I want that on my conscience. It's why I'm hoping you'll see something in the water."

She patted Konstantin's arm, not quite sure what to say. They had to return to Earth and make a good faith effort to stem the tide of destruction she was certain hung over it like a pall. But none of the other shifters were under any compunction to follow them. Earth wasn't their problem. Neither were dragons or serpents.

"I've been trying to reach Y Ddraigh Goch," Kon went on,

"but he's probably sick of bailing me out. Regardless, he's not answering."

"The dinosaurs have a way of managing the renegade dragons," she reminded her brother. Resurrecting how closely Johan had skirted destruction was unsettling.

"Yes, but it takes a lot of them, and it wouldn't be practical if we ran into more than the three on that last world. Even with all of us, it took a very long time to rid ourselves of them.

"That's not the worst part," Konstantin continued. "I'm assuming this is a two-way street."

"What do you mean?"

"We already know dragons can absorb—and utilize—serpent magic. Since serpents appear to be the perpetrators in that unholy alliance, they've discovered how to avail themselves of our power as well. Their use of dragons as broodmares confirms my hypothesis. The ones we left back on Earth hadn't yet gotten that far, but they may have by now."

She'd already considered and discarded that possibility. "How?" she demanded. "They'd need willing dragons. Dragons who were ripe for corruption. How many of those could there be?"

"We just found four," he reminded her and ducked through a clump of marsh grass. A clear, still pool sat on the far side. "Will this work?"

Katya nodded. "It's perfect. What shall I ask?"

"Any clues you come up with about what we face, and

our immediate future, would be a tremendous help. Take whatever time you need."

"What about the round robin with everyone?"

"I'll begin soliciting ideas, but we shan't draw conclusions until you return."

"You do realize this might not work," she told her twin.

He offered a crooked half grin. "Then you'll be back soon. The way I figure things, Sister, there's nothing to lose by having you attempt to lever your scrying magic, and everything to gain."

With a jaunty wave, he vanished back through the thick clumps of grass.

She knelt next to the pool and stilled her mind, or tried to. The loss of her psychic ability disturbed her far more than she'd let on. If she cast future-seeking magic, and failed again...

Katya raked curved fingers through her hair, wincing as they snagged on tangles. Best not to even consider failure. It might tempt the gods, and not in good ways. Perhaps that was what had gone wrong her last few tries. She'd been so despondent about her beast's absence, she'd anticipated a fiasco, and it had become a self-fulfilling prophecy.

Kicking her shoulders back, she inhaled to the very bottom of her lungs, blew out the breath, and repeated the action a few times to clear her mind of everything but the task ahead. With her hands turned palms up atop her knees, she stared at the still surface of the pond. Its blue-green water soothed her.

As ready as she was likely to be, she began to chant. The

familiar words of the scrying spell spilled through her as if they'd been anxiously waiting in the wings for her call. Before, she'd had to pull each spell element out of sticky mud. Hope soared this attempt would be different.

Her chant shifted to a series of notes from low to high and back again. She merged her magic with the surface of the water, urging it to cede to her casting and show her the future.

She'd chosen to keep her request vague. Any future was better than none, and scrying often displayed many futures. She wouldn't know until they occurred which one was real. Time was a funny thing. Multiple timelines spread out from a central location like spokes on a wagon wheel. Some came to be, intersecting with other spokes as time lurched forward. Others lay in wait, not in play, but not out of the picture entirely, either.

She'd often wondered whose hand played at manipulating the various possibilities time presented. Who decided which future would be primary? One of the dinosaurs had said he was a seer. Perhaps he knew the answers to her questions. She'd have to ask him.

The water's surface remained stubbornly quiet. Maybe because her mind was wandering. Was she so afraid of failing, she was sowing the seeds of her own ineptitude by not giving the spell her full magical attention?

"Help me," she begged her beast.

Her inner beacon, repository of her power, brightened.

Once again, she picked up her chant and focused

everything in her on the surface of the pool. Drawn by her magic, small creatures crept close. Mice. Squirrels. A vole.

Determined to reclaim her ability, Katya poured everything in her into her casting. Inner doors burst open as she held nothing back. Finally, the water swirled into a familiar vortex, twirling downward as water spiraled into a chute. The blue color darkened to first gray and then black.

Her breath quickened, and she scooted forward until her knees touched the water's edge. "Tell me," she exhorted. "What will be?"

Images crashed against one another, taking shape and ceding to the next in line. Part of her magic was interpreting the cavalcade of illustrations painting the water's surface before they were sucked into the vortex and replaced by another sketch.

The initial image was their grotto deep beneath Antarctica. Relief filled her to find it unchanged. Serpents hadn't desecrated it, apparently hadn't discovered it, but she hadn't expected them to.

Not really.

The next picture showed the headlands and beach above their lair. Serpents lolled on ice-covered water and ice-crusted rocks on shore. Hundreds of them, stretching as far as she could see. The next image added several ships bobbing in brash ice in the Weddell Sea.

She moved the lens closer and made out bodies spread across every visible deck. Bodies and blood. Was this how the serpents had strengthened themselves? By capturing ships and eating the humans?

Stomach roiling, she cast her net farther, needing to see if the serpents had spread to other lands on Earth. Two research stations looked unoccupied. A third had been turned into a fort. She sensed humans barricaded within, but no serpents lurked anywhere near. A large, apparently empty, ship was moored in a nearby bay.

Had word gone out?

Probably. Considering their lack of telepathy, humans had decent communications systems. She considered searching Argentina, New Zealand, and South Africa but didn't want to take the time. Now she had her scrying ability back, that quest could wait for another day.

Since her magic was cooperating, she returned to the headlands. This time they were empty. Not a serpent in sight. Where had all of them gone? Or had the first vision been of a future that might not occur?

She searched for other dragons but didn't find any. Surely that boded well. No dragons meant no one for the serpents to seduce, although how they'd managed to convince any dragon to merge magic with them remained a mystery.

Katya was about to close off her spell. She'd seen enough to reassure her twin they probably weren't teleporting into a trap. As she scanned the empty headlands, the absence of marine life jabbed her. Seals should be barking. Penguins prancing, yet neither was present.

What did it mean?

The ocean turned black, ice cracking into dark shards. Unable to look away, she stared as a chiaroscuro curtain gradually obliterated everything. She blinked, but the darkness was absolute.

Because her attention wavered, the spell blew up in front of her, showering her with pond water. Katya gasped. She'd never had a scrying spell end this way. Ever. Almost as if this world sensed she dallied with evil and had slammed the gateway fast.

She scooted back from the edge of the pond and wrapped her arms around her knees. An edgy weariness filled her, along with dark thoughts. Destruction. Despair.

Her dragon bugled. The sound broke through inertia wrapping her in hopelessness, and she understood fragments of evil had traveled through her spell. She shot to her feet and immersed herself in the purification ritual to dispel the last of them.

"*I didn't like that,*" her beast muttered. "*Something sly is afoot. We must be careful.*"

Katya's eyes widened. Careful wasn't even a word in her bondmate's vocabulary. Until now.

"What on earth will I tell Konstantin?" she mused.

"*The truth.*" Her beast puffed smoke and ash. "*What else?*"

Sure, but if the truth was what she thought she'd seen, none of them would ever be safe again. She crossed her arms beneath her breasts determined to come up with something more coherent than amorphous fear when she talked with her brother and the other shifters.

CHAPTER 17

I'd been keeping an eye on the direction where Katya and her brother had gone. Obviously, Kon was long since back, but I was waiting for Katya. My heart was so full of love and gratitude she loved me back, I fear I was rather a blithering idiot whenever anyone tried to talk with me.

She was gone far longer than I anticipated from her blithe assessment that if her magic worked, things would unfold quickly. Konstantin had gathered everyone and was evaluating theories about how to neutralize the serpents with the least damage to us. And the most to them.

I was coming to appreciate how inconvenient immortal enemies were. I didn't say anything, but I was hoping they were still vulnerable in their human bodies. Drawing them out was time-consuming, but at least it ensured they wouldn't jump on some sneaky backdoor magic no one knew about and rise to fight another day.

I knew Kon was worried about his sister because he often glanced the same way I was looking, but it didn't keep him from funneling and distilling suggestions. So far, the best ideas had come from the dinosaurs. They had access to an ancient vein of magic. From the sound of it, perhaps the bedrock all other magic had sprung from.

The dragon shifters didn't care much for the dinosaurs' explanation; they'd always assumed their magic was the prototype for what came later. At least they were civil, though. Not as if they had a lot of choice in the matter. Word of how the dinosaurs managed the renegade dragons had spread, and if any doubt remained, Konstantin provided an instant replay of our battle.

He was a competent leader, understanding it paid to give credit where it was due. Many commanders simply grabbed all the glory for themselves, but Konstantin actually minimized his role with Loran's brothers. I suspect he was ashamed any dragon had hearkened to evil's inducements.

I felt Katya's unique energy drawing near before she came into view. Breath rattled from me, mixed with steam. I'd been worried about her, but so had my beast. He was just as happy to see her as I was. She strode purposefully toward us, her face set in determined lines.

I'd seen that combination of grim determination and grit on her face before. Apparently, so had Konstantin. He broke off midsentence and walked toward his sister, gripping her forearms as soon as he got close enough. She shook her head, perhaps in reaction to private telepathy from him.

"I am only going to say this once." Her tone was neutral, as if she were making an effort to suppress any feelings she might have about how things had gone with her scrying spell.

My beast urged me to go to her, stand by her side, but I was close enough. It appeared she'd had a rough time, and she didn't need me crowding her. Katya wasn't asking for emotional support, and I wouldn't insult her by assuming she couldn't stand on her own. Rushing to her like an overprotective husband would be the wrong thing to do. She'd been managing her own life for a very long time.

Konstantin motioned his twin forward, and she took his place at the head of the gathering. "Before I begin," she said, "I have a question for the dinosaurs' seer."

A pterodactyl flew close, shifting in midair and somersaulting to the ground as the silver-haired shifter. His eyes glowed, appearing almost as eerie as dragons' eyes. How long would it take before I looked at a normal human and found them lackluster, boring. No glowing magical nimbus. Pedestrian eyes. The transition would happen, and probably sooner rather than later.

"You were successful." Yle didn't pose it as a question.

"If the measure of success is my scrying spell worked, then, yes, I was successful. Do you know who controls time's various iterations?"

"What do you mean?" Yle narrowed his eyes.

"I'm not certain how scrying goes for you, but I see

multiple versions of the future. I never know until it comes to pass which of the variants won. My question to you is this: Is there some entity—perhaps a god—behind the scenes controlling outcomes? If so, have you any idea how he or she determines which timeline will be primary?"

"If any such being exists, they haven't made themselves known to me." Yle frowned, creating a deep furrow between his silver brows. "My issue has always been figuring out which vision is years in the future, and which is likely to unfold in the next few moments. Sometimes, they are very similar."

"What did you see?" Apparently unwilling to wait any longer, Konstantin had moved close to his twin.

"Several possibilities. Our home has not yet been disturbed, but in one set of images, serpents were thick around our headlands. In another set, boats littered with dead floated quite a way offshore. Depending on which theory about the source of the ice is correct, Earth could be fighting back because both the ocean and beach areas were frozen."

"Go on," many of the shifters urged.

"Still more images showed our headlands undisturbed, but the water had turned brackish and darker. I expanded my scan to include some of the research stations. Humans appeared to have barricaded themselves into one of them."

"They must know they're in danger," Erin spoke up.

"I assumed the same." Katya nodded. "They have communication via satellites and would have recognized they were imperiled after many ships were set upon.

"My last vision..." She stopped, perhaps regrouping, before talking again. "The headlands were empty. The sea was black. The ice shattered, but nothing poked through. I'm certain this next is metaphor since it doesn't match any physical phenomena, but darkness fell across the land, closing it in blackness so absolute I couldn't penetrate it.

"Right afterward, my spell snapped back on me like a boomerang. Something wicked followed me, but between my beast and me, we made short work of it."

Yle's gaze had never left her. "It may not be as bad as you assume," he began.

I waited. Her recitation had sounded pretty frightening to me. Not that we wouldn't return to Earth and do the best we could, but evil that could latch onto a spell and follow it to another location had to be powerful as hell.

A corner of Katya's mouth turned downward. "I wasn't aware I'd voiced any judgment on my experience."

"You didn't have to," Yle retorted. "A spell or two has chased me back to my point of origin. It's unnerving, and it happens when the world you're on senses a threat from what you're doing and slams the door shut on your casting."

"The entire Fleisher system is on high alert," Konstantin affirmed. "These lands are angry. They feel taken advantage of and are determined to mount a better defense." He hesitated. "When I initially touched the land with my magic, it rebuffed me. Its trust in dragons has been severely compromised after the debacle on the third world and the extent of the breeding farms on the ninth."

Katya raised her arms to quell side conversations that

were cropping up. "I'm nearly done. My overarching sense was that darkness and evil are growing, but they have a long way to go before Earth succumbs."

"Do you believe it's only serpents?" Nikolai asked.

Katya's brow furrowed. "That's a sound question. It doesn't seem possible the serpents could have grown strong enough to set up brood farm operations here and invade Earth too. Perhaps something worse is behind them, directing their actions."

"Like what?" Melara asked.

"Besides their dragon allies perhaps a bored dark god or two? We haven't heard much from any of the gods beyond Y Ddraigh Goch—and the shifter gods who helped us clear the seventh world—since Mu fell," Konstantin growled. Before anyone could posit more theories, he went on. "I traveled to this system of borderworlds to solicit aid from others with magic, but the barefaced truth is dragons aren't your problem. Neither are sea-serpents. Returning to Earth and mounting a defense against whatever faces us will be dangerous."

He rocked back on the balls of his feet before continuing. "I welcome assistance from anyone who wishes to offer it, but one of my core assumptions is no longer true. When we teleported here, I figured all of us were immortal. It's clear the serpents—and their dragon allies—have found a way to steal our magic and end our lives. Think long and hard before committing to a cause that doesn't impact you directly. Your altruism could cost far more than you have in mind."

"But the serpents do impact us directly," Gustaf said. "They inveigled their way into our worlds. Had you not shown up, we would have been much slower figuring that out. The ones who pretended to be like us may well have gotten away with it. By the time we understood what they were up to, it would have been too late. I'm not clear why we didn't recognize them for what they were, but we accepted their illusion as reality."

"They tricked you with dragon coercion." Katya's words were stark.

"Same way they lulled the land into not raising hell about their presence," Konstantin said darkly. "Regardless, we've set things to rights here. The land is more savvy than it was and will hold vigil too, now that it knows to be on the lookout for dragons who are not what they seem."

He thinned his mouth into a harsh line. "Every single time I utter the word dragon in close proximity to the word serpent, a part of me dies. I will not rest until I've rid every world of serpents. Before they were a scourge, but they've made it personal."

My beast trumpeted, along with every dragon there. The mesa filled with fire, smoke, and ash.

When it cleared, Konstantin said, "Think on what you wish to do. Once we've firmed up who will accompany us, we'll be on our way."

"The dinosaurs are fully committed," Yle said without hesitation. "Our magic has been underutilized for centuries. You've offered us an appealing project, plus we do not seem to be vulnerable to your brand of magic. It will make us valuable since the serpents cannot harm us."

"Thank you." Kon bowed low. "I admit I'm relieved since your ability is a lynchpin for every strategy we came up with."

"The time to thank us," Yle said, "is when we are done and the serpents vanquished."

I noticed he didn't add traitorous dragons to the vanquished list. Probably wise. My dragon was angry at the betrayal of his kinsmen, and I suspected every single dragon shifter's beast was muttering the same dark curses and urging immediate retribution for those who wore false faces.

Katya strode toward me. I opened my arms; she walked into them and closed hers around my back. She felt so good in my embrace. So right. Fierce protectiveness seared me. "How are you?" I asked.

"Better than I was. I've never had a spell blow up in my face like that."

"Could it have injured you?" Alarmed by the possibility, I stroked her hair.

"No. At least I don't believe so." She tilted her head back and looked at me, her golden eyes serious. "Magic is changing. I'm not certain when it began to alter itself, but I wonder what the outcome will be."

"What do you mean changing?" I didn't know enough about enchantments in the first place to understand what she was suggesting.

"There was a time long ago when it wasn't possible for dark power to corrupt anyone wielding dragon magic. As I think on it, the beginnings of where we now find ourselves probably occurred when the serpents tortured Y Ddraigh Goch's children. The children were tainted by evil. Rather than compelling them to commit foul deeds, though, dark power drove them mad."

"Too bad the dragon god did not do away with the serpents then," I mumbled.

A soft smile played at the edges of Katya's full lips. "It isn't easy to destroy your creations. Up until that time, serpents and dragons were one and the same. Kinship ties and magic are hard to lay aside."

I continued to stroke her curls, moving stray locks out of her face. I understood full well how painful it was to jettison work you'd sunk your soul into. For me, it had been theories that hadn't paid out. How much harder would it be to make the choice to kill off living beings?

"I understand," I told her. "Easy to judge when you are not in another man's shoes. How far afield did you travel from the southern pole?"

"With my spell?" After I nodded, she went on, "Not far. I'll extend my reach another day. It appears the serpents' damage has been localized, but it won't take them long to spread out."

I moved a hand to tap my breastbone. "My bondmate is outraged."

"Mine too. She wants us to get moving."

"How likely is it we'll find dragons on Earth who are no longer working the good side of the street?" I asked.

"What a quaint way to put it." She smiled wanly. "If you'd

asked me that question even a week ago, I'd have said zero. And meant it. Now I'm not so sure. What we don't know is what's in it for the dragons. Why any of them would align themselves with serpents is an enormous unknown."

"You said magic is changing," I reminded her. "Worlds are dying. Perhaps some cosmic balance has shifted beyond a tipping point."

Her face crumpled until distress carved lines into it. "Tipping point means there's no coming back, right?"

I nodded. "Earth is—or was—a dying world. Thanks to a continued onslaught from men who prioritized money over wisdom, it heated to a point many species were dying out. Oceans have become less able to support life. Depending on whom you talked with, Earth was either doomed or well on its way."

"We sensed as much, Konstantin and me. So did the other dragon shifters who lived in our underground grotto. I have no idea what happened to them. Always thought it odd we never heard one word after they left."

"Let us hope they relocated far away," I told her.

It would be demoralizing as fuck if she ended up knowing some of the dragons who'd joined up with the serpents. I was getting way ahead of myself, though. When we'd left Earth—and it was only a few days ago—the serpents had been weak and on their own. As I thought about it, I was fairly certain they hadn't glommed onto any dragons. If they had, the first thing they'd have done was reclaim their immortality.

A sizable circle had formed around Konstantin. Part of it

was dinosaurs who took up quite a bit of space, but at least fifty other shifters beyond the dragons we'd found on the third world had clearly signed on for our undertaking.

"We will teleport to a vast plateau roughly four kilometers beneath the Antarctic ice shelf," Konstantin told everyone. "That way, we can plan our first offensive in relative safety. I've sent each of you a rough idea of teleport coordinates."

"Is there water?" Nikolai asked.

"Yes. A string of freshwater lakes, some of them quite large," Kon replied. "Why?"

"Water is the serpents' natural element. Means we must be vigilant."

"We will be. See you all very soon." The air around Konstantin and Erin took on a liquid, glistening aspect right before they vanished.

I let go of Katya. "Let me manage the teleport spell this time. I need practice."

"All right."

She didn't seem particularly happy about returning home, but then I reminded myself she'd never really viewed Earth as her home. It had merely been a place to reside while she and her brother sorted what to do next.

"Are the scrying visions still bothering you?" I asked as I opened a channel to my power.

"Of course. I'd be a fool not to be disturbed by them." She shook her head until hair danced around her shoulders. "Sorry. I sounded bitchy, but I'm not angry at you. I'll feel better once we have this task well under way."

"We all will." Because her grotto was familiar to me, it was simple enough to set it as our endpoint. The high plains world around us ceded to darkness, and we shot through whatever wrinkle in the space-time continuum allowed shuttling between worlds.

"I hope everyone who is coming along is what they seem," she said.

"Why would you suspect they are not?"

I'd woven my arms around her, and she leaned into me. "Suspect is too strong a word. After today, though, I'm not completely sure of anyone. Except for you and Kon and Erin, of course."

"And probably the dinosaurs."

She laughed. "They seem too solid to be anything but trustworthy."

I did what I thought might be the magical equivalent of a course correction. When I stretched my power it seemed we weren't any closer to Earth than we'd been when we left the sixth world. I share most men's antipathy for asking directions. I'd rather figure things out for myself, but after a few more minutes dripped by, I shelved my pride.

"Could you check where we are, please?"

Katya had been drowsing against me. Her scrying spell seemed to have taken a lot more out of her than her confidence in the future. Her eyes fluttered open. "Sure. Hold on."

The characteristic tang of her magic wrapped around us, and she stiffened in my arms. "Dragon's balls! How did we drift so far off course?"

Defensiveness ran hot, but I managed to say, "I have no idea. I did exactly what you taught me to do. Set a course and confirmed it from time to time."

"When did you notice things weren't right?"

"About five minutes before I asked you to check."

Her jaw muscles tensed; I wasn't the only one keeping blistering words from leaking out. Her magic strengthened as she did something I wasn't totally following.

"Help me." The controlled terror in her words dug deep. Shit! I hadn't been on top of my game, and now we were caught in some magical cesspool.

"Anything," I said.

"Open your magic to me. Mine isn't doing it."

I redirected power away from my failed teleport spell, and funneled it into Katya. I had a lot of questions, most of them revolving around what was wrong and where we were. She took every scrap of magic I offered and then some until I was running on fumes.

Maybe I could gather information without bothering her concentration. I turned my attention inward to my beast. The place I associated with him was empty. Was that what had happened? My dragon assumed all was simpatico and had gone on an errand of his own?

"This will be rough," Katya said through clenched teeth. "We'll come out on the headland, but at least we'll be on Earth. We can travel to the grotto once we've broken through from the place between worlds."

I've always had solid intuition. What if my missing

bondmate wasn't coincidental? "Where is your dragon?" I asked.

"Why does it matter?" She sounded annoyed. And exhausted. I felt like a chump. I'd meant to make her life easier, and had ended up draining both our power banks down to their foundations.

"Mine seems to be gone."

Katya's magic that had been propelling us through darkness halted so abruptly my teeth clanged together. She was panting. "Solid observation. Mine is missing as well. Calls for a dramatic course correction."

I fed her magic from my dwindling supply. Now that I'd become more familiar with it, I'd learned to assess about how much I had to work with. I had a lot of questions, but they could wait until we'd gained safe harbor. Or harbor, anyway. Probably none of them were safe.

We flashed through a barrier and dropped through wet, drizzly skies onto an icy moor. I landed harder than I would have liked; it knocked the wind out of me. The unmistakable smells of wet heather and gorse bushes bombarded me. "Scotland? We are in the Highlands, are we not?"

"Good guess." She started across spongy, frozen grass toward a spot where power flared. I followed her through some kind of gateway into a rounded cavern. At least it was dry in here.

"It was not a guess," I said. "Why here? And what happened to our dragons?"

A bluish mage light kindled next to her, turning her eyes

into luminous pools. "Magic is very near the surface in the Highlands. We can replenish ourselves easily. Your second question isn't as simple. Something—perhaps a lingering mischief—separated us from our bondmates. Not permanently because the bond is intact. My guess is our dragons were sent one direction while we traveled in another."

She shook water out of her hair. "If I'm right, they'll find us."

"Ja, but we must ensure this never happens again." I should have been terrified. Instead, indignation ruled.

"It's not as if this was random. Shots out of left field are hard to plan for." Katya rubbed the side of her face with one hand. Her fingers left grimy streaks down her cheek.

"Do you suppose everyone else made it back?"

Rather than answering, she said, "Draw power from the earth into your body. Imagine setting up a flow and then keeping it active. This is much like warming yourself, except you're replenishing your magic."

My connection with the earth soothed and invigorated me at the same time. The lethargy that had dogged me since the bloody dragon nearly killed me finally receded. When my dragon slammed into me, it felt like I'd been kicked in the chest, but I welcomed him.

Bugling rang from my mouth. Steam followed. *"You're safe,"* my beast crowed. *"You're safe."*

Katya sank into a crouch, smiling. The timbre of her magic changed pitch, so I figured her dragon was back too. Looking up, Katya met my gaze. "This could have been so much worse. We're whole again, and it didn't take nearly as long as I feared it would."

More bugling, this time from two dragons, filled the cavern, along with buckets of steam. Because I was reveling in relief I didn't notice we had company until a man with a staunch Scottish brogue said, "Ye're making enough racket to wake the dead. Tell me what two dragon shifters are doing in my realm, and make it snappy."

Katya redirected her mage light until it illuminated two tall, ethereal-looking, barefooted men wearing fawn-colored robes. Slender silvery circlets sat over their brows. One's eyes were very blue. The other's were dark. Masses of golden hair shot with silver sparkled around them.

"Sidhe." Katya breathed the word.

One inclined his head. "Aye. Daione Sidhe. Now tell me why two dragon shifters are tapping magic that rightfully belongs to the *Dreaming*."

"It is entirely my fault," I said. "I am who failed to guide our traveling spell."

"A Dutchman?" The blue-eyed faery sounded more than surprised.

"At your service." I bowed.

"Which adds another question to my first," the man went on. "There are no Dutch dragon shifters. Holland wasn't a country when—"

"I was h—" I began.

"*Uh-uh!*" Katya's warning was timely. I'd been about to blurt the truth.

I cleared my throat before I said, "I was separated from

my beast for a while and spent much time in the Netherlands."

Two sets of Sidhe eyes lit with curiosity. "Separated from your dragon? Surely 'tis a tale worth hearing," the dark-eyed one said. "Begin at the beginning."

"We lack the time for this." I aimed for a respectful tone. I'd made enough mistakes for one day and felt certain dragon business wasn't to be shared.

Magic dripping with the scent of the Highlands wrapped around me. Even I, green as I was, recognized a compulsion spell.

"Begin at the beginning," the faery repeated, and I understood it wasn't a request, but a command. Power, ancient and gilt-edged, flared around him, and I fell headlong into his magic.

CHAPTER 18

Katya was of two minds about the Sidhe. They might become allies in an all-out war, but anyone—magical or otherwise—who trusted a Sidhe generally lived to regret it. Granted she and Johan had been noisier than they should have been, and the noise—and probably their magic—had drawn the faeries' attention.

No one to blame but ourselves.

She inclined her head intent on chopping through the spell threading itself about Johan.

"With all due respect, Brothers, we were diverted from our intended destination. I brought us here to replenish our magic. Apologies for taking what was not ours, but our plight is desperate. We are in the midst of a war. If we lose, dark magic will overrun Earth and obliterate everything and everyone who calls this world home."

"A war with whom?" the dark-dyed Sidhe asked, adding, "I am Gavin; his name is Keir."

"Katya and Johan," she said. Trading names was traditional, and it would have been rude of her to withhold theirs. At least the spell that had Johan in its sights was dissipating. The Sidhe had short attention spans, particularly compared with dragons.

"Our war is with sea-serpents," Johan replied.

"The selfsame beasts linked to dragonkind by blood?" Gavin asked.

Katya nodded.

"We felt...something," Keir muttered, "but convinced ourselves we'd imagined it."

"Their entry point is far from here," Johan said. "The Southern Ocean to put a finer point on it."

"Och, the beasties would surely be drawn to a spot with plenty of icy water." Gavin sucked his mouth into a disapproving moue.

"What is your plan for ridding Earth of the serpents?" Keir asked.

Katya blew out a breath. Her revelation—coupled with a subtle shot of magic—had diverted the Sidhe from their insistence on hearing every last detail about Johan and his dragon and the Netherlands. Somewhere along the line, the Sidhe would figure out they were being fed half-truths. Humans could not discover the transformation was possible, though, or there'd be a rush of people wanting to become something they could never understand.

The Sidhe were a bunch of gossipmongers. The less they knew, the better.

"We have only the barest bones of a plan in place," she replied. "As I said, something diverted our travel spell. As soon as I realized we were in trouble, I altered destinations. It's how we ended up here. We'll be on our way very soon."

"But ye must discuss this with our council." Gavin regarded them through narrowed eyes.

Katya planted herself in front of him. "As my companion said, we have no time. My brother is Konstantin, and he will turn the world upside down hunting for us if we don't return immediately. We must not squander our magic. Whatever he expends hunting for me will make us that much less effective fighting the serpents."

"Konstantin, as in the dragon shifters' liege? The one who speaks to the land?" Keir raised a golden eyebrow.

"The same," Katya concurred. How was it these faeries knew so much about dragon shifters?

"We understand." Gavin glanced at Keir.

"Tell your brother we shall come to him." Keir nodded firmly, as if the matter were settled.

"I'm certain he would deem it a great honor." Katya chose her words carefully. "And we can plan an enormous celebration including all magic wielders—once the serpent threat is behind us."

She hurried on before the Sidhe could launch their own agenda. "Surely the goddess's hand is in our chance meeting. Mobilize all with magic in this region. Be vigilant. Strike down evil with neither jury nor trial."

"You do not command us." Gavin's tone held a warning note.

"Nor do I wish to," she agreed smoothly. "If you choose to be the beacon that keeps these lands from falling to wickedness, we very much appreciate your aid."

"Dinosaurs stand with us," Johan spoke up.

Surprise radiated from the Sidhe. "They left their borderworlds? What magic did ye cast to accomplish such a feat?" Keir's eyebrows crawled back down his forehead.

"None. A select few left one of their worlds willingly," Katya murmured. She blew out a tense breath, but she had to tell them. "Um, some dragons have joined with the serpents. The illusion shielding what they are is cunning."

"How do we know ye're not in that camp?" Gavin dropped a truth spell over her. He didn't bother with subtlety. She felt the prick of its weave.

Her beast was infuriated. *"How dare he?"* the dragon raged. Fire shot from her mouth, mixed with ash.

Katya shook her head. "Sorry. You offended my dragon. Were we aligned with serpents, we'd scarcely have told you to be on the lookout for such dragons."

"The lass has a point," Gavin mumbled, but stopped short of an actual apology.

"We must leave," Katya said. "When next we see you, I shall pay for the magic we withdrew from the *Dreaming* with gold from my hoard."

"I shall make certain that message is passed to Oberon and Titania," Keir said. "We will also discuss your war with the serpents and see if we might help."

"It is not 'our' war," Johan cut in, making Katya proud of him. "If we fail, the only life left on Earth will be powered by dark magic."

"Regardless. Until we decide it's worth our magic to join your cause," Keir said, "it is still your war." The air around the two Sidhe took on a warm, golden glow. When it cleared, they were gone.

"Well. That was a surprise," Katya said, blinking at the afterglow left by the Sidhe. "I haven't seen any faery-folk in the last millennia."

"Moving past my amazement the Sidhe are real, you might be onto something." Johan creased his forehead thoughtfully.

"We're real," she reminded him, followed by, "What do you mean?"

"I am coming to understand not much that happens in a magical world is accidental. We were directed off course by an unseen hand. We assumed malevolent intent, but perhaps whoever was behind our unexpected side trip orchestrated precisely what just occurred. You said a lot of magic resides in the UK. Now everyone with power will know of the serpents' insidious plot."

"Maybe. The Sidhe are quite insular. It would surprise me if they did anything beyond discussing the serpents. If they told anyone about them, it would be a bonus. Ready to leave?"

"I am, but why are you so certain the Sidhe aren't behind the magic that diverted us here? Seems quite convenient and coincidental to me."

She smiled. "When you put it that way, I'm not certain at all. Want to try again with the teleport spell?"

Johan hesitated. When he finally nodded, she was pleased. Magic was like anything else. Sometimes things didn't work out, but failure didn't excuse you from getting back on the horse and trying again. She resisted an urge to walk through the steps of the spell with him.

If he needed something, he'd ask. Having his last attempt roll off the rails would add a layer of caution.

"This will go fast, right?" Magic bubbled around Johan as he laid the foundations for his spell a piece at a time.

"Yes. Very fast. The place between worlds is the limiting factor in teleporting."

"I would like to know why, but not just now."

His spell closed around them, snapping them into its trajectory. Before she had an opportunity to quietly double-check his destination vector, they emerged on the far side of the lake nearest her home. She cushioned their descent with a shot of magic. In the distance, dinosaurs grazed. They were quite spread out, and she assumed they were making the best of this world beneath Earth. It would work for the herbivores, but the others would find it lacking.

Johan shook his head. "My spells either work too well or not at all. I must plan for both ends of the continuum."

Their feet touched down, and she draped an arm around his shoulders. "Nicely done. It gets easier."

Konstantin ran toward them with Erin right behind him. "Where were you?"

"We ended up in Scotland and ran into some Sidhe. At least they know about the serpents now. And the war," Katya said. Maybe Kon would leave things there and not mine for details. Until she figured out exactly what had diverted them, she didn't want to waste energy on guesswork.

"Sidhe? As in faery folk?" Erin asked. "Don't they live underneath Scotland in like hills and barrows or something?"

"The faery part is correct." Konstantin turned toward her. "They live in a separate world, rather like a borderworld except it shares many elements with Earth, so travel back and forth is straightforward."

"I am sorry we were detained. What did we miss?" Johan tipped his head in Kon's direction.

"Very little," Erin said. "Shifters only just now stopped arriving. Good thing this place"—she spread her arms to the sides—"used to house a whole lot of dragons. Kon has been assigning shifters to the different levels here."

"I wish them to rest and refresh themselves," Konstantin clarified.

"Have you been to the surface?" Katya asked, sensing her twin knew more than he was letting on.

"I have. It's not pretty, but neither is it much worse than when we left. The ocean is frozen. The land is covered in ice. We will face the serpents, but not before everyone's magic is in tiptop condition. Also not before I establish a link to the land. What did the Sidhe have to say?"

"They wished us to remain," Johan said.

Konstantin snorted ash and smoke. "I just bet they did. Inquisitive bunch of bastards. And born troublemakers." He cast a speculative glance Katya's way.

She held up a hand. "All right. Our transport spell was rerouted. Both our dragons went missing for a brief time. As soon as Johan told me his beast was gone, I knew mischief was afoot and sent us straight to the Highlands. My plan was to refresh our magic and leave."

"Let me guess," Konstantin said. "The dragons returned, and while you were drawing power from the *Dreaming*, the Sidhe conveniently showed up."

"Ja, but how could you know?" Johan said. "You were not there."

"Never underestimate their power," Konstantin said. "They make it look as if they're playing at magic, but they are strong and ancient. Particularly their royalty. I suspect they've had problems and set scouts to keep a close eye on the primary traveling channels. They found you and Katya and jumped on a chance to tap into your minds."

"They didn't need to," Katya said, annoyed she hadn't put two and two together. "I told them about the serpents."

"We did not tell them about me," Johan said.

"You didn't need to," Konstantin said. "While they played at chatting with you, they were siphoning information out of your heads."

"That's just rude," Erin said.

"Meh. It's more annoying than rude. Sidhe have their own customs, most of which I've forgotten," Katya muttered. She gave her twin a quick hug. "The faeries did threaten to visit. It seems unlikely, but I thought you should know in case I'm wrong, and Oberon and Titania decide to drop in. If it's all the same to you, Brother, Johan and I will retire within."

"I need more library time," Johan said.

"Funny, but that's where I've been." Erin rolled her blue eyes. "Human habits are hard to shake."

"I envy your study time. You have probably moved many steps beyond me." Johan laughed. "I may never catch up."

Katya laced her fingers with his. "Books and scrolls weren't exactly what I had in mind, but we'll manage."

"You have a few hours," Kon told her.

Johan squeezed her hand. "I can absorb a lot in that time."

"See you in the library." Erin waved as they walked toward the stone entry doors.

Katya leaned into Johan. He felt solid and right next to her. Her dragon puffed steam, the equivalent of a cat purring. A shot of magic pulled one of the doors open. They walked through and down one flight to the level holding sleeping chambers. He stopped and turned to face her at the top of the next flight of stairs. A smile illuminated his face. "Are you going to tell me what you had in mind?"

She grinned back. "No, but I'll show you." She led the way to the last sleeping area at the end of the hall and ducked inside. Once he'd joined her, she sealed the entryway with magic.

"Locking us in, eh?" He winked broadly.

"Can't risk you getting away," she countered. "Those books and scrolls might win."

"Not a chance." He wrapped his arms around her from behind and filled his hands with her breasts. She arched against him, loving the feel of his body next to hers. The stretch of skin over bone and muscle. The rise of his cock where it pressed into her ass. He nuzzled beneath her hair and kissed the side of her neck, mixing nips with his kisses.

Her nipples stiffened into peaks where he rubbed them between his fingers and thumbs. She wanted to savor the moment, remember every single thing about how his body felt jammed against hers. The mingled scents of their arousal—sunbaked clay and wildflowers and herbs—eddied about them.

He was murmuring endearments in Dutch in between kisses. She reached behind her and curved her fingers around his cock, remembering the taste of him, the nectar of his semen jetting into her mouth. He bit her shoulder; his penis twitched in her hand.

She let go of him and twisted in his arms until she faced him. Heat spilled through her, turning her brain to a delightful lusty haze, but she had to know if he was ready to formalize their mating bond. The dark secret place between her legs cried out to be filled. For long moments, she drank him in. Strands of shiny black hair fell to his shoulders. The severe planes of his face, the ones that made him so beautiful it nearly stopped her heart, had softened with wanting her.

"Are we?" she began and then tried again. "Will we be mates?"

"Is that what you want?" His gaze—dark eyes rimmed with gold—seared her, made her shiver all the way to her toes.

"Yes. More than I've ever wanted anything."

A smile formed in his eyes before it spread to his lips. "Then we shall be mates."

She should have been satisfied with his assertion, but she felt compelled to add. "Are you certain? No divorce."

"So you have told me, Liebchen. Ja, I am very certain."

Katya threw her arms around him and plastered her lips over his, thrusting her tongue inside his mouth. He sparred with it and gripped her ass while dipping his forearms beneath her thighs and lifting her. It surprised her, but she'd always been a quick study.

Katya threaded her legs around his waist. The motion spread her labia, and his cockhead seated itself at the entrance to her vault. "No going back now," he said and sank into her body.

Her muscles clung to him, dancing around his cock, as he stretched her with his girth. Once he was fully encased in the heat of her, he stopped moving beyond tiny little contractions that sent shudders of delight through her.

She rocked against him and tore her mouth from his. "Move, damn you!"

He repositioned her body so her nub rested directly on his pubic bone and pushed forward. She writhed against him as waves of delight shot outward from her sensitive center.

Slowly, ever so slowly, he lifted her until just the tip of him brushed her labia before lowering her back onto his hot hardness. The slow part didn't last long. He was as aroused as she. Every stroke ignited a different special spot within her until her entire body vibrated with lust and love and need for the man in her arms.

He lifted her all the way off his cock, carried her to a soft pallet, and set her down, kneeling between her legs. His member jutted outward from his body, glistening with their combined secretions. She wanted to lick him clean, but the mating ritual wasn't yet complete.

With a very male groan, peppered with a possessiveness that sang to her heart, he sank back to the hilt. She propped her legs on his shoulders and opened herself as fully as she could.

As he thrust into her, his nipples puckered into copper buds of desire. "Put your arms above your head," he said, his voice harsh with passion.

He clasped a hand around both her wrists and held her while he drove himself into her, rocking at the bottom of each stroke to tease her nub. The sexual haze thickened until the only thing in her world was the orgasm swirling deep in her belly.

It crashed over her, followed by another, and still one more. Somewhere between her second and third orgasms, she felt him release. Rhythmic contractions followed by blistering heat as semen painted the inside of her body.

Her dragon bugled, singing her joy that the deed was finally done. Her bondmate was no longer alone, and so neither was she.

Johan's dragon bugled back. The bedchamber filled with steam.

Panting, breath raspy, Johan lowered himself until he lay full-length on top of her. He'd let go of her wrists, so she wrapped her arms around him. Once their breathing quieted, he rolled them onto their sides.

"I love you," he said.

"I love you too." She brushed hair back from his face. "Such a beautiful man."

"You are the beautiful one." He laughed softly. "I love your dragon too. She sang to us, and mine returned her song."

"She's delighted. She never believed I'd settle on a mate."

He made a snorting noise. "My dragon does not know me well enough to have come to any such conclusions."

"But if he did?"

"He would have feared the same. I was a confirmed bachelor. Until I met you."

They held one another for long moments.

"I wish we could remain here forever, Liebchen, but I truly do need to add to my knowledge base." Johan nuzzled her neck.

"I understand." Katya untangled herself from his embrace and set herself to rights as best as she could without a dip in the lake. Taking time to formalize their mating bond was critical; bathing could wait.

He got to his feet and offered her a hand up. She clasped it, and together they walked from the room.

Happy, satiated, mated, Katya tucked her head into Johan's shoulder as they strode downstairs to the library. War still loomed ahead of them. Nothing about that had changed, but everything in her world had shifted on its axis. Johan was hers. Forever. She was mated, and her dragon couldn't stop producing steam and squealing, a very undragonlike thing to do. She made a strong bid for the mating flight to happen right now, but Katya explained they should have other dragons and a ceremony.

Her beast understood. Now that the bond was unbreakable, the dragon could be patient. To a point.

Katya cut through the library's illusory wall with a focused shot of power.

"There you are!" Erin looked up from a pile of dusty scrolls.

Kon sat next to her, clearly hunting for something in a large tome with a cracked brown leather binding. His nostrils flared, and he shot to his feet grinning like a madman.

"Congratulations!" he trumpeted. Fire shot from his mouth, followed by billows of steam.

"Ooohhh!" Erin scrambled upright, beaming. "You did it. You're mated. My dragon just told me. Best of luck to you both." She rushed forward and hugged Katya and then Johan.

Konstantin pumped Johan's hand then changed his mind

and wrapped his arms around him. "Welcome to the family. Treat her like a queen."

"No worries on that front," Johan said and laughed. "If I do not, you would have my hide."

"There is that." Kon let go of Johan and hugged Katya. When he stepped back, he said, "We will have a celebration, once this mess with the serpents is concluded."

Katya smiled at her twin. "We should make it a double mating flight."

"Perhaps we will." He knelt next to Erin. "What about it, darling?"

"I'm almost there." She smiled fondly at Konstantin and held her thumb and forefinger a centimeter or so apart. "Almost."

"No more sex play until you say yes."

Laughter bubbled from Erin. "You've got my number, sweetie, but right now I have to study. You'd feel really bad if I got snagged by a serpent because I didn't quite get to a critical element in my magical training."

"She makes it hard to argue with her," Konstantin said and took up his vigil with the imposing book.

"And she also brings up a most excellent point." Johan sat on the floor near enough to Erin to drag a couple of scrolls off the stack of her discards.

Katya settled next to him. "Practice is the heart and soul of magic," she lectured. They'd had their intimate time. Now was when she'd make double damn certain her mate knew enough to protect himself.

They'd be in the thick of a battle in a few hours' time. And it would only be the first. Because the serpents were so much like dragons, this war could drag on for weeks. Or months.

It probably wouldn't last years. By then, Earth would be such a shambles from magical fallout, dragons and their shifter allies would have no choice but to locate elsewhere.

She redirected her attention to the scroll in Johan's lap. He was mumbling about titrating air into fire to focus destructive magic. "Don't just read about it," she said. "Get up and feel how it actually works."

"But I could hurt something in here," he protested.

"Bring the book. We'll move one more level down. Some of the dragons who are no longer here built a workspace specifically to hone fighting skills."

"I need practice too," Erin spoke up.

"We'll all go," Konstantin said and clapped Katya across the shoulders. "I'd forgotten about the workshop. Thanks for the timely reminder."

"Anytime, Brother. Anytime." She got to her feet and joined Johan, her heart, her life, her future.

"Which way?" he asked.

"Let's see if you can find it on your own," she countered.

He gifted her with a smile that made her heart sing. "First I visualize the level below us, right?"

She smiled back. "Trust yourself. Trust your magic. Trust your dragon. Between those three, it's hard to go too far astray."

"What if I wish to add my mate to the mix?"

"Makes it that much stronger." Katya's smile broadened,

and her dragon puffed enough steam that at first she didn't recognize the dusty, unused practice studio.

She clapped her hands smartly and paired off with Konstantin. "Johan and Erin, levy offensive power. We'll parry it. Once you have the offense side underway, we'll trade."

Konstantin laughed. "I should make you my master-at-arms, Sister. Who'd ever have guessed you had such a flare for tossing orders about?"

She bowed low. "I shall serve wherever you have need of me, Brother, but mates must remain together."

Her twin regarded her, trying to look serious but humor danced in his eyes. "Method to your madness, eh?"

"Always. Now let's get this sparring session underway."

She blew a kiss to Johan before squaring off against him. It would be good practice—and a confidence builder—for him and Erin to figure out as much as they could within the relative safety of the grotto.

What came next in the world a few kilometers above would challenge them all. She dodged a volley of magic and sent a quick prayer to Y Ddraigh Goch to see them through the days ahead.

You've reached the end of the second book in the Ice Dragon Trilogy. While it's fresh in your mind, please leave a review for *Cursed Ice*. It doesn't have to be fancy, a couple of sentences about why you enjoyed it would be so appreciated.

The next book, *Primal Ice*, is everyone's story. All the

characters you've come to know and care about. It begins at 110 percent where this story left off and doesn't let up until... well until the end. No spoilers, but be ready for nonstop action as the war with the sea-serpents and dragon traitors moves into its endgame.

Read on for a sample of *Primal Ice*.

ABOUT THE AUTHOR

Ann Gimpel is a USA Today bestselling author. A lifelong aficionado of the unusual, she began writing speculative fiction a few years ago. Since then her short fiction has appeared in many webzines and anthologies. Her longer books run the gamut from urban fantasy to paranormal romance. Once upon a time, she nurtured clients. Now she nurtures dark, gritty fantasy stories that push hard against reality. When she's not writing, she's in the backcountry getting down and dirty with her camera. She's published over 70 books to date, with several more planned for 2019 and beyond. A husband, grown children, grandchildren, and wolf hybrids round out her family.

Keep up with her at www.anngimpel.com or http://anngimpel.blogspot.com

If you enjoyed what you read, get in line for special offers and pre-release special reads. Newsletter Signup!

PRIMAL ICE, DRAGON TIME

Konstantin's dragon here, folks. We're two-thirds of the way through what is, essentially, my story. Yet none of you know me at all. I'm about to correct that. Not to be outdone, Katya's dragon wants a voice as well.

"What about us?" Johan and Erin's dragons bugled from where they'd just broken through into the dragons' borderworld.

The "us" took on echoes as dragons appeared from every quadrant and moved closer. Worse than a pack of hyenas scenting a feast, everyone wanted a piece of the action, but it was impossible.

For a whole lot of very good reasons.

"Are any of you part of the serpent battle?" I demanded, blowing fire. I swear, these insurrections can spiral out of hand if you don't get a jump on them right away. Dragons are born warriors, though, so the possibility of battle has more allure than a fresh, bloody carcass.

"We could be part of it." A beefy dark red male lumbered closer, his golden eyes spinning like pinwheels.

"Seems to me, you'd welcome more help," a white dragon bugled. White is rare among our kind. This particular female is only the third white dragon I've seen during my rather lengthy life.

I stood taller and asked her, "How do you envision that working?"

She shrugged amid the rattling of scales. "We show up and fight."

If I'd been in Konstantin's body, I'd have dipped my head into my hands. All we needed were a bunch of mateless dragons steeped in bloodlust. Lacking a human bondmate's cooler head, they'd become impossible to control in short order.

Katya's dragon nudged me. *"Maybe it's not such a bad idea as all that,"* she hissed in shielded mindspeech.

I chose to ignore her. Turns out it was a mistake because she fanned her golden wings and clacked her double rows of teeth together to get everyone's attention. "The thing about battles," she said, punctuating her words with ash and smoke, "is there are always leaders. When Y Ddraigh Goch gathers his minions for an undertaking, they do as he orders them."

"Aye, but he's a god," a blue dragon pointed out dryly. "The rest of us have equal standing."

Cries of, "We are dragonkind. We answer to no one," filled the air.

I wondered if our god, Y Ddraigh Goch, was listening. If not, he ought to be. He'd swoop down and disabuse this crowd of their notions of independence damned fast.

I bumped Katya's dragon to make certain she heeded my words. "Good place to stop," I muttered, not bothering with telepathy.

"But I never even got to the part about asking them if they could see their way clear to following you." She turned her whirling gaze my way but not for long.

Facing the growing crowd of dragons again, she said, "This is precisely why those of you who are not bonded with humans cannot help us fight the serpents. Battles are choreographed, planned ahead of time. Yet they oftentimes slew sideways. Whoever commands the action must make decisions that impact everyone. You would be expected— nay, required—to do precisely as you were ordered."

Grumbling and fire filled the air, along with more, "We answer to no ones."

I stared at the assemblage, willing them to disperse. I knew better than to try for an out-and-out command. Me telling them to find something else to do would make things worse. They'd never leave then.

Done glaring at my brethren, I scanned rock-studded sand. Our borderworld is a barren place, marked by a string of active volcanoes. At any given time, one or more are erupting. They keep the place hot and ashy, but it's our home, and we love it. Several subterranean caverns house underground springs. Water makes it possible for us to raise game animals, but most of us prefer to travel to neighboring worlds where there's always been exceptional hunting.

Magical creatures enjoy eating, but we can go for long periods without food. Unless we select a human to bond with. Dragon shifters require a lot of calories, so it gives us an excuse to hunt.

Dragon ire was increasing. The smoke eddying about me thickened. I felt like thumping Katya's dragon soundly. She'd made it appear the topic of the upcoming war was up for discussion. It wasn't.

"Silence!" I bellowed and followed the single word with judiciously applied shots of magic into the center of the crowd.

Once the dragons had quieted some, I said, "I appreciate your warriors' hearts, but shy of talking Y Ddraigh Goch into leading a troop of dragons against the serpents, you'd be more trouble than help. Each dragon would have its own plan, and many of them would run counter to the common good."

"We'd all be there killing serpents," the red explained. "How could that not shorten the—"

"How would we kill them? They're immortal. You know, like us," another dragon, this one green, spoke over him.

Eyes whirled faster. Scales rattled. Bugles and trumpets nearly deafened me. The crux of the problem with the serpent war had hit home. We couldn't kill them. Worse, a few renegade dragons had jumped ship and now worked alongside the serpents.

It made them ridiculously strong since they could blend serpent power with our own brand of magic. From what we'd seen so far, it also allowed them to hide themselves behind powerful illusion.

"Sorry I got them stirred up," Katya's dragon mumbled.

I didn't answer. Dragons are hot-headed by nature. Nothing I could say would alter that tendency to shoot from the hip and think about it later. As quickly as they'd formed a crowd, the dragons drifted away.

Soon only the four of us remained.

Good.

Perhaps we can get through introductions—which should have happened far earlier in this tale. The only reason I have a spot of time on my hands is because Konstantin is in wait mode. The shifters who volunteered to help with the serpents are maximizing their magic, so when we launch our first strike it gives our enemy something to think about.

I chafed at any delays at all. They offered the serpents time to shore up their own magic, but I could see Kon's side of things too. If we lost too badly during the initial skirmish, it would be all that much harder to recapture lost ground. Beyond that, none of us has any true idea how many dragons are part of the serpents' cadre.

Konstantin and I made certain Y Ddraig Goch knew we harbored turncoats in our midst. While we can't kill serpents or dragons, our god is capable of doing away with them. If we only had serpents to deal with—and not our own kind— we might have a chance. I'm off on a bit of a tangent here, but if I were running the show, I'd leave the serpents to do whatever with Earth. Once they'd killed off everyone, we could appeal to other gods—the ones who manage all universes—to ensure Earth meets the same fate as Mu.

Blown up, and then sucked into magnetic holes deep in space.

But it's not my call. Konstantin rarely explains himself to me. He doesn't have to because I can read his mind. Not that he harbors any fondness for Earth, but Erin, the dragon shifter he's almost, almost mated to, used to be human. Earth was her home, and she would be sad to leave it.

I believe he's taking on the serpents to protect Erin's home, but that might only be part of it. He's never been one to walk away from a challenge, or to allow evil free rein. It's one of the reasons I bonded with him before he was born. I saw his strength, his potential. And I knew he would be a solid bondmate for me.

Sometimes, a mateless dragon will ask why I shackled myself to a human. There are downsides, but my human half exerts a modulating effect. My life is far richer for sharing it with Konstantin. I had no idea he would grow to be the dragons' princeling, but even if that hadn't happened, I would still be satisfied with my choice.

Those days—when dragons eagerly chose human bondmates—are long behind us. Not many new dragon shifters are born anymore. I'm not certain why that is, but I bet it has something to do with men no longer believing in magic. Science has displaced it, and not to anyone's betterment.

When you stop believing in the impossible, your world grows far smaller, duller, less exciting. People's days are filled with drudgery rather than possibilities. I have no clue why they settle for so little, but that's another story, and truly a digression. Not at all what I planned for my special time with you, our readers.

"I want to talk about Katya," her dragon spoke up.

"Yes, and I can tell them about Erin," the red dragon offered. "Not that I know her well, but they should know why I agreed to bond with her."

"Same for Johan." The green dragon bobbed his head.

"Lead out," I invited. Saving Konstantin for last was a good idea. He was the closest thing dragon shifters had to royalty, mostly because of his link to the land, but more about that neat piece of magic later.

Katya's golden dragon flared her wings. Tongues of flame shot from her nostrils. "Katya is unique among women," the dragon began. "Of course, I may be prejudiced because she is mine, but I fell in love with her when she was but a seedling in her mother's womb. A space she and Konstantin shared, although not without the occasional squabble.

"I used to worry we would never have a mate of our own, but we do now." Smoke curled from her nostrils and open mouth. "My only two complaints were no mate and our long tenure on Earth. From what I've seen, it's not a good place for dragons or anything magical. Men are steeped in phony science. Phony because they dredge up arguments to line their pockets with worthless money. No one cares about learning anything.

"I left Katya for a while because I couldn't pry her away from Earth. Luckily, we got past that. She has no idea why I returned. The bare truth is Konstantin's dragon rounded me up. We exchanged a few harsh words, but he was right that my place was with Katya."

She turned toward the green dragon, newly bonded to Johan. "Your turn. As our new mate, your tale should dovetail with mine."

The green dragon stood taller. His gaze slid across our small group. "I never thought to bond with anyone, but one day our god showed up. He didn't force me by any means. Merely told me he thought I would make a good bondmate for a worthy human."

The dragon shook his head until his scales rattled. "I tell you, if I'd had any idea how horrible Johan's first shift would be—how little he knew—I'd not have been so quick to agree. Katya showed up in the nick of time. Without her and her dragon, Johan would have died. And left me feeling like a miserable failure. I admit, I was angry with him even after he finessed that first shift.

"It made no sense, and it was unconscionable of me to blame him for being what he was—human. It took us a while to find common ground after that little incident." He puffed smoke and ash. "I readily acknowledge I am young for a dragon, but it doesn't excuse my behavior. After my faux pas with Johan, I made an unforgivable error—defied a direct command from Konstantin—and nearly ended both myself and Johan."

"Humility is the beginning of wisdom," I muttered,

wincing as I remembered that incident. We'd nearly lost Johan. It had taken all Konstantin's skill to bring him back.

Johan's dragon blatted laughter, laced with smoke. "Humility and dragon don't belong in the same bunch of words."

I chuckled and then laughed. "Right you are." I clapped him on the back and looked at the red dragon bonded with Erin.

"One more thing." Johan's dragon aimed his next words at Katya's dragon. "I am very much anticipating our mating flight."

She puffed steam until it billowed around both her and Johan's green. He added more to the mix. Before they decided on their own mating flight, absent their human counterparts, I pushed my body between them murmuring, "I'm certain it will happen soon."

"Not until we have a better handle on the serpent problem," Katya's dragon said resolutely.

"That could take a while." Johan's dragon sounded resigned, and not especially pleased about his mate's position.

I understood the unhappy part. While Erin was almost promised to us, she and Konstantin had yet to make love in either form. Until that happened, she could still change her mind. "Your turn," I nodded toward Erin's dragon. I longed to tell her how beautiful she was, but perhaps she'd be as skittish as her bondmate.

She tilted her head. "I'm not certain what I can add. Erin had just as hard a time with her first shift as Johan. I feared she wouldn't survive, yet I wouldn't have blamed myself."

"Why not?" I was curious after what Johan's dragon had disclosed.

"Y Ddraigh Goch was there. I assumed if the human woman died, it was his will."

I recalled the scene on the borderworld all too well. Konstantin's desolation and his certainty it would be his fault if Erin perished. Yet she'd figured things out, and I'd been relieved and grateful—two very undragonlike emotions. Kon would have ripped the world apart if Erin died, and I'd have been there every step of the way trying to mitigate his grief and guilt.

Getting back on an even keel would have taken centuries. Our opportunity to take on the serpents would have gone by the wayside.

"Anyway," the red dragon went on, "I like Erin Ryan. She has pluck, grit, and a spark that shines from within. No one takes advantage of her, not without her dressing them down. She and I are well mated." Lashes brushed her scaled cheeks. "It is my hope one day you and I will be mates as well," she told me.

Surprise ratcheted through me. I hadn't expected her to acknowledge the almost-complete mating ritual. I bowed before her and took care to puff steam. "Such is my hope as well." I sounded horribly formal, but tucked away where no one could see it, my cock swelled and curved against my scaled belly.

To divert my attention away from jumping skyward and

dragging Erin's dragon with me—a forbidden act since our humans had yet to formalize their troth—I let a purifying blast of fire escape my jaws. Unbonded dragons could have all the sex they wished, but once we joined our lives with a dragon shifter, that aspect of our free will dissolved.

"I would tell you of my bondmate, Konstantin," I began. "His link to the land is poorly understood, so I will start there. All worlds hold untold power within their core. Many of them began as flaming balls of heat that turned to primal ice as they cooled. Over eons the ice ceded to a rich diversity of living creatures. From time to time, ice returned. It is a world's way of cleansing itself of taint."

I blew out more fire. "Konstantin can merge his mind with the land's deep knowledge. Watching him work his land-linked magic is fascinating—and humbling. He has infinite patience. Many a time, we have sat for months waiting for a stubborn world to notice us. Mu was like that. It did not reveal its secrets easily, nor did it trust Kon's intent. Probably because he did not truly believe he possessed land-linked power."

"He doubted himself," Katya's dragon concurred. "It was us—me and my bondmate—who convinced him to keep trying."

I scowled, but she spoke true. Dragons could lie, but it wasn't easy. "A needed boost," I murmured. "And one we are forever grateful for."

"Pfft." Katya's dragon puffed smoke and ash and fire. "Dragons are rarely grateful. It's not part of who we are."

I kept my mouth shut. It might not be part of who we

claimed to be, or the image we projected, but I'd experienced my share of gratitude. Like when Erin hadn't died on the borderworld where she met her dragon.

"Konstantin should be establishing a link with Earth," I went on. "By the time we return, it may well be intact. It is one element that could work in our favor—"

"We need you back here now!" Kon's voice blasted into my mind.

The other dragons' heads shot up. Clearly, they'd either received a similar summons from their bondmates. Or they'd heard Konstantin.

"Did we accomplish enough?" Katya's dragon asked me.

"I believe so," I replied and shaped magic to return us to the grotto deep beneath the ice sheet covering the southern end of Earth. As I worked, I thought about humans. And dragons. We're good for one another. Dragons encourage their humans to reach for the stars. Humans are good for selecting which stars are most likely to yield fruit.

On that whimsical note, I shall cede my centerstage spot to Konstantin. If I can finagle my way back to talk with you again, I shall. Dragons do like to have the last word. And now, I have battles to plan, enemies to slay, and a world to conquer.

Draping the edges of my spell around the other dragons, I headed all of us toward our bondmates. I can't speak for my companions, but merging with Konstantin fills me with joy. Every single time. No matter how bad a mood he's in or how out of sorts. I love him. He is mine, and I am his.

It's the miracle of the shifter mate bond.